A LURCHER IN THE HOUSE

WHAT THE REVIEWERS SAY . . .

The merriest, funniest first novel. A romping political satire, the book is also a touching love-story . . . The dog hero is based on Willie's noble, beautiful lurcher Kaid, who never left his bedside during his last days. *Semper fidelis*

JILLY COOPER, *The Daily Mail*

A gentle political thriller which I could describe as being 'by Dick Francis out of Jilly Cooper'. It has political skulduggery, romance, country life and dogs — lots of dogs. It is also very funny, and had me shaking with laughter.

R. W. F. POOLE, *The Daily Telegraph*

Posthumous masterpiece . . . terribly funny and politically incorrect.

DAVID RENNIE, *The Evening Standard*

Present fit for the Queen.

REG LITTLE, *Oxford Mail*

Kaid the lurcher gives wonderful asides through the book about his masters varied and amusing life. I do hope that *A Lurcher in the House* will become a film on the lines of *Four Weddings and a Funeral*. It has all the ingredients of a Box Office winner.

MAJOR RONALD FERGUSON, *The Field*

This Jilly Cooperesque novel is a marvellous posthumous tribute . . . there is plenty of hunting, polo, Army and Etonian anecdotes to bring back the memories.

DIANA BUTLER, *Horse and Hound*

WHAT THE REVIEWERS SAY . . .

This thoroughly readable short novel is at once light hearted and poignant . . . it is great fun.

DAVID EDELSTEN, *Country Life*

Loyd's light, romantic tale is set in the Vale of Evenlode, a sort of Lake Woebegon of the British Countryside where women are strong, the men are good-looking and the dogs are above average.
David wages his underdog's campaign with faithful Überdog Kaid and fiancée Lara at his side.

MARTY LE GRAND, *Polo (USA)*

Set in the Nineties, it has the feeling of the easy going, civilised and more relaxed time of the inter-war years and sub-plots and dalliances are portrayed with wit and authenticity. Engagingly delightful.

CHARLES GOODSON-WICKES, *Country Sports*

A charming mix of farce, romance and political satire. Loyd's style is that of a raconteur, a brisk efficient prose spiced with some nicely pithy asides. The revenge of the shires may well prove prophetic. Good entertaining company.

MARTIN GIBSON, *The Oldie*

A LURCHER IN THE HOUSE

BY WILLIAM LOYD

Everyone prefers dogs to politicians
A.N. WILSON

The more I see of men, the more I love dogs
MADAME MANON ROWLAND (XVIII CENTURY)

NYALI PRESS
EYNSHAM

First published in Great Britain in Oct 1994 by
Nyali Press,
Pinkhill Farm, Eynsham, Oxon OX8 1JO

2nd impression, November 1994
3rd impression, February 1995

A CIP catalogue record for this book is available
from the British Library.

ISBN 0 9524188 0 0

Typeset by Electronic Type & Design, Oxford
in 12pt Garamond Book

Printed by Mayfield Press (Oxford) Ltd.,
Oxford

CONTENTS

		page
Chapter 1	Kaid	1
Chapter 2	David	16
Chapter 3	Lara	31
Chapter 4	The Warm-up	48
Chapter 5	The Starter's Gun	66
Chapter 6	The Hustings	86
Chapter 7	An Interlude at Eton	100
Chapter 8	A Mile to Run	111
Chapter 9	The Queen's Cup	123
Chapter 10	The Final Furlong	132
Chapter 11	The Finishing Post	149
Chapter 12	Winner's Enclosure	167
Chapter 13	Wedding Plans	184
Chapter 14	And Granny came too	198
Chapter 15	A Lurcher in the House	217

To Lilo, who helped so much, with Love

ACKNOWLEDGMENTS

I would like to thank the following people for their help, either wittingly or unwittingly given, in preparing the background to this book. Mr David Blunkett, MP, and Mr Ivor Stanbrook for much of the parliamentary material; the Lycée Français Charles de Gaulle and Miss Philippa Grace for, respectively, information on the education in the Lycée and at Eton; Miss Nicola Stoy for her advice on rock concerts; and Mr Jonathan Grosvenor, JP, for correcting my text on matters pertaining to law and order.

Most of all I would like to thank Yvette Goulden for her kind advice and Jilly Cooper for her unstinting support.

CHARACTERS

Carmen diaz Alberdi	A beautiful Ecuadorian heiress
Georgina Ardkinglas	David Vyvian's elder sister and an accomplished sportswoman
Hamish Ardkinglas	An Etonian son of Dougal and Georgina
The Master of Ardkinglas	Georgina's husband, and heir to a large slice of Scotland
The Bladon	The local pack of foxhounds
Buraq	'Sonny', a flippant Lurcher owned by Lara Graham and son of Kaid
Major John Crispin	Bucolic Master of the Bladon
Sir Peregrine d'Artois, Bt	Former Lord Lieutenant for the County
Lady Maris 'Stella' d'Artois	His wife
Ivor Digney	A freelance butler
Dr Paul Enstone	Labour candidate for the Vale of Evenlode
Evenlode Brigade	Local ex-soldiers' drinking club
Flicka	A greyhound bitch
Ilona Graham	Slovene-born wife of Simon and mother of Lara
Lara Graham	PA to a film producer Robert Summer
Lt Col Simon Graham, OBE	A former Green Jacket
Virginia Graham	Lara's maiden aunt
Stanton Harcourt	A Land agent
Joanna	An Eton housemaster's daughter
Kaid	A hairy and heroic long-coated brindled Lurcher owned by David Vyvian
Mrs Kerr	Devoted Housekeeper to David Vyvian, and Village Gossip
Jack Kestrel	Tractor driver and part-time gamekeeper at the Windrush Hall
Roy Large	News Editor on the local paper
Esther Livkin	Strident feminist wife of Norman
Norman Livkin	Official Conservative candidate for the Vale of Evenlode. Junior partner in the law firm of Schuster and Schneider in Cheapside

Brig. 'Buff' Mainwaring, MC	A randy member of the Cavalry & Guards Club
Roger Mileham	Liberal Democrat candidate for the Vale of Evenlode
Teresa Mileham	His wife
Luigi Montecuccoli	An Italian playboy
Nikki and Tracy	Two super-efficient secretaries working for Clyne Films
Pearl	An exotic and discreet whore
Richard Riley, QC	An Independent MP
Sidi	A Deerhound, since departed
Mirza Sind	An Indian polo-playing and dog loving friend of David Vyvian, currently working for the BBC
Tony Stark	Former Farrier Corporal in the King's Lancers
Robert Summer	An American-born film producer
Franzesca Tavcar	Ilona Graham's widowed mother
Terri	Immaculate Stud Groom at Windrush Hall, and fond of the odd 'jar'
Father Timothy	Anglo-Catholic vicar of St Leonard's, on the road to Rome
Cat Thrust	10-year-old son of Mandy and Lance
Lance Thrust	Lead guitarist with the group 'Rock and the Hard Place'
Mandy Thrust	Lance Thrust's wife
Sir Reggie Token	Late (Cons) MP for The Vale of Evenlode
Vale of Evenlode	Midland constituency
Spring Ur	A new-age yob
Veronica	David Vyvian's ex-wife and a prize bitch
Caspar Vyvian	David's father and an elderly rake
David Vyvian	An Oxfordshire landowner and aspiring politician
Mary Vyvian	David's late mother
Mrs Watt	A part-time secretary
Yvette	Caspar's young Companion

Chapter 1

KAID

"Oh Anubis! Oh God! What has the Boss got himself into now? It really does look like being one of those days. To start with, I am too hot. Yes, I know that I chose to lie on the lawn in the sun, rather than in the shade of one of the apple trees, and as a result I am panting. I also know that Mrs Kerr, the Boss's housekeeper, has put Domestos into all the downstairs loos ('poisoning the wells', I call it) and closed the lids, so that my only alternative for a drink is either the rather common bowl with 'DOG' written on its side in the boot room, or the bird-bath. No thanks! I'll wait for the Boss to open the garden gate when he goes out to the stables and then have a slurp from the horse trough in the yard.

No, the main cause of worry on this warm May morning is that he seems about to go into politics. He is usually quite sane, but Stanton Harcourt, his agent, 'Stan' to him and me, has been spending quite a lot of time with the Boss, known to the outside world as David Vyvian, recently and they weren't just talking about linseed acreages. Politics bore me — indeed, the Boss hasn't been over-keen on them in the past. Whenever a Party Political broadcast has come on the television, he always nips out to get a drink, or to telephone Lara, his girl-friend, or whatever.

Not that I am that keen on television, you understand (apart from when I appeared on it, but we will come to that in due course). Basically, I enjoy the wildlife programmes, especially a recent one about wolves which was really sexually explicit at times, and the Boss tries to get me to watch *One Man and his Dog* from time to time. A bunch of common smart-arsed collies performing tricks with some stupid sheep, I ask you!

But I digress. The French windows which lead from the lawn to the office are always open by day in summer, so I could hear the Boss talking on the telephone to Stan quite easily. The key words seemed to be: 'I've slept on the idea and have decided to give it a try, Where and when do we start?' Where and when indeed! Since Lara stayed here last night anyway, 'sleeping on the idea' is a new euphemism to me.

Kaid rolled over onto his back and wriggled on the close-cut grass to have a good itch at a tender spot behind his left shoulder blade. A bumble bee droned past his nose, annoying him. He rolled back onto his side, resting his head on a cool clump of bluebells.

"I suppose that, at this stage, I had better fill you in on the background to my full and interesting life. As you know, we Lurchers, or our forebears, adopted man at around Stone Age times. A bit later on, but very much before your Jesus was around, some more enlightened humans in the Eastern Mediterranean countries actually worshipped Anubis, the Dog-God son of Osiris and Isis. Interesting, that. Since the Boss always refers to his ex-wife, Veronica, as 'that bitch', it is perhaps as well that there was no off-spring of their union, so to speak.

Anyway, I come from a long line of well-bred Lurchers, although there was some talk of my great-grandmother having a fling with a travelling chap. That resulted in my grandfather Bertie, twice champion at Lambourn in the Seventies. I was born in a rather grand country house near Salisbury and had a happy childhood with my brothers and sisters. I was the only one of the litter to be long-coated, which led to some rather unkind remarks at times. Mother was also getting a bit bored with us all as time went on, so at around eight weeks we broke up as a family, not that I ever saw my father. Another travelling man, perhaps?

The Boss came to pick me up in his car. He had been down a couple of weeks earlier and had chosen me, which I suppose was flattering. In fact the trouble that Mum's owner took to vet all the applicants for us puppies was truly impressive. 'Rather like getting a son down for a good house at Eton,' I heard the Boss telling Lara sometime later. My new home was, and is, very dog-friendly, with stone floors — we all make mistakes when we are young — and a bean-bag at either end on which to relax. Being deep-chested I often lie on my back with my legs in the air, which prompts Mrs Kerr to make her disapproving tutting noise and complain to Terri, the stud groom, that I have been exposing my rude bits again.

I met Sidi on arrival, an old deerhound who was kindness itself. He had endured a rough time with the dreadful Veronica who, being a cat-lover, had banished him to the tack-room. This did not suit Sidi, who felt rejected, nor Terri; for Uncle, as I used to call him, was prone to fart a bit, rather like old humans come to think of it, consequently the atmosphere in there tended to be a bit, well, fruity come Reveille. Once Veronica had left, taking her cats, the matrimonial bed and her adultery with her, Sidi came back into the library, which was where he was when I came upon the scene. Poor Uncle. He was suffering from angina towards the end, then one day he just wasn't there any more.

I missed him a bit initially, but quite honestly I really prefer humans. I do see other dogs of course, even other Lurchers at the occasional informal coursing meetings, but they tend to be rather a rough bunch who are jealous of my silky coat. We even went down for a day at my first home where a family get-together had been planned. The Boss has a nice saying about 'being able to choose your friends, but not your relations'. How apt! My only consolation, apart from being the fastest of them all when a hare was put up, was when the family cook came out after lunch and said that I was the most handsome of the litter. Great taste, that cook.

On the subject of coursing, I feel that I better make my position clear: us Lurchers have been bred for the chase of hares (and deer, though I have never had one myself, and was kicked when I chased a muntjac) for a very long time. If I see a hare, I go, whatever the Boss might be shouting at me (usually encouragement, unless he thinks that I am knackered from a previous course). Sometimes I kill the hare (in which case Mrs Kerr cooks it, Terri having skinned it after Harry has been hung for about a week); sometimes not, in which case it gets clean away. In any event, I can handle it, for that is the way that I am. I also try for the odd pheasant (to give them flying practice) and, when young, had a couple of Marans in the yard in a fit of misplaced exuberance."

The heat was now such as to drive Kaid indoors in search of a drink. He found Mrs Kerr in the kitchen and panted at her, wagging his tail. She, of course, knew perfectly well that her employer condoned the dog's habit of drinking from the downstairs loos, — indeed she had often caught the Captain following her around and flushing the Domestos out of them. However she was fond of Kaid, so filled a mixing bowl from the tap and set it on the floor. The dog drank noisily, gave a slight belch, and returned to the garden.

"I have also been to London — once, which was quite enough for me, and quite traumatic to boot. That was in early days when the Boss was trying to get me used to car travel, not that it has ever been a problem for me, unlike some that I could name. His Diesel Merc had gone in for service and he had to go to London to see his lawyers (about the divorce, I expect) so we went in the farm Land Rover, me wearing my smart collar with the Boss's regimental badge on it. We parked in some basement garage in Brick Street, just off Park Lane; then any idea of a walk in this exciting new place, full of strange smells, was dashed as the Boss shoved me in the back and buckled down the canvass flap to keep me in.

After about an hour I was thoroughly bored and quite frankly, a bit pissed off as well. After nosing around the canvass cover, I soon found a spot where the side cord was not properly done up, so forced my way out, landing rather uncomfortably on the hard floor. Nobody was around, so I trotted up the ramp and into the low February sunlight. I hadn't a clue where I was, of course, and not being a blasted Bloodhound, no way could I pick up the Boss's spoor. So I followed my nose and found myself in what I now know to have been Shepherd Market, not that there were many sheep around.

There were one or two dogs on leads, sort of poodle types, and the variety of humans put market day in Banbury right into the shade! I wandered around for a while and an old lady gave me a bit of cake that she was eating with her coffee at a pavement cafe. After a time I started to feel that perhaps my adventure hadn't been such a brilliant idea after all, and all that I wanted was out. I wandered down to the end of the market where there was a flower and vegetable stall. There I found my saviour. He was buying a flower for his button-hole and was deep in conversation with a pretty young black girl.

He was an elderly chap, smartly dressed, and I suppose the fact that he smelled of Penhaligon's Blenheim Bouquet, like the Boss, drew me to him. I wagged my tail and looked pathetic. It worked. He grinned at me and held out the back of his hand towards me. Emboldened that I didn't remove said hand at the wrist, he examined the badge on my collar. 'Good God!' he exclaimed. 'The Plonkers!' (This, I happen to know, was a rather unfortunate nickname given to the Boss's former regiment by lesser cavalry regiments.) 'Only one place for you, Old Lad, and that's the Club,' he added.

And so it was that Brigadier 'Buff' Mainwaring, MC, with me trotting along at his side on the end of his silk scarf, marched down to Piccadilly and along to the Cavalry and Guards Club near Hyde Park Corner. (The pretty black girl did not come with us, in fact she had become rather bored when the Brigadier became more interested in me than he had been in her.) Luckily it was lunch time, so the Club was fairly full. The Boss has been a member for years, and by chance there were one or two in there on this occasion, braying at each other, who had shot at Windrush, my home, over the winter, and made the connection between him, the cap-badge and me.

Someone telephoned the Hall and spoke to Mrs Kerr, who was always left with details of the Boss's movements, not all of them perhaps. To cut a long story short, she provided the telephone number of his lawyers in Gresham Street, where he was still hard at it over the lunch-hour, and he came by taxi to rescue me. I was so excited that I inadvertently pee-ed on the Hall Porter's box. 'Keeps the wood-worm at bay,' was Brigadier Buff's only comment, reflecting that his kindness to animals might have cost him a pre-lunch *apéritif* with Pearl, the girl in Shepherd Market, but he could always reschedule the rendezvous as a post-prandial gallop.

We made it back to the Hall without further incident — believe me, there really is no place like home — and the Boss telephoned Stan to fix up a meeting for the following day. Stan is the Agricultural Consultant to a big London-based firm of Estate Agents, and the Boss is one of his clients. I suppose that he knows what he is doing, as he advises several other large landowners in the area and has a string of initials after his

5

name. His brief on the following day was short and to the point. 'With the alimony payments that I have been landed with,' said the Boss. 'This estate has got to pay for itself, and more.' Fine words, but they were to lead to a time of real embarrassment for me and a change for the better in the Boss's lifestyle."

The love-chat of two red-legged partridges interrupted the dog's reflections. The Frenchmen were sitting on the wall, oblivious of Kaid who wanted to mark their nest for future reference. He was partial to a fresh partridge egg.

"It all started pleasantly enough. A week or so after their meeting Stan called round to say that the Locations Director for Clyne Films had approached him over a suitable site for a television commercial. The money was generous and film crews had quite a good record for leaving their locations clean and tidy, presumably so that they would be welcomed if they ever wished to return. Stan had suggested that the pond (being an estate agent, he called it a lake) would be ideal, with the Boss's herd of Charolais cows in the field beyond. The advertisement itself was for some instant coffee, which was to feature in a picnic scene that they needed to film in March. Something about schedules.

Although the Boss had some reservations initially, he eventually came round to the idea ('Think of it as a month's alimony, David,' said Stan). So, a couple of weeks later, at some fantastically early hour, the film crew turned up. What a crowd to make a thirty-second commercial! There were sound men, lighting men, camera men, the producer and his retinue, the director and his numerous assistants, the props crew, continuity girl and — joy oh joy — a catering bus. The actors, all resting between films, turned up a bit later in a luxury caravan.

The Boss was as fascinated as I was, and although he went back to the delights of Mrs Kerr's cooking (from the smell, jugged hare), and a stiff drink, the film set being 'dry', at lunch time, I hung around and was given so much to eat that I felt rather sick. I wandered over to where the filming had been taking place and saw a particularly inviting cake, Dundee, I think, which was part of the picnic set-up. I certainly wasn't hungry, but I nicked it all the same. The continuity girl saw what I was doing and straight away gave chase, followed by most of the crew.

I was beginning to get rather perturbed by all these cross people chasing me, though they couldn't catch me of course, when the Boss re-appeared and told me to drop it, so honour was saved. The continuity girl made a big fuss, and the cake had to be repositioned to show the unbitten side, but filming continued. It was at that point that the Boss saw one of the crew climbing across the post-and-rail fence into the field with the Charolais. 'Get out!' he yelled. 'Leave the cows alone. They are all about to calve.'

'I can see that,' replied the girl. 'And you have a breach-birth with this cow, unless I am much mistaken.'

'I'll call the Vet.'

'No time. Just give me a hand.'

For choice the Boss always leaves this messy calving business to his cowman, though he is prepared to get involved if needed. The girl clearly knew what she was doing as, with Barbour discarded and jersey sleeves rolled up, she proceeded to feel for the calf's slippery hind legs (rather like a scene from *All Creatures Great and Small*). With enlisted help from the Boss, they managed to extract the bull-calf before if suffocated, or whatever calves do when they are the wrong way round

The girl turned to the Boss, who immediately asked her back to the Hall to clean up. 'I'm Lara Graham,' she said. 'You must be David Vyvian. I don't think that we've met, but my father knew yours when he farmed here. Mummy and Daddy live over the other side of Chipping Norton.'

There then followed that boring ritual of name-dropping between them both which ascertained that they had various friends in common, in other words, Blah, Blah, Blah!. Lara was shown up to one of the upstairs bathrooms and the Boss provided a clean jersey. When she came down (Mrs Kerr, smiling to herself that this would make the rounds in the Post Office tomorrow, had already made some tea) Lara affected to notice me for the first time. 'So there's the cake-stealer,' she said. 'Have you ever bred from him? I'd love a puppy of his.'

'No,' says the Boss, and I could sense his mind working on the angles. 'But I think I will soon.'

Well, thanks a million! Thanks very much! So who is expected to provide the action, then! As a breed we are not all that keen on sex, indeed Stan once said that Lurchers had about as much sex-drive as giant pandas! Sure, we go through the motions when bitches are around, tale wagging in double time and strutting stiff-legged around the lady, peeing copiously on anything upright. Also, with other dogs, once we have finished the ritual growling at one another, there are the usual remarks of: 'Grr, wouldn't mind getting my leg over there!' when a pretty bitch passes. But, to be perfectly candid, that is about it.

No more was said about it at the time, and I rather hoped that the Boss had forgotten all about it, though he started seeing Lara quite often. We had a quiet summer, during which we went to watch polo at Cirencester Park from time to time. To be honest, half a chukka is about my limit, after which I get bored. Cirencester is a bit special however, as there are quite a few genuine country dogs around and, unlike on Smith's Lawn, we are allowed into the clubhouse. I even met Jilly Cooper's dogs during the treading-in session at half time on one occasion, but I don't think that her dogs liked me all that much, though she gave me a really nice cuddle.

I don't chase hares during the summer — apart from anything else I can't find them when the crops are standing prior to harvest. If I do have a course, I tend to lose Harry pretty soon, by which time I am so hot that I have to have a wallow in the pond, or in one of the streams. Then, about a year later, we were into that hectic period of the autumn harvest, the drilling of the winter crops and the local hunt, the Bladon, started cubbing. Prince Charles even came out with them when they met here at the start of the proper season in November. To be honest, I wouldn't have known about it but for the fact that the Master, Major John Crispin, started to make a fearful fuss when a couple of press photographers turned up."

Kaid, having drunk deeply earlier in the kitchen, now needed to have a pee. This he did, out of habit, on the parsley that grew with some other herbs in the south-facing border. He knew that Mrs Kerr always admired the dew on the parsley and washed everything that she took from the garden anyway, but this was his secret joke. He then resumed his position.

"Then the blow fell. Lara came over on a Saturday morning and they then both drove off in the Boss's Merc. Sometimes I get taken along in the car, at other times not, so I was not particularly bothered and went out riding with Terri, who was exercising the Boss's hunters, clad in her normal porkpie hat with a jay's feather in the band. The car came back at around midday, and I immediately sensed that something was wrong. Then I saw it. There was another dog in my seat in the back! The Boss parked the car next to Lara's and decanted the interloper onto the drive. 'Come on Kaid,' says he, sounding rather like a salesman who knows that the product is dodgy. 'Come and meet Flicka!'

Well, at least it seemed that I wasn't required to perform there and then. Flicka, who was a sort of foxy colour with huge brown eyes, was friendly enough, though institutionalised from a life in kennels and an inglorious career on the track. This suited quite well as, after one disastrous night in the house, she was firmly banished to the stables. An iron mesh grill had to be fixed over the door frame of a loose box to stop her from gnawing her way out. Also, after a lifetime of chasing a fluffy toy around a circular track, she went bananas when she met the real thing. I grant you that she could move, but her first (and last) course resulted in a broken toe and a cut foreleg. No common sense, in spite of her going on the whole time about her breeding and her papers.

From this you will have gathered that Flicka, after the flurry of her arrival, didn't really intrude on my life that much. This happy state of affairs was rudely interrupted about four weeks later when I heard Terri telling the Boss that the bitch was about ready for me. You will note that no mention was made about me being ready for the bitch, or anything like that. Also, whatever Terri's views on her state of readiness, nobody had told Flicka. Consequently, when I first laid a tentative paw across her back, she as near as damn it removed my wedding tackle in a frenzied attack on my person!

As Stud Groom, Terri was in charge of all of this and promptly muzzled my reluctant bride and tied her to the apple-tree beside which I am at present relaxing. Not that the bondage did anything for me, you understand, but at least it kept the target fairly static and pacified. Even so I couldn't get it together with her, and after a while I went and hid in the stables, overcome with mortification.

Round Two was held on the following day, and only after Terri had visited the Chemists in the village to buy something that humans use with similar problems. I heard her telling Mrs Kerr about it later on: apparently the girl in the shop didn't buy the story that the preparation was for canine use and suspected that Terri, who must be in her late 20s, wanted it for her own needs! Mrs Kerr thought that this was a capital joke and laughed immoderately. Anyway, a combination of bondage, the lubricant and Terri practically lifting me into the correct position finally worked. I had a couple of further encounters, and was just about getting it worked out for myself, when Flicka was pronounced to be past it, or something, and that was that. Sex may indeed make the world go round, but as for me, a brisk course, a good meal and a sleep on the sofa in front of a log fire beat it any day.

Nothing much happened for the next couple of months. Flicka grew increasingly mumsy; the Boss knocked up a wooden bench for her in the loose box; and Jack Kestrel, who does everything on the farm from running the shooting days to tractor driving, rigged up a red light above the bench. Then, early in the New Year, all hell broke loose one morning. Poor Flicka, she really was a no-hoper. A loser on the track, she was hardly a dream lover and now was an inadequate mother. Her screams during labour were adequate proof, the Boss told Lara later, if indeed proof was needed, that a man's place during childbirth is in his club. Those men, who insisted in 'sharing the experience' with their wives, he tended to write off as 'Afterbirth Bores'.

On this occasion we walked across to one of the game belts to discuss the drives for the following week with Jack. For this was to be the last shoot of the season at home and the Boss had invited down Buff Mainwaring, my chum from the Cavalry and Guards club. By the time that we came back at lunch time, it was all over, Flicka and Terri were both exhausted and I was a daddy six times over! Not that I could stand the little buggers, mark you, who were mercifully confined to the loose box, little walks apart, for their eight-week stay. There was, needless to say, one exception. Lara had been over on the day after the birth to chose her puppy. Her choice made (a dog), the Boss promptly named it Buraq, an Arabic moniker such as I, and indeed my late uncle, bear.

To me the little runt will always be 'Sonny'. True, Lara took him away with her after a couple of months, but since she seems to be spending an increasing amount of time over here, and since she has become as fond of him as I am of the Boss, everywhere that Lara goes, so does Sonny. He is now over a year old, but still chews my ruff when he comes over and still has that irritating 'Da-ad!' whine. Every time I see him I am reminded of his late mother and of that vastly overrated and highly embarrassing performance under the apple-tree. 'For as you sow, ye are to reap' as the Vicar said in church the other day (we are tolerated providing that we sit towards the back). Indeed!"

His proximity to the tree clearly brought back unhappy memories to Kaid, who now moved to the office and lay down on the cool flags.

"We will now come to the incident to which I alluded earlier, namely my deed of such bravery that I appeared on prime-time television and in all of the national papers. I saved the life of a pop star's son! Not that I had a clue as to who he was at the time, but this is what happened.

It was a pretty miserable Sunday afternoon a couple of months ago, nevertheless the Boss and I went for our daily walk around the estate. We don't walk round the whole estate on the same day, of course, but he likes to ring the changes, and uses it as an opportunity to check his fences and things. We had crossed into Cowarth Mead, which is fairly wet at that time of year and is anyway bordered by the Thames on the far side. By habit, I usually run over to the towpath to see if there

is the odd swan to sharpen up, but on this occasion there was nothing, just some small cabin cruiser disappearing downstream. So I trotted along the path, keeping an eye on the Boss who was walking up the fence between the Mead and the next field away from the river, when I realised that something was wrong.

My hackles rose and all of my senses went onto full alert. Then I felt, as much as heard, that some living thing was in trouble nearby. By instinct I raced to an old willow upstream that was more in the river than on the bank; there was a small child in a yellow flotation vest, like many river users wear, clinging with one hand to a root in the fast-flowing river and looking blue with cold. No, I didn't dive in, pick up the child in my mouth and leap, porpoise-like, back onto the bank, as the *Sunday Sport* apparently later suggested. What I did do was to race up and down the bank by the tree, barking furiously.

The Boss knows that I don't bark capriciously so, seeing my performance now, he ran over and took in what was the problem. Now I am not denigrating the part that the Boss took in this rescue or anything — indeed he had to lower himself down the bank and, immersed to the waist, work his way round the exposed roots until he could grab the child's collar. He then had to pull himself and the child up the bank. By this stage the child was unconscious, so he had to wrap it in his Barbour and start to carry it the quarter of a mile back to the Hall. But it was me who found the child in the first place.

Luckily Terri, who had been feeding the young stock out in the neighbouring field from the Land Rover, realised that something was up and drove over. So back at home the redoubtable Mrs Kerr took charge. She stripped off the child (it appeared to be a boy) and with the application of some vigorous towelling in front of the Aga in the kitchen, and some hot milk once the little chap started coming to, everything seemed to be in hand. The Boss, who had removed his own sodden lower clothing and had wrapped himself in a towel, was having a hard time with the police. No child had yet been reported as missing, and because our foundling was firstly alive, and secondly as yet of no name, they were not that interested.

The Boss returned to the kitchen to find Mrs Kerr, and Terri who had stayed to help, feeding a much revived victim ginger biscuits, and more hot milk to which she had added a tot of cooking brandy. His name, they told him, was something like 'Cat Trust'. When he telephoned the Witney duty officer again to tell him the boy's name, the world seemed to go a little mad. Twenty minutes later a police car arrived at speed, and a distraught and weeping blonde in leggings and a fur coat, together with a female police sergeant, swept into the house and removed Cat, woolly towel and all, without so much as a word of thanks. The boy just managed to say: 'Bye Kide!' and they were off. Half an hour later the telephone started ringing, and hardly stopped for the rest of the evening. Our rescuee was Cat Thrust, only son of the veteran rock star Lance Thrust who was still lead guitarist with the group 'Rock and the Hard Place' who were currently on tour in the North. The Press were onto the scent!

At about 11 o'clock, past my bedtime, I watched from the library windows as a long, black American-style limmo drove up and the great man himself climbed out of the back. The Boss let him in, introduced himself and offered the living legend a drink. Lance settled for neat whiskey and proceeded to sink the half-tumbler that he was given in quick time. He was a small man, icy calm and smoking a huge cigar.

'Mate,' he said, looking the Boss straight in the eye, 'I won't waste our time. Besides, I want to get back to Cat. He has been ordered to bed for a few days by our Medic. Mandy is a bit, ah, upset, too.'

'You and your mutt (I suppose that he meant me) have saved the one person in this world who really means something to me,' he added. 'I owe you one. Always remember that, and call me if there is ever anything that I can do for you.'

He turned to go, adding as an afterthought that if the Press became too bad on the following day, he would send over a couple of his boys to help keep order. And so to bed. It had been a long day for us all.

Monday was pretty frantic, too. Correctly anticipating a lot of media interest, the Boss laid on some hot soup, beer and sandwiches in the forage barn. (The soup was kept hot in the feed boiler, which was ideal for the purpose.) This went down well with the press, a few of whom had been down before Christmas last year when Prince Charles had come to our meet. Of course, they all wanted my photograph, especially as Cat was confined to bed and so could not be present. Also Mrs Kerr, apple-cheeked and homely, was pictured before her Aga ('The little mite was like a block of ice when the Captain brought him in,'). Terri also got in on the act, being taken at the wheel of the Land Rover as she had been during the critical dash across the fields.

The photographers were a little disappointed by the actual site of the rescue, so moved downstream to where the banks were even steeper and the water swirled and eddied in a more convincing way to suit their purpose. The Boss told Lara (whom else?) later that it was lucky that Cat couldn't be there, as they would probably have demanded a re-enactment of the drama. The television crews, both from the BBC and Central News, came around lunch time, so I showed off a bit by running at full speed into the pond and out again. And that, really, was about that. I like Lara, who I think is good for the Boss, but I was glad that she was away working and didn't arrive until later on, as that idiot Sonny would otherwise have tried to muscle in on the act. As it was, I was on two channels that evening and was pictured in most of the tabloids on Tuesday."

Remembering the attractive images of himself both on television and in print motivated Kaid to attend to his personal toilette. He concentrated on a manicure of his fore-paws.

"Gratifying really. All of that, as I said, was about two months ago. *Hello!* magazine interest followed, and there was some talk about being nominated for the Dog of the Year award, but at the moment I am resting on my laurels. Eat your heart out, Lassie, I'm for real!"

Chapter 2

DAVID

"I suppose that I really need my head examining, and I am certain that my grandfather will be turning in his grave. Stanton Harcourt, my agent and my friend, has just persuaded me to stand for parliament on an Independent ticket. His reasoning is positively Byzantine and goes something like this. Reggie Token, one of the few remaining knights of the shires and our local MP, is dying. Though his detractors might say that he has been brain-dead for some decades, he has always been returned by the voters in the Vale of Evenlode with a comfortable majority, because he is sound on such matters as agriculture, defence and hunting.

Stan, with his peculiar Fifties-style haircut (I call it the Brylcream look), has always been a bit of a political animal, but prefers to work behind the scenes on behalf of the Conservatives. Thus he is kept well informed on dear old Reggie's progress, or regress, in the Intensive Care ward at the John Radcliffe by one of the few doctors (in this case, being Stan, a lady doctor) left in the country who support the Tory party. The prognosis, he is told, is downhill all the way, so the prospect of a by-election is looming up. The local party have Perry d'Artois, a near neighbour of mine, lined up. Another knight of the shires (in his case a baronet), a former Lord Lieutenant of the county and another, if a bit long in the tooth, who is unwavering about the things that matter to the Vale.

But Stan has another female contact, this time in Central Office in Smith Square, who tells him that the local party are to be foisted with a candidate on dogmatic grounds. Norman Livkin, although reducing the swing to Labour in a spectacular way in a north London constituency in the 1992 election, is so unsuited to the Vale as to risk losing it, most probably to the Liberal Democrats. Party HQ obviously can't announce their plans while there is still breath left in poor Reggie, but once he has gone, they are liable to call a by-election at fairly short notice in an effort to safeguard their wafer-thin overall majority of three seats.

Stan's reasoning, although he is a little short on names, is that he has taken soundings with the 'people who matter' in the constituency, and that they are prepared to back a local independent candidate, who in turn would be expected to follow the party line, in order to keep the Tories in power for the remaining two years of their term. The alternative, as they all saw it, would be to risk losing the seat to the opposition and for a possible Dissolution of Parliament. With much of their legislation yet to be seen to be bearing fruit, the government dare not go to the country in mid-term without risking a humiliating defeat.

Stan is fully aware that my interest in politics is microscopic — indeed though a traditional Tory voter, the only reason that I supported them last time around was as the lesser of the other evils on offer. I have also made it clear to him that I am not prepared to stand as an Independent Conservative against Livkin, but will fight for my own party (whatever we decide to call it) and on my own ticket. For his part he has told me that I will be able to count on financial support from his 'names' in order to fight the established parties in what will be probably no more than a four-week campaign. Since the basic upper limit for a by-election is £18,572, with a *per capita* rate of around 20 pence per elector, this is something of a relief. Short of selling the family silver, with the alimony that I am obliged to pay Veronica, no way have I got that sort of money sitting idly around."

He glanced out onto the lawn where Kaid, who had earlier been playing with his teddy bear, was panting in the heat. Lara had been over on the previous evening and had inevitably brought Sonny, hence Kaid was still sulking.

"I suppose that I am quite well known in the area, though it is not for me to say if I am well liked enough for people to vote for me. I was born at Windrush Hall, my home, as were my father and grandfather before me. I have an elder sister, Georgie, who is married to Dougal Ardkinglas, heir to a large slice of Scotland which is largely inhabited by red deer and assorted game birds. Looking back on it, we must have had an idyllic childhood here with dogs, ponies and all of the estate's 3,000 acres in hand.

My father, whom I always think of by his ridiculous Christian name of Caspar, was born just in time for the Second World War. Enlisting in the King's Lancers, a regiment in which we Vyvians traditionally shed our blood, Caspar had managed to keep most of his within his own skin. With the regiment, he had gone to France as part of the British Expeditionary Force. Come Dunkirk, the regiment was selected for evacuation and Caspar was back at the bar of the Cavalry Club with his war stories while most of the BEF were still up to their armpits in the sea awaiting the little ships.

His luck held in the desert, too. Far out on the left flank of Montgomery's 8th Army at El Alamein, C Squadron, of which he was now Second-in-Command, breached the minefields, with Sapper help, in record time and so captured an embarrassing amount of Italians. Back in Cairo at Shepheard's Hotel it was once more Caspar, still in his sweaty and dusty khaki drill shirt, slacks and worn desert boots, who was being stood drinks by envious men who had yet to 'get their knees brown'.

From there the regiment went back to England to prepare for the eventual invasion of Europe. There was some gossip, I heard much later, about Caspar and the colonel's wife which probably cost him a DSO in the advance to the Rhine after the Normandy landings. Caspar, by now a major and commanding his squadron, handled his command in much the same way as he was later to handle the Bladon when he was amateur huntsman to the pack in the Fifties. He had to be content with a more humble Mention in Despatches. Eventually reaching Berlin soon after VE Day, Caspar had a sybaritic time in the battered capital before being discharged some eighteen months later.

He then moved back home to run the estate — my grandfather had died from pneumonia during the war after a night exercise with the Home Guard — and married Mary, my mother and apparently a great beauty in her youth, a few years later. Both of them were enthusiastic riders and keen supporters of the Bladon, the local hunt. Caspar, as I mentioned earlier, hunted the hounds himself and was a joint master for a time when I was very young, but he soon found the commitment of three days a week was at the expense of his shooting. It naturally followed that both Georgie and I hunted from an early age and were both wearing the Hunt Button by the time that we left school.

I have never regarded my school days as the happiest period of my life, though I have fond memories of them. The fondest of them all was the crush that I had on Joanna, the teenage daughter of my tutor at Eton. She was my first love, and although our relationship was largely confined to chaste embraces when she came home at weekends, the situation was misunderstood by her father who became positively Victorian. I can still remember the feel of her smooth young skin, the taste of her kisses, and her wonderful long legs, but I digress.

Although National Service had ended while I was in my last year at Eton, it had always been accepted that I would join the King's Lancers when I left. There was no talk of any 'gap' year in those days, so it was off to Sandhurst for the following term. Mercifully, the course for would-be regular officers had recently been shortened from two years to one. I passed out without mishap, apart from some slight bother with the Military Police after a party in Aldershot, and after Special to Arm training at the Royal Armoured Corps' centre in Dorset, joined my regiment at Tidworth.

In the end, I only served for twelve years, but can say with all honesty that I enjoyed every minute of it. While we were at Tidworth we had to send a squadron to Cyprus as part of the United Nations' Force for six months, and the squadron which went was the one in which I was a troop leader. The Turks had recently invaded the northern half of the island, so, together with Danes, Austrians and Swedes, we had a fairly busy time in keeping the Turkish Cypriots and the Greek Cypriots apart. The British garrison forces, largely RAF, were really surprisingly hospitable — or perhaps it was our blue berets that turned their women on — so it was hardly a punishment posting.

Again, when we converted from the armoured reconnaissance role to that of armour and moved to the Rhine

Army, the monotony of driving around the same limited training areas was relieved by an emergency tour, as motorised infantry, in Ulster. We were lucky not to lose any soldiers to the mines that were constantly being detonated by remote control in the path of our vehicles. None of the joys of Cyprus here, but the constant danger certainly concentrated the mind.

I also found early on that the King's Lancers were a polo regiment. Other cavalry regiments concentrated on racing and some, like the Household Cavalry, ran their own pack of hounds. Caspar, ever indulgent to a son who was following in the family footsteps, financed me to the extent of three very reasonable ponies, and my ability to ride, coupled with a good eye for a ball, saw me playing off a three-goal handicap by the time that I was 25.

I was picked for an army polo team to visit Rajasthan where we were looked after like kings! (no nautch-girls, alas!) It was there that I struck up a friendship with Mirza Sind, who is currently based in London and working for BBC television as a freelance reporter. He came down for lunch the other day, largely to see Kaid whom he adores. He was quite amusing about being asked to commentate at the Ham polo club. Being an educated Indian, his accent is flawless, rather better than those of most of my friends.

In the early Eighties I went to the Ministry of Defence for a two-year stint. Although a trifle old for the deb circuit, quite a few friends from school and indeed from the Army were in London, so the time passed quickly. This was hardly convenient though for polo at Tidworth, so I kept my ponies at Windsor and played at the Guards polo club for two seasons. At the start of the second season Ronald Ferguson, who was then polo manager to the Prince of Wales, invited me to play with the Prince's Windsor Park team for the low-goal Archie David cup. We didn't get as far as the final, but had a good crack at it. Nor did it in any way justify the tag later given to me by the gossip columns of 'Polo-playing friend of Prince Charles'. 'Good afternoon, David' and 'Good afternoon, Sir' were about as far as we got.

Mother had died in 1980, having broken her neck out hunting with the Bladon. This was quite an achievement in itself, as the Bladon is not a very demanding country, the majority of the obstacles being either straightforward post-and-rail fences or, down in the Vale, drainage ditches. Anyway, in driving sleet and with a certain amount of bone in the ground, she elected to take on about the only combination of both types of obstacles in the entire Saturday country, pecked on the timber and crashed into the far bank of the ditch beyond. I flew back from Germany for the funeral, as did Georgie and Dougal from Scotland.

John Crispin went rather over the top, what with having 'Gone away!' blown over the grave and telling everyone that 'she had gone as she would have wished'. That I rather doubted, as Mother was only in her fifties, in good health and enjoying a very happy marriage with Caspar. Besides, being a generous woman, she would certainly not have wanted the Saturday field to have been deprived of what promised to have been a good run by John ordering his huntsman to blow for home, which he felt obliged so to do in the circumstances. The little medieval church of St Leonhart was freezing cold and it was snowing during the interment, so Georgie and I took Caspar home as soon as we decently could. He had, of course, to follow the ritual of inviting the mourners back to the Hall for a drink. I like to think that Mother was somewhere around, no doubt having a chuckle at all of her hunting friends snivelling into their sherry.

Georgie and I were both very sad at Mother's death, perhaps I most of all as, being still single, I tended to spend my leave at home as often as not; Georgie, with a young family at foot, saw her less often on her rare visits south of the border. The one who was most cut up of us all was Caspar. Although I had gathered that he had quite a reputation as a young man, I believe that he had been faithful to Mother during their marriage, as indeed had she to him. I went back to Germany after the funeral, and Georgie went back to Scotland, but we soon started to hear reports from friends that Caspar was really burning the candle at both ends, with constant house parties at the Hall and a bewildering assortment of companions. It was as if he was frantically trying to recapture his one true love."

Kaid really was being a pain this morning, thought David. He had seen him peeing in the herb border and now he was panting on the stone flags in the office, looking at him accusingly, as if to say that he thought it time that his Boss went out to the stable yard. Giving in to the canine blackmail, he went out to the yard only to find Jack Kestrel chatting up Terri who, being of a very independent nature, was sweeping the yard in a dismissively brisk fashion. David returned to his office. He would see her later.

"I suppose it didn't come as a great surprise to any of us when Caspar had a stroke. I was on a course near Salisbury at the at the time, so drove over to the hospital that evening to see him. Luckily, it was not too bad, but from his rather shaken manner a week later, it was clear that the doctors had warned as to his future conduct, so to speak. He had, he told me, decided to retire to the South of France on medical advice, and was already negotiating to buy a comfortable villa in the foothills of the Alpes Maritimes between Valbonne and Grasse. It was time, he added, that I came home to manage my inheritance.

On a point of detail, grandfather, shortly before he died, had, perhaps rather wisely, tied up the Hall, all of the land and much of the family fortune in a family trust of such complexity that subsequent generations were mere custodians, rather than outright owners, of the estate. Caspar told me that he would naturally hold the fort while I handed in my papers, and also while I attended the year-long farming course at the Royal Agricultural College at Cirencester.

I was sorry to leave the Regiment of course; although they dined me out in traditional style, it was more especially galling as I had passed the promotion exam from captain to major. But I had realised all along that I had been living on borrowed time, and that sooner or later I would be called to carry out my duties at the Hall. Anyway, I formally resigned and within three months was learning at Cirencester about the ph values in the soil and the precautions to be taken with sheep-dip. It was at this stage that I decided to give up polo, tempting as it was to have one last season at the Cirencester Park polo club. Without the subsidies that I had enjoyed as a serving officer, and with the expenses anyway of hunting, one of them had to go.

All too soon my year was up and, brimming with new ideas, I came home. I was glad to see that Caspar had steadied down somewhat, and he had acquired a French woman of about my own age. I didn't resent Yvette in any way, not that I saw all that much of her since they left for France about three weeks later. She had enormous brown eyes, long flowing black hair and a tiny waist. In different circumstances I could have quite fancied her myself. She seems to be splendid for Caspar and is still with him, some five years on. She is also a brilliant cook, and her lobster thermidor is a gastronomic triumph. Unfortunately Veronica couldn't stand her (it was mutual) so I really didn't see much of them during my three years of marriage.

I suppose that I was now very lonely for the first time in my life. Hitherto there had been my parents and my sister at home, then Eton, Sandhurst and the Regiment. Even Cirencester had been quite social, but now I was on my own. The days were busy enough with the farm, as I battled with Stan, who had done the full Cirencester three-year course about fifteen years before I had done my crash course. Not that he wasn't progressive or anything, but he had experienced the practical problems involved in the past over implementing some of Cirencester's new ideas. But the nights were lonely. My twelve years away had left me with few close friends locally and, to be frank, I became a little fed up with being invited to dinner parties or the odd dance as a spare man. I drove up to London from time to time to let off steam, but that meant that I would stay up at the club (or elsewhere if I got lucky!) and not be functioning again at home much before midday.

Then Stan persuaded me to join a party that he was getting up for the Bladon hunt ball. Like the annual point-to-point, the hunt ball is a major source of revenue for any hunt and is attended by many people from outside the country of the particular pack. On this occasion is was held to be Perry's turn to stage the event, so after a good dinner given by Stan in Oxford's Randolph Hotel, we drove out to d'Artois Court where Perry and Maris — we call her Stella behind her back — were greeting the guests.

It was there that I met Veronica, the friend of a friend. Even now I will give her that she was attractive, sophisticated and could be very funny. She had red hair, red lips and a figure that would have been a joy to Rubens. Her stockbroker father, and her mother, lived near Weybridge in Surrey, though she, so she told me, worked in London for an advertising agency. She appeared to have no particular boyfriend in tow, and at the end of the evening I had arranged to see her in London two days later. After what I believe could be described as a whirlwind courtship, we were married within six months in London. Thereafter it was downhill all the way, and three years later we were divorced.

I feel no guilt about it, though I suppose that I was wildly over-optimistic in my expectations. For at heart she was a townie, and as such soon found that life at Windrush Hall, my hunting and shooting friends and the worthy inhabitants of the Vale of Evenlode too provincial for her cosmopolitan tastes. She promptly acquired two cats, to the dismay of my part-time keeper, Jack, and of Sidi, Caspar's old deerhound, who was banished to the stables; the enthusiasm that she had shown in bed during our engagement seemed to diminish after our marriage; and her occasional day trips to London soon became overnight stays with, she said, a variety of bachelor girlfriends.

Soon my friends, doubtless meaning well, started to hint to me that Veronica was being rather free with her favours in Kensington and Belgravia, and *Private Eye* started to refer to her as the 'fun-loving Veronica Vyvian'. No man can enjoy wearing the cuckold's horns, with the inevitable suggestion that he is failing to satisfy his woman, and so I went to see my lawyers. In a final effort to save our marriage, I confronted Veronica with the evidence that they eventually provided.

She appeared not too surprised and told me that the only way that she saw our marriage surviving was for me to sell up and to buy some large house, say, on Sunningdale's Wentworth Estate. Again, it was probably my fault that she had not fully appreciated the nature of the family trust. When I pointed out that there was no way could I ever sell Windrush nor, more to the point, could she ever have a legal claim to it, she went ballistic. (She had been a bit off colour anyway, as I suspect that a rat had died under the floorboards of what she called her boudoir. It smelled!) She stormed out of the house and, lawyers and the eventual divorce hearing apart, out of my life. As it was, out of some mistaken sense of chivalry, I allowed her to divorce me and I was stuck with alimony anyway. Thank God there were no children. At least the cats were gone, together with the fancy bed that she had bought from some London designer friend. Also, poor old Sidi came back to his rightful place in the library.

Then I acquired Kaid. We had dogs at home when I was young, of course, but Kaid was the first dog that was truly my own. He was disobedient as a puppy, naturally, and still is now for that matter, and I am not really sure that he can understand more than a few simple commands. He does sense my moods to an extent and as such is of great comfort to me when I am feeling low. Although I don't take him to dances, and we are talking here about perhaps two a year, one of which is a hunt ball, he comes everywhere else with me. At local branch meetings of the National Farmers' Union and the Country Landowners' Association he lies quietly in a corner, fixing me with an unblinking stare. He also is a great favourite at the fortnightly meetings of the Evenlode Brigade, which requires some explanation.

One of Perry d'Artois's forebears was so sickened by the lack of aftercare for locally enlisted men who were wounded at Waterloo that he donated a large sum of money to found a charity. Named the Evenlode Brigade, it was to be for the benefit of any man who had seen Army Service and who lived in the Vale of Evenlode. Women soldiers, and indeed the Royal Air Force, were not envisaged by the founder, and Royal Naval personnel were discounted anyway, having taken no part at Waterloo. I had been a bit diffident about joining the organisation, with my modest two campaign medals, as most of the members were veterans of the Second World War, but Perry, who was a trustee, had been most insistent.

The charity had survived attempts by the Royal British Legion to take it over and, although the cases of genuine hardship had lessened with the advent of the Welfare State, it flourished as a subsidised fortnightly drinking club for former soldiers. I, together with Kaid, resplendent with his King's Lancers' cap-badge on his collar, would try to look in at least once a month. I think that the old soldiers were more pleased to see Kaid than they were to see me!

Kaid also came with me to local dinner parties, to the annoyance of some hostesses, though I drew the line at taking him to London after nearly losing him once in Mayfair. Luckily that old rake 'Buff' Mainwaring, who had just slipped out of the club for a carnal encounter with Pearl, whom I can honestly say I have not met for a few years now, spotted him.

Then came the filming of the coffee commercial by Clyne Films, enlivened by Kaid making off with one of the props during their lunch break. I had just returned from my own lunch at the Hall (jugged hare, apple pie and a glass or two of claret) prepared by the excellent Mrs Kerr when I saw a girl from the film crew climbing in with the cows. What followed was a little embarrassing; she had noticed, and I had not, that one of the cows was in trouble calving. She also proved rather more adept in dealing with the problem, Cirencester not withstanding, than me, but together we delivered the calf. I took her back to the Hall to clean up afterwards, and she turned out to be Lara Graham, the daughter of a chum of Caspar who lived at the other end of the Vale. She was working as the personal assistant to the producer of Clyne Films. It so happens that Lara has turned out to be the best thing that has happened to me in my life, but I am getting ahead of myself

Mrs Kerr, antennae twitching, produced some tea after Lara had been upstairs (it seemed that Robert Summer, the producer, was fairly happy on his own once shooting had started) and she started admiring Kaid. The thought of breeding from him had not crossed my mind, to be honest, as long dogs are notoriously shy about that sort of thing, but yes, I said, I had been thinking of the idea, when she brought the subject up.

I saw her occasionally over the summer, though with her hectic filming schedule and early starts it was normally at weekends or on the few days when Robert was between films. Commercials for television were his bread and butter, and usually involved two days' work, but when he produced a feature film, he could be involved for weeks at a time. Lara was

26

ten years younger than me and, thank God, had very little in common with Veronica.

She was fair, above average height and had almost classical features, though tinged with more than a touch of Slav. She was serious and thoughtful, where Veronica had been shallow, and was, as I later found out, passionate where my former wife had been, well, a trifle frigid. Lara had hunted with the Bladon as a child, but after University abroad had gone to work full-time, so now only hunted when offered a horse. This suited me, as having two hunters up during the season for perhaps three half-days a fortnight was rather a luxury. So she eventually more or less took over Tanya, my second hunter and a mare with an incredible jump in her.

We rode out together when time allowed in the autumn and went cubbing with the Bladon a few times. Lara was also out at the lawn meet the following season that we traditionally held at the Hall in mid-November. John Crispin, the master, telephoned on the previous evening to warn me that Prince Charles intended to come out with us and, unusually in that he normally joined at the first draw, to be at the meet as well.

I still believe that it was John himself who tipped off the press photographers, despite his vehement denials later on. A public footpath crosses the field below the Hall, so the half dozen gentlemen with the long lenses had a perfect right to be there. John went through the motions of rage, puce in the face and handling his hunting whip aggressively, and the Prince looked a trifle put out, but it was Lara who saved the day. Terri, pork-pie hat at a jaunty angle, Mrs Kerr, who was, as ever tut-tutting and a bit flustered by the Royal Presence, and the ubiquitous Jack were handing around glasses of shooting port and fruit cake to the mounted field. Lara, whom I had earlier introduced to the Prince — he had presumably been briefed that his host was me — diverted Terri towards the photographers. Terri plied them with food, drink and her ready wit for the duration of the meet, so much so that such coverage that appeared in the tabloids on the following day was muted and quite friendly.

When Lara had come over once during the previous winter, we had driven over to Maidenhead where a friend had a greyhound bitch for me to collect. Flicka was off the track, now only of use for breeding which in my case meant for Kaid. Although, come the early spring, it led to Lara ending up with Buraq, one of the litter of six, I don't think that either Kaid or Flicka enjoyed any aspect of the whole performance. He didn't have a clue what to do and she was extremely unenthusiastic from the start. I left it all to Terri to sort out, including the eventual whelping down, but I don't think that either dog thanked me for it."

'Too bloody right we didn't,' thought Kaid, still lying on the cool flagstones. He had been reminded of the whole hideously embarrassing performance only the night before by the presence of the dreadful Sonny. Although he became confused when the Boss started an abstract line, he could normally follow his thoughts quite easily.

"I must admit at this point that Lara and I did not became lovers until the second winter, nearly two years after we had first met. Both of us had been hurt in the past, so certainly weren't seeking any involvement or commitment in a hurry. Moreover, she is a devout but pragmatic Roman Catholic (her mother came from Slovenia), a new experience for me which I didn't quite know how to handle. Neither of us had anyone else in our lives, and eventually it just, well, happened. Lara had stayed over for supper one evening after hunting. She had told me that she was doing location work nearby on the following morning, so I lightly suggested, since it was late, that it would make more sense to stay here, rather than to go to her parents or back to her basement flat in London. She agreed, and that was that. Later on, she told me that she thought making love was a form of sacrament. I think I can understand what she meant .

Lara had left for London that fateful Sunday about a couple of months ago when Kaid and I rescued the child from the river. We were walking in Cowarth Mead. He was over by the Thames towpath and I was checking the fences on the other side of the field, when he started barking in a most frenzied way at something in the river. I had seen a river cruiser going down-stream earlier, but had thought nothing of it. Now, when I arrived on the bank, there was this small child who had been swept into the bank and was holding on to a willow root. It had a sort of lifejacket on, but candidly, with no one else about and with the river running quite high and cold, wouldn't have lasted that long. As it was, it was only with some difficulty that I managed to get the child (it was a boy, as we discovered later) out, and thank God, Terri, who had been feeding hay to the young stock from the Land Rover in the next field, saw that something was up. She drove us back home where I left the boy in Mrs Kerr's capable hands and telephoned the police.

Quite frankly they treated the whole business as a non-event until, later on, we managed to find out that the boy's name was Trust, or something similar. Thereafter the sky fell in. I had heard of Lance Thrust and his group, Rock and the Hard Place, indeed they had been around for almost as long as I had. We seemed to have fished his only son, Cat, out of the water. First his mother, Mandy, slightly hysterical and her face streaked with mascara, arrived in a police car and removed the boy, without much thanks I may say. Then the press were on the telephone, tipped off no doubt by the police. Luckily, it was near their deadline for a Sunday evening, so that didn't last too long, before the pop star himself arrived. Born Neil Carter in Liverpool, he was one of Merseyside's success stories in the rock and roll world and, it turned out, one hell of a nice guy.

He was on tour in the north and had left his wife (his third), small son Cat and minders at home near Abingdon. Mandy had told a minder to take Cat out on the river, so he had hired a boat at Oxford, driven upstream for a while, then turned back for the boat station. Cat had fallen over the stern on the return trip and the minder, happily smoking a joint and with the headset of his Walkman firmly in place, hadn't noticed his loss for a time. He had then panicked, and instead of retracing his route, had driven on.

Lance had already been home, sacked the minder and let Mandy have the sharp side of his tongue. Now he had taken the trouble to come over there and then to thank Kaid and me. He swallowed a quick drink, warned me what to expect the next day from the media, and was on his way. I gave Lara a call at her flat, and she said that she would try to get away from filming as soon as possible on the following day.

Monday was chaos. Luckily, it did not suit the tabloids to have a landed Old Etonian as a hero, so Kaid was built up to be the star of the story, with Terri, Mrs Kerr, and Lara, when she turned up at around midday, as the supporting cast. We had a glimpse of the headlines from Jeremy Paxman on *Newsnight*, then on Tuesday Jack was sent out to buy all the papers. Kaid was in every one of them. 'Dog saves Cat' proclaimed the *Daily Mirror*, while 'Gotcha!' was the *Sun's* contribution, a repeat from the time of the sinking of the *General Belgrano* in 1982. *The Daily Telegraph's* Peterborough column, which had run a piece 'War Hero arrests Kerb-crawling Canine' at the time of Kaid's absence in Mayfair nearly two years before, ran a follow-up on the lines of 'Piccadilly Pooch turns Lifeguard'.

Lara, whose picture appeared a few times because she is so very beautiful, was variously described as a family friend, and once as my fiancée. Hmm. Food for thought, there. And now I appear to be going into politics! *Ex Oxfordshire semper aliquid novi*, to misquote Pliny."

Chapter 3

LARA

'Ave Maria, gratia plena, Dominus tecum, benedicta tu in mulieribus . . .' Automatically Lara, having narrowly missed some lunatic man in a Montego who had cut in on her, mumbled a quick Hail Mary.

She was driving, fortunately well ahead of the rush-hour, in her white BMW cabriolet, to Sunningdale, where Clyne Films were due to shoot a toothpaste commercial. The talented locations manager had apparently found a perfectly shaped oak, which was to signify the importance of caring for the roots of viewers' teeth, so his reasoning went. She left the M40 at High Wycombe, drove down past Marlow and through Maidenhead Thicket, thence through Holyport and Winkfield Row, towards Sunningdale, or the 'Cocktail Belt', as David described it.

Buraq sat smugly on his rug on the back seat with what Lara called his pink 'comfort teddy'. He was now a seasoned traveller, having been prone to car-sickness in early days.

"I really do not trust Stanton Harcourt. I know that he has been giving David good advice over diversification in his agricultural enterprises at Windrush, as he did to Caspar Vyvian. I also know that Stan, who made a vague pass at me, part of his act I suppose, when David and I first got together, has been seeing Veronica from time to time. He would naturally have met her when she and David were married, and since he is single, and she is divorced, there is no reason why not. He hasn't told David, and since my information, though reliable, is second-hand, it remains his secret.

It is this political thing which sets my alarm bells going. I love David with all my heart, body and soul, and he is crammed full of virtues, but political awareness is not one of them. Stan, who has failed in the past on several occasions to get even onto the District Council on a Conservative ticket, has somehow convinced my darling that he should stand as an Independent in the forthcoming by-election in the Vale. This is sure to follow the imminent demise of Sir Reggie Token, the current MP, who is, I gather, breathing his last in the John Radcliffe.

We talked about it far into last night, and David is convinced, by the persuasive Stan, with his stupid greasy hair-style, that he will be doing the right thing by the local people if he allows his name to go forward. Thus I can only support him as much as I can, and hope that he doesn't get his fingers burned.

It all seems a far cry from my childhood. Why Lara? *Doctor Zhivago* was on release at the Army cinema when Mummy was carrying me and Lara's theme rather got to her. It is usually shown on television around Christmas and watching it has become part of the festive ritual. In fact I rather like watching old films on the video. I tease David that he looks like a mixture of a young Richard Burton and a young Stewart Granger, which always is good for a rise.

My father, Simon Graham, was a Lieutenant Colonel in the Green Jackets. He had picked up an OBE when commanding his battalion in the Malayan Emergency, but didn't receive good enough reports to hold out much hope for a further field command. He found himself in due course as Military Attaché to the British Embassy in Belgrade, then the capital of Tito's Yugoslavia. Poor Daddy! He used to joke that he held the record for being the slowest officer ever to pick up the necessary basic Serbo-Croat. He met my Slovene mother, Ilona, at some embassy function, and after a great deal of difficulty, they were married in England before he was posted to the Rhine Army in 1964. I followed a year later, being born at the British Military Hospital, Rinteln.

Daddy's marriage to a woman whose nation, though not Communist, had been perhaps a little too enthusiastic in their support of the Third Reich, cost him his Positive Vetting with MI5; so he had to be content for the remainder of his service with non-sensitive Staff jobs within the Ministry of Defence. So my first memories are of being pushed in a pram around the Round Pond in Kensington Gardens. Although a Yugoslav by birth, Mummy's family were more Austrian (or Habsburg, as she put it) than anything else, so I grew up reasonably fluent in

German and Slovene with a smattering of Italian, though English was obviously my first language. Although I was an only child (unspecified complications surrounded my birth) I have memories of a very jolly kindergarten in Kensington near to Mummy and Daddy's small terraced house, and of children's tea-parties.

Later, I was enrolled in the *Lycée Français Charles de Gaulle* in the Cromwell Road, where I stayed for the next thirteen years. This really was the most magnificent school for me, being of a fairly complicated ethnic mix anyway. During my time there were children from some sixty-five different countries represented, quite a few of whom were English, but most came from the large amount of expatriate diplomatic or commercial families living in or near London. Apart from a very good education, it meant two further languages for me (Latin and French) neither of which presented any problem.

When I was about seven, I received my First Holy Communion. Since Mummy was a Roman Catholic, Daddy had agreed with good grace on marriage that any children (in the event, only me) would be raised in the faith. We were in the majority at the Lycée anyway, so there were quite a few of us that attended the service at the French church of Notre Dame off Leicester Square. Mummy has a picture of me somewhere at home which was taken at the time. We girls all looked rather sweet, clutching our rosaries and candles, and clad in white dresses with garlands of marguerites in our hair.

I remember that I found the whole experience immensely moving. I almost fainted at one point, due to nearly being overpowered by the clouds of incense, and a couple of Venetian girls actually did, but us Slovenes are made of sterner stuff! This, and my Confirmation (by Cardinal Hume, no less) four years later have been a great strength to me in later years when things went wrong. I don't make a big deal out of it, but I go to Mass, and even to Confession, from time to time. Nonetheless it is my personal belief that we all, including heretics and even heathens, have a direct line to Him when we need to call. Mummy, who instilled in me the pragmatic approach to the Holy Father's teachings, demonstrated this in a practical way by giving me advice about the pill before I went to University.

Daddy left the Army when I was about thirteen, and bought a small farm down in the Vale of Evenlode, in Oxfordshire. So I stayed with his unmarried sister, Virginia, who lived in decaying splendour in Elizabeth Street, next to the Victoria bus station. This was not ideal, in that I only saw my parents at weekends and in the holidays, but Aunt Virginia was very kind. I had the whole of the basement to myself which was great. Besides, by now I had a whole host of friends of my own age, and London then appeared to be much safer for the young than it is today.

I really prefer the country to London, so the farm made a pleasant break. Daddy had a fair amount of money of his own (slave trade in the last century, he would tell me, but I think that it was something more boring, like tea) so, together with his pension we were quite comfortable. He had an old cob, and I a sort of all-purpose pony, both of which lived out for most of the time, but carried us for the odd half-day if the Bladon met nearby. Mummy was far better with the stock, and started to breed some exotic pedigree cattle which, fortunately as it later turned out, proved to be a real money-spinner."

Lara arrived at the location and parked her car with those of such other members of the film-crew who had already arrived. Buraq, who by now had learned that the assistant director's cries of 'Action!' did not require his participation, trotted at her heels as she started to check as to who had turned up, and who was yet to come.

He was well behaved for routine work, but needed to be shut in the car should other animals be involved.

"When I was seventeen I was accepted, on my baccalaureate and my languages, to go to the University of Trieste in the following October. There seemed little point, in those circumstances, in staying on at the Lycée so I opted to go to Eton, not that I needed to really, for their so-called 'Oxbridge Half'. Eton had been already allowing the brighter daughters of existing assistant masters to attend their sixth form. They had now expanded this, only as it turned out briefly, to allow a few selected girls to attend their Michaelmas Half prior to going on to University. We lived out (this time it was a married cousin of Daddy who put me up in her home near Ascot) and had our own table in Bekynton, the cafeteria where about half of the school ate, for lunch. By now I had passed my driving test and had my own VW Beetle, so drove in by day.

They were some of the most enjoyable months of my life although, of course, totally artificial. We all had the feeling that we were being put on a pedestal and being placed under a microscope at the same time, For instance, whomever one was seen talking to, and whatever was allegedly said, would. regularly be reported in the *Eton Chronicle*. The academic work was really tough though, and as a break we played a little hockey amongst ourselves on the half-days.

One of our number, Carmen diaz Alberdi from Ecuador, was so stunning that the boys almost spread their morning-coats in her path as she walked by. A few others weren't up to the level of heavy teasing that the Etonians were constantly practising among each other, so dropped out. I made a great friend of Pippa Grace, whose New Zealander father ran an exotic polo school at the Guards Polo club the other side of Windsor. Because we were both unfazed by the 'mobbing up' and, as well as being attractive (so it seemed) to the boys and having our own cars, we both had a great time.

We were individually allowed, providing we gave notice, to have tea with the boys in their house Libraries, and to attend their house dinners which were rare occasions. The whole house would rise to its feet as any of us entered the Dining Room — quite an ego trip! Dinner in College, with all the silver on the long tables, and the portraits glaring down from the walls, was most spectacular. Some of us took part in the '83 Leavers' Play at the Farrer Theatre which, needless to say, got somewhat out of hand on the final evening. (A boy opened some of the champagne cider, intended for celebrations after the curtain had come down, before it had even been raised!) In all it was an unforgettable experience. David tells me that I am his favourite Old Etonienne!

After spending a white Christmas at home (the Boxing Day meet was frozen off, much to the chagrin of the Bladon's hunt secretary) I went off to Lech. A mixed group of us had fixed it up from Eton, and I had coerced some Lycée friends to come as well, so we took a chalet for a fortnight. I think that we all enjoyed it. Skiing apart, the evenings were wild though, in retrospect, there was no tremendous drunkenness, nor sex, the odd flirtation aside. To be honest, the thought of anything heavy with boys with whom we had recently been seated in the same lecture hall or class-room struck most of the girls as being a bit ridiculous.

Back at home, I felt that it was time for me to spread my wings and fly. To be sure, I would still be relying on an allowance from Daddy until I left University and found a job, and I still dearly loved Mummy and Daddy, as I believed they so loved me. But it was time to leave the nest. I had eight months to kill before Trieste, so planned to inflict myself on my grand-parents for a change.

March is not really the best time to see Scotland, where Grandpa and Granny Graham, he a Scot by birth, and she by marriage, live near Kings Muir, by Peebles. They were kind enough during the rather long week for which I had proposed myself, and made some effort in introducing me to their friends, but I fear that the Lycée and Eton were very different from life in the Borders. I am afraid that I upset them both by expressing a wish to go to Mass on the Sunday of my visit.

Then it was the turn of Granny Tavcar in Slovenia, then part of Yugoslavia. Grandpa, like all Slovenes, had backed the wrong horse in the Second World War, but had surrendered, together with his regiment, to the British in Carinthia during the closing days. They were all interned in reasonable comfort near Klagenfurt, together with various Cossacks and others in a similar predicament, while the Allies tried to work out what to do with them. There was some court case about it all a few years ago, but Tito and his Chetniks on the one hand, and Stalin and his butchers on the other, both demanded their nationals back. The British gave in, so neither Franzesca nor her small daughter, my mother Ilona, ever saw or heard from Josip again.

Granny, with whom I had stayed quite often during the holidays, had recently moved from her small and rather decrepit hunting lodge in the foothills of the Steiner Alpen to Kranj, or Krainburg as she would call it, remembering forgotten days when the area had been a Habsburg Dukedom for 600 years. After a lifetime of working her small cattle farm, admittedly with help from the village, she had decided to take it easy in the autumn of her life. As a result, she was bored to tears and welcomed her only grandchild into her modest house.

I had taken my faithful Beetle out with me, and as often as not Granny would accompany me on voyages (for me) of exploration around the beautiful countryside. I felt that I had, to an extent, found my roots. Nor was it any bad thing for me to return to a life of basic values after my rather hot-house upbringing. Though life in general had obviously improved dramatically in the forty-odd years since the end of the war, I could now understand how Mummy and Granny, with no man in the house, had led a life of bare subsistence in the late Forties and early Fifties. Granny also taught me such now largely forgotten skills of how to bake bread, make sheep's cheese and delicious sausages, and how to cure and smoke hams.

Kranj was fairly near to the Italian border, and indeed to my eventual destination of Trieste. I had never been to Rome, so I went there for a week (by train, on Granny's advice). I behaved like the straight-forward tourist that I suppose that I was. I stayed at a small hotel off the Via Veneto and went on practically every tour that was on offer. The catacombs, Villa D'Este, the coliseum, the forum and Mussolini's balcony were but a few of the sights that I crammed in. The most impressive of all, naturally, was a visit to the Vatican, and in particular to Saint Peter's, when the Holy Father, then as now Pope John Paul II, gave his weekly public audience. The most stupid thing that I did, it so turned out, was to toss a coin into the Trevi fountain.

Then in late summer Carmen, my fellow Old Etonienne, invited me for a cruise on her father's yacht around the Mediterranean. Papa diaz Alberdi held some sort of undefined job with the United Nations, and either he had discovered the alchemist's dream of turning base metal into gold, or he was very well paid indeed. He spent most of the summer on the yacht which, though not quite in the class of Aristotle Onassis's *Christina*, was not far off. I was quite happy to play second fiddle to Carmen, whether it was with the boys on board, or in the night-clubs ashore. She was such fun but, like me at that time, wasn't after any deep commitments, so flirted outrageously with the field. After three glorious weeks and with a superb tan, they dropped me off in Venice and it was back to Granny to prepare for University.

Trieste, in the Istrian peninsular, itself had been part of the Habsburg Empire since the 14th Century, only being ceded to the Italians in 1919. Further troubles at the end of the Second World War led to its occupation by Anglo-American forces until 1954 when it was returned to Italy. Thus the University only dated back to 1924. Unlike in British seats of higher learning, all of the students live out from the start. I was placed with three other girls in an apartment on the Via del Campanile, overlooking the Grand Canal."

Robert Summer had arrived on the set, together with the talented director, Bob Bierman. Although Clyne Films was Robert's company, he and Lara were the only regulars on the set, all of the remainder being recruited according to availability when the need arose.

Buraq, who had pee-ed on the front off-side tyre of his car as a standard form of greeting, rubbed against his legs.

Robert, who had lusted after Lara ever since he had first offered her a job, tolerated the dog: it fitted in with his image of Lara as Princess Daisy in Judith Krantz's novel of that name.

"I had enrolled in the faculty of Literature and Philosophy to read European History and Literature. Like other girls in my year, I developed a fantastic, though totally unrequited, passion for one of our professors, Claudio Magris. He was in the process of putting the finishing touches to his future best seller, *Danube*, so no detail was too tiny or too insignificant for us to research for the Master.

The racial mix made the Lycée look parochial, for as well as the largely European blend that I had encountered in the Cromwell Road, there were now Iranians, Libyans and a certain amount of Africans from Italy's former colonies. Even with hindsight, it must have been a mind-broadening experience for any girl. None of us was that well-off, and most months were divided into a fortnight of plenty, after the allowances or grants had come through, followed by a fortnight of lean days when the money was running out fast. After six semesters, I set my sights on my thesis, which was to be on the influence of Sigmund Freud on the novels of Stefan Zweig.

I suppose that I was Trilby to his Svengali, and the point where Luigi Montecuccoli and I met was certainly one of the milestones, and a painful one at that, in my life. We had all seen him around, of course, for Luigi drove a Ferrari, was obviously very rich and was the son of a Papal Count. This latter entitled him to call himself a count as well, which in fairness he didn't do while at Trieste. He was a few years older than most of his year and at first we couldn't work out what such an obvious playboy, though with a brilliant brain, was doing amongst us all.

He was in his last year and was in the process of completing a thesis on a comparison of the role of sexuality in the poetry of Baudelaire, Rimbaud and Swinburne. That should have warned me! He told me later that his intention was to go into politics, and in particular the neo-Fascist MSI party for whom Mussolini's grand-daughter, a former actress called Alessandra, was already active. Dottore il Conte Luigi di Montecuccoli would give him the credibility that the title on its own, so he thought, would not.

He really was fantastically beautiful, brown wavy hair, liquid eyes and sensuous lips that only partially concealed perfect teeth. He had a permanent tan, that I am afraid was due in part to his sun-bed, and a tremendous line in patter. Hardly surprisingly, girls lay down and rolled over, figuratively, in his path. He sailed and water-skied during the summer, when not flying down to Rome for a little polo, hunted with the Roman Fox Hounds, or with the drag near Milan in the autumn, and skied for most of the winter. When nightfall brought temporary suspension to his sporting activities, there was always some party of which he tended to be the pivot.

With hindsight, I suppose that I would have made life a lot easier for myself had I just succumbed to his charms, when he got round to making a pass at me, rather than trying to resist the irresistible force. But at the time I thought that he was too good to be true and besides, strange as it may seem, I was still *intacta* up until then. He wined me and he dined me and gave me pearls; we went skiing in the Spring and sailing in the summer, with occasional interruptions while he finished his

39

thesis. Then one hot, lazy afternoon we were drifting in his boat far off the Ligurian coast. We had taken with us a delicious lunch of Salade Niçoise, cheese and wild raspberries, together with a couple of bottles of cold, rough rosé.

I was amused to watch Luigi, who had deliberately held back on the Pont l'Evêque until he saw that I was having some myself, before helping himself to a slice. Sunbathing topless after lunch, and feeling drowsy and replete, I squinted at Luigi's Renaissance body. It seemed unkind to refuse him any longer.

Luigi was a very skilful lover and after the first bitter-sweet encounter on his boat, from then on I needed him like a drug. I completely neglected my studies and moved in with him, he of course having his own apartment. In July his thesis was accepted, thus ensuring in due course his precious doctorate. When he suggested that I should move to Rome with him, now that his time in Trieste was up, I can say now with some regret that I accepted without a second thought, and was soon living in some comfort with him near the Spanish Steps .

My professors were stoic over my abrupt and premature departure on account of a man — they had seen it all before, many times. I think that Mummy and Daddy were worried about me. Although their own love had crossed racial boundaries, it had led to an outstandingly happy marriage. Now here was their only daughter who had dropped out of University and was living, to all intents and purposes, as the kept woman of some bogus Italian count. The most cross of them all was Granny Tavcar. I saw her quite a bit over the next ten months, as I found that I needed periodic breaks from the hectic pace of the *Dolce Vita* with the Roman jet-set. She had little love for the Italians at the best of times, and the fact that I was living with one without the blessing of the Church was a bitter pill for her to swallow. She made it abundantly clear that I would always continue to be welcomed at her house, but not with 'him'.

Luigi had no obvious gainful employment in Rome, but a large circle of very rich friends. Marriage didn't seem to feature with many of them anyway, and it was just taken for granted that I was Luigi's girlfriend. He had to go up to Milan from time to time on unspecified family business, which was when I took off to stay with Granny, or to look up old school friends, some of

whom were now married. Luigi was always a bit evasive when I asked him about his parents, merely saying that they were boring, but how happy they were that he had found a steady girlfriend. So we went to Deauville in August for the racing and the polo, to Acapulco for Christmas and to St Moritz in the New Year. I also acquired my addiction to Gucci shirts! By now Luigi must have been around thirty years old, and I was twenty-three.

Then, in May, the blow fell. I was having my hair done and was idly looking at a society magazine when I saw my lover and some rather plain girl (she already had the downy moustache which requires depilatory treatment for some Italian women). The caption underneath suggested that this was the promising politician, Count Luigi Montecuccoli, and his fiancée, an industrialist's daughter and a childhood sweetheart, to whom he was to be married later in the summer in Milan. The bottom fell out of my stupid, self-created, world. Now it was clear why he had never introduced me to his family, and had to be away in Milan so often. Perhaps, had I not been so dependent on his body, I might have seen that I was never more than a fancy Anglo-Slovene mistress to him.

For one so clever, he must have known that I would have to find out sooner or later. No, he had never spoken of marriage to me, and I had my doubts about his suitability as a mate for life anyway. Even if he had come clean with me from the start, I would probably still have chucked in my studies and come to Rome with him, albeit for a limited duration. It was the deceit that had been behind all of that fun that we had together which hurt me the most. He had the grace to squeeze out the odd tear when we parted later that day. But his revolting suggestion that I could always stay on as his mistress after his wedding really made the parting a lot easier."

Buraq was getting bored. One of his party tricks in the summer, when Lara had the hood of the car down, was to jump straight onto the back seat from outside. This was a slight nuisance, as she had to keep all the tools of her trade, the call-sheets, the filofax and even the mobile telephone, in the boot.

In he jumped, only to pop out again with his pink teddy in his mouth. Strangled-sounding grunts were an invitation to the crew to throw the bear for him, as one might with a ball for a terrier.

"I really couldn't face my family, especially not Granny. She would have been loving and comforting I knew, but there would have been a constant bubble over her head with 'I told you so' written in it. I had moved to a small hotel outside the city in the Via dei Campi Sportivi, which although a trifle close to the polo club and Luigi's friends, gave me breathing space. On impulse, I telephoned Carmen, who had by now finished at the Sorbonne, and was, when I had last heard from her a few weeks before, having a final summer in Europe.

I finally traced her to the yacht. Her father, tipped by some to be in the running for the next Secretary General of the United Nations, was busy in New York, so had let her have the boat to entertain her own friends for a farewell cruise for the summer. It turned out that I knew quite a few of them when Carmen and the MY *Sybarite* picked me up from Ostia a few days later. Although there was a strong temptation to curl up quietly in a corner and die, life must go on. Besides, quite a few of the others seemed to have had recent problems with their love-lives, not the least of whom was Carmen herself. She was still very beautiful and had featured in the gossip columns across Europe over the past couple of years in some well publicised affairs. But, as an heiress with an overprotective Latin father, either she had been paranoid about fortune-hunters, or the predators had been frightened off by Papa.

She certainly had no intention of spending the rest of her life in her native Ecuador, doubtless married to some Criollo lad of 'good family' and being obliged to produce numerous bambini, she told me later. We were meandering among the Greek Islands (God, there are a lot of them) and had anchored off a fair-sized fishing port. She and I, plus a couple of others, had gone ashore in the launch and were drinking local wine in a quay-side taverna. A rather pleasant middle-aged American, who appeared to be on his own, asked, in that gregarious way that they have, if he could join us. This was Robert Summer, the England-based film producer who had earlier been filming on the island.

He had clearly seen us arrive from the enormous yacht and, although he certainly wasn't angling for an invitation, accepted with alacrity when Carmen asked him for supper on board. He was an amusing guest. Out of deference to his rather limited linguistic ability, we all spoke English that evening. I suppose that someone filled him in on my background at some stage, for before the party was over, he drew me to one side and had offered me a job as his personal assistant! He might have been hoping, in early days, for something more, and I think it was that he found me attractive as much for my looks as for my languages (and my still-born doctorate at Trieste). He offered me a wage that made me gasp, and the opportunity to travel, so four years later, here I still am. Commercials occupied much of Robert's time, but they, too, paid well and he rarely lacked for work.

I had decided, before I even returned to England, that I was by now a bit old to stay with Aunt Virginia. Anyway, she had taken one Brigadier Mainwaring, a widower on whom she had vague designs, as a PG for my old basement flat. Through the *Evening Standard* I found the opportunity to share a tiny place in Hays Mews, off Berkeley Square, which had the advantage of a garage for my Beetle, soon to be replaced with the BMW by courtesy of my munificent salary. It was also in walking distance of Clyne Films' office in Greek Street, where two super-efficient girls, Nikki and Tracy, coped with all of the administration. I went in when needed to help with anything foreign, but was mainly on location with Robert. I enjoy my work, but hope not to be doing the same thing in five years time.

Once I had been in the job for a month or two, and met many of the experts who joined us from time to time for different shoots, I had found my feet. We filmed mainly in England, occasionally in Europe and rarely further afield. In 1991 we went briefly to Colombia and were royally entertained by Carmen, who was finding life at home, in some large estançia in the hills behind Quito in neighbouring Ecuador, a little restricting.

Then came the shoot at Windrush Hall, fairly near to home. I had never been there, it being out of hacking distance for meets of the Bladon. Daddy had shot there in the past with one Caspar Vyvian, who had now moved away, leaving his son in charge. I knew where it was, so was there in good time to set things up for Robert. Shooting started on schedule.

I had been watching the big Charolais cow since mid-morning. First she had been standing well away from the rest of the herd, who were grazing peacefully, with her tail slightly raised, — always a sign of imminent calving. Then she kept on lying down and getting up in a restless fashion. I just had a feeling that things weren't going quite right. Having climbed over the fence into her field, I walked up to her and she made no effort to get away from me. Her bag had already broken and two black hind feet were just visible, rather than the normal presentation of a nose between two front feet.

A tall youngish man in worn cords and an old army sweater was walking quickly towards me. He looked as angry as he was handsome. However, he grudgingly agreed to help me deliver his calf and made up in strength what he lacked in skill. By the time that the cow was licking her calf dry, I had already fallen in love with David — not that I admitted it to myself, of course.

He was rather endearing in his embarrassment afterwards and became very polite and solicitous, asking me to come back to the house and giving me a clean jersey. I had always loved Lurchers and Kaid, his dog, certainly was stunning, with his silky brindled coat and enormous wide grin. How I would love to have a puppy of his! Though Daddy always had some sort of shooting retriever at home, I had never had a dog of my own.

I didn't see much of David that year, but we kept in touch, and in the late autumn he invited me to come along and pick up a greyhound bitch for Kaid, which some friend of his had surplus to requirements. David was very funny in his description of Kaid's embarrassment of being cast in the role of a stud dog! Anyway, early in the New Year Flicka produced six puppies and I was allowed the pick of the litter. David, in his quite unconsciously authoritarian manner, named him Buraq — after the Prophet Mohammed's horse — without consulting me.

Actually, I find the combination of reticence and authority really rather attractive — but then I came to realise, as time went by, I found virtually everything about David attractive. The trouble was, I could not make head nor tail about his attitude towards me. He clearly enjoyed my company; last autumn he had practically given me the full use of Tanya, the most exciting horse that I have ever hunted. But, apart from the odd peck on the cheek, nothing. Did he and his dog share the same distaste for physical love? I had a nagging suspicion that he had some rather warped ideas about Roman Catholics and chastity — English Catholics can be a bit odd.

One evening, after Tanya had cast a shoe out hunting when far from home, I had stayed on for supper. We were both tired and hungry and were still clad in our breeches, though in stockinged feet, having helped each other in removing our muddy boots. Neither of us had got around to taking our silk hunting ties off, but David had replaced his waistcoat with an ancient cashmere jersey; I just unbuttoned mine after letting my hair loose from the tight chignon that it had been confined in all day. David, I remember, had a streak of encrusted blood across the bridge of his nose and his cheekbones from an encounter with some brambles during the day.

He asked me, shyly, if I would like to stay the night. He was looking rather miserable, clutching a big glass of whiskey and avoiding my eyes. 'I love you, David,' I said quietly before I could stop making a fool of myself, David stood up, put down his tumbler and gently pulled me off the sofa into his arms, 'Darling, darling Lara, oh my darling!' he murmured over and over again, kissing my still mud-spattered face. He grasped my hand and, like a little boy pulling his teddy bear behind him, led me upstairs to his bedroom. I had gathered from Mrs Kerr that this had been the Captain's dressing-room during his short-lived marriage. I had seen glimpses of a beautiful golden 18th century bed, piled high with discarded clothing, before.

Now, David impatiently tipped most of the clothes onto the floor and somehow managed to get undressed while I was defeated by the knot in my tie; so when David first made love to me, I was modestly still clad in my cotton shirt and silk tie.

Much later on we remembered Kaid and Buraq. In some old towelling dressing-gowns we tiptoed down stairs and, having slipped some gumboots on, walked briefly out with the two Lurchers into the frosty December night. Orion had risen in the east and, with Sirius at heel,was pursuing the Seven Sisters across the midnight sky.

I was a fairly regular visitor thereafter to Windrush. Poor Kaid had to put up with Buraq, who always came with me, though, unlike Kaid, he was temperamentally unsuited for meetings and parties. We started to be asked to functions together (variations on 'Captain David Vyvian and Miss Lara Graham') and even Mrs Kerr, after a week or so of heavy tut-tutting, accepted that I shared her employer's bed. David, who had met Robert at the time of the coffee commercial, had him down for lunch one Sunday, together with a rather amusing Indian, Mirza Sind, whom he had met on a polo trip to India some time ago. It was a great success.

Then we had the drama of Cat Thrust falling in the river. I was on the way back to London prior to a shoot on the following morning in Essex, so didn't know about it before David telephoned that evening, sounding slightly in need of moral support. I told Robert about it when we met on location the following morning and he let me off to go and help. Luckily, the M25 and M40 were fairly clear, so I was at the Hall to help to charm the press by midday. One of the papers on the following day described me, beneath a rather flattering picture, as David's fiancée. Secretly, I was pleased by it.

But I am worried that David is being used by the devious Stan. Daddy, with huge recent losses at Lloyds, hardly a judge of character, always says: 'Never trust a Wykehamist.' "

Chapter 4

THE WARM-UP

'Sir Reginald Token, who died yesterday in hospital after a long illness aged 74, gave a lifetime of service to Oxfordshire and in particular to the Vale of Evenlode. He had represented the constituency for the Conservative party since 1950,' read David in *The Daily Telegraph* at breakfast on the following day. He wondered what had happened to Stan's mole in the John Radcliffe hospital. He read on.

'War service with the Ox and Bucks (43rd and 52nd) . . . Town Major in Leoben . . . British Legion, Red Cross, NFU, High Sheriff . . .' All of his worthy, if slightly dull achievements were listed, and there was rather a good photograph of Reggie in his younger days. David smiled as recalled the story repeated *ad nauseam* in the Evenlode Brigade. Reggie had enlisted in 1939 and had promptly engaged in a dalliance with the daughter of the Depot's deputy chief instructor. Obliged to take leave of her in rather a hurry — an irate father was coming up the stairs at speed, fearing the worst — he leaped from her bedroom window, only to suffer a highly embarrassing and lasting injury when landing on a bamboo cane that supported one of the hollyhocks in the border beneath.

Front-line material no longer, he was not allowed across the Channel until after VE Day, and then only to administer an Austrian town while civil government was being restored. He regarded his post-war award of the Territorial Decoration, when many of his friends were sporting the blue and white ribbon of the Military Cross, as so shaming that he had used neither decoration nor his war-time rank subsequently. It used to be said, to misquote a line from HH Munro, that a Barbary ape could get elected for Evenlode, providing it stood on a Tory ticket, and Sir Reginald, as Reggie was later to become (Services to Politics) proved no exception when he stood for the seat.

David's paper usually did not run obituaries until after the funeral of the individual had taken place, unlike some of the other broad-sheets, but the political ramifications of Reggie's passing were such that even the tabloids carried the news. (No tabloids were delivered to the Hall itself, but David always had his attention drawn to relevant items in Mrs Kerr's *Daily Mail*, or in Terri's *Sun*.) So where was Stan, David wondered again, and why had he not heard yesterday's news from him, rather than reading about it over his scrambled eggs, collected on the previous evening from his surviving Marans?

Stanton Harcourt had been badly wrong-footed by the news. His contact in the hospital had left the vital information on his answering machine at his cottage, but he, intent on an evening of fun with the red-lipped Veronica in London, had not bothered to check for any messages. Consequently, the first that he knew of the turn of events was when he had heard it on the *Today* programme on Radio 4 while he was driving back down the M40. He would hardly have described his relationship with Veronica as an affair. Indeed, he realised that he was but one of many who shared her favours. Nor did he feel any disloyalty to David, his client, even though the carnal friendship with the latter's wife had started when she was still married to David. Nevertheless he sensed that the election campaign had not begun ideally.

David took his second cup of coffee (Kenya, as Mrs Kerr would countenance none other) into the garden with Kaid and sat on a stone bench in the morning sun. For perhaps the first time in his life, he really did not know what to do next, apart from telephoning Lara. God, how he loved that girl, he thought. Her father had almost been wiped out by his losses with Lloyds, and it was only his wife's enormous successes with her Bazadais bulls at Perth that had saved them from having to sell up. Lara, as a result, was financially fully independent of her parents but, he feared, wedded to her nomadic film producing career as a result.

He went back into the house to telephone, and paged Lara on her car-phone. He had hardly put down before Stan was on the line. He would be over that evening, he said, in the meantime could David please come up with some ideas as to what ticket he wanted to run on, being as how he had declined to be an Independent Conservative. David had already given the matter some thought. The British National Party would have been pleasing, though that had been high-jacked by the remnants of the National Front a few years earlier. He had also thought, capriciously, about the National Dog Lovers' Party, but had a vague idea that Auberon Waugh had stood on a similar ticket in the Seventies.

He had finally decided on the County Party, if for no better reason than, city dwellers apart, everyone lived in a county, so hopefully, could identify with the name. It was just as well that he had taken a decision, as his next caller was the news editor of the weekly *Evenlode Echo*. David had met the genial Roy Large on a few occasions before, the last time being when he gave him an interview after the Cat Thrust and Kaid story.

"Is there any truth in the rumour, Captain Vyvian" asked Large formally, "that you intend to fight for Sir Reginald's seat on an independent ticket?"

"Yes, Mr Large," replied David in kind. "But I will be representing the County Party. Our aim is to restore and retain the quality of life of Britons, and to give people pride in their country once again. We will be printing our manifesto as soon as the by-election has been called," he added hastily, playing for time. "You will be among the first to receive a copy."

The newsman checked on one or two details about David, then rang off. David remembered that he had promised Terri to telephone Tony Stark, the former Farrier Corporal of the King's Lancers, who now did all the shoeing at Windrush. The feet of the young stock needed trimming. Besides, Terri quite liked playing the burly farrier off against Jack Kestrel, or Jack-the-lad as she always thought of him. No sooner was that call made than the crunch of tyres upon gravel denoted the arrival, at speed, of a visitor.

"Do you know what those shits in Central Office have done?" bellowed Sir Peregrine d'Artois, ninth baronet, as he stormed into the house. "They have appointed some smart-arsed Essex lawyer to stand for the Vale, overruling the local party who have always had their eyes on me! They won't announce the day of the by-election until Reggie is planted on Friday, but Mr bloody Livkin will be their man."

David took his near-neighbour into the library, seated him in Caspar's old leather armchair and poured him a stiff vodka-and-tonic. The combination seemed to settle Perry, who then became more rational. He started to talk about the unofficial approaches that had already been made to him, and to others, by Stan; he ended up by saying that he would not only be prepared to fling his weight, and that of the Evenlode Brigade, behind David, but also would be happy to act as local chairman to any party under whose banner he cared to fight; and, perhaps most importantly, that David could count on him for election expenses of up to £10,000.

"It is about time that we had a few more Old Etonians in the House," he pronounced. "Let the bag-men stay where they belong!" Grateful as he was to his generous backer, David hoped that such election-losing utterances would be kept to a minimum for the duration of the campaign.

By half past twelve David felt that he had earned a pre-lunch drink, so prepared one of his own concoctions. The 'Lurcher's Revenge' is a mixture of Vodka and freshly pressed pink grapefruit in about equal parts, with a dash of sloe vodka for good measure. (Mrs Kerr was not a fan of this concoction: her employer always made a frightful mess when pressing the fruit.) The sloes had been picked from the hedges during the autumn by him and Lara and, although the mix with the vodka and sugar was not mature enough to satisfy purists, it added a certain something to David's mixture. One glass was enough for anyone, but it had to have been Perry's stupid wife, Maris, who had insisted on two last summer, thinking that it was a form of pure fruit juice. To call her condition on her subsequent departure 'tired and emotional' would have been an understatement. He took a long pull at his drink and glanced down at Kaid.

'The trouble is,' thought the dog, 'that whenever the Boss has a drink like that before lunch, he wastes valuable walking time after lunch by snoozing with his paper.' He shifted crossly: it had been rather a stressful day so far once again.

Lara telephoned in response to his paged message of the morning before lunch, and in the circumstances agreed to come down after shooting to help David to plan his campaign, and to stay for the night. Accordingly, after lunch he told Mrs Kerr that there would be three for supper, and that Miss Graham would be staying overnight. Mrs Kerr liked Lara, especially as even the Witch of Endor would have been an improvement on Veronica; she would make up the bed in the main guest room automatically, although she knew full well that the sheets would be unruffled come the morning.

Although the prospect of half an hour with his paper in the sun was tempting, the proximity to the telephone before he had his act together was not. David strode off to look at the hay meadows, which should be ready for cutting in around a month's time, and at the winter corn to inspect for rust. Kaid trotted along behind him, pausing to investigate any particularly interesting smell that he encountered on their route. After stopping for a chat over the boundary fence with his neighbour's keeper and checking on the contractors who were clearing some dead timber for him, it was well after five o'clock that the pair returned. David took Kaid to the kitchen where he gave him his supper and then had a quick bath before coming down to watch the *News at Six*.

Stanton Harcourt was working to a hidden agenda that he intended at all costs to keep secret. An intelligent and well-educated man, who had lived through both the winter of discontent under the Socialists and the boom of the Thatcher years, he had come to the recent conclusion that the only hope for the country lay in a return to Thatcherism. Therefore if he could devise a plan to split the Tory vote, thus allowing the Liberal Democrats victory, in the by-election, on the pretext of trying to save it by running a right-of-centre independent against the official Tory candidate, the present government's days really would be numbered.

A spell in opposition, while a Labour-Liberal Democrat coalition dug its own grave, would enable the Tories to get rid of some of the dross that had accumulated whilst in government and to return before too long with a big majority, but no Major. His views were shared by many of his friends, including some fringe members of the Tory 1922 Committee.

He had, he admitted to himself, slight qualms about using David, a client whom he liked, as a cat's paw in this Machiavellian scheme. He certainly would do his level best to see that David would not lose his deposit and would attract a reasonable proportion of the vote. With this in mind and with his past experience on the fringes he had spent a busy day already with preparatory work. As the agricultural consultant to his London firm of estate agents, he told head office to count him out for the next five weeks, barring emergencies. He also prepared a large map of the constituency on which he had marked likely village halls and other suitable venues for public meetings. He knew that this would appeal to the military mind. Above all, he, Stan, must maintain the initiative.

He found David alone in the drawing-room when he arrived at the Hall. After accepting a drink he went straight into a prepared speech on what was allowed and what was not. He reminded David that every penny spent in any connection with his campaign must be accounted for and be within the prescribed limits. He finished rather harshly, as he had intended.

"Finally, David, you must get rid of the kraut car for the next few weeks," he declared. "Also, and I am sorry to put it like this, having an unmarried left-footer from Yugoslavia hanging around will not do your campaign any good at all. I suggest that you don't see Lara again until after polling day. It is bad enough that you are divorced." It immediately became apparent that he had badly misjudged his candidate.

"Look Stan," said David quietly, "you talked me into this, and now I will do it my way or not at all. We are in Europe now, for better or worse, so the Mercedes stays. As for Lara, I would have thought that her Yugoslav blood would attract sympathy, rather than prejudice, at this time. Anyway, I intend to marry her."

Further discussion was interrupted by the arrival of Lara herself. She dropped her car keys onto the console table in the hall and went straight to the drawing-room with Buraq skipping behind. Both men had half risen to their feet

"Please don't move," she said, kissing David warmly and giving Stan a sharp glance. Then she, too launched into her rehearsed speech. Her line was even more positive and forceful than Stan's.

"David, I am speaking as a professional communicator now, so please listen to me carefully." She spoke slowly, looking steadily at him. "You must have a trump card for your campaign, or you will end up as just another nice guy who lost his deposit in a by-election on a fringe ticket. Luckily you have the answer sitting under your nose."

Oh no! thought Kaid, who was sitting at his Boss's feet and resting his head on the Boss's knees, having pointedly ignored Sonny's arrival. She means me!'

"You don't mean the dog," snorted Stan, following Lara's gaze and deeply resentful of her intrusion. "I want David to win this damned seat, and he will if he follows my advice, and that doesn't include canine gimmicks."

"Why do you think that Clyne Films are so much in demand for commercials?" retorted Lara, flushing with annoyance. "Because Robert Summer, and the successful directors that he employs, know how to sell products. Kaid is not a Rottweiler: he is visually attractive and he is still fresh in the minds of our public as the local dog-hero."

'Flattery will get you everywhere, Darling!' thought Kaid.

David diplomatically suggested that they break off for supper at this point, but Stan, his nose firmly out of joint, said that he had things to do, so he left.

"By the way," he called over his shoulder to Lara as he climbed into his car. "Congratulations! I hope that you will both be very happy!"

"What on earth does he mean?" Lara turned to David as Stan's car sped off down the drive.

"Darling, I told him that we were going to be married," David confessed. "He was riling me about you and the Mercedes being electoral liabilities, so I wanted to shut him up."

Lara froze on the spot. Joy, annoyance, incredulity and anger followed each other through her mind. David, of course, sensed nothing of it, having cravenly returned to the drawing-room to fetch Lara a drink. When he came back to her at the front door, spilling the odd drop of whiskey and soda on the way, she was overcome by mirth.

"David, if that is a form of indirect marriage proposal, it must be the least romantic in history," she said, laughing helplessly. "But if it is a politically correct move for this by-election, then you can take a running jump!" She repressed the thought that this was not David's first proposal on record, and made a note that Stan was a bigger bastard than she had hitherto thought.

"I'm sorry that it had to come out like this, Darling," stammered a truly mortified David. "But please marry me and make me the happiest man on earth. I've wanted to ask you this for some weeks, but have been frightened that you were so keen on your filming work that you'd say no."

And so David Vyvian and Lara Graham became engaged to be wed. Later on, and after they had supped and each had telephoned their respective parents, David went to the safe in his office; he took out the ring, a small emerald surrounded by a cluster of diamonds, that Caspar had given to his mother over forty years ago. (Veronica, needless to say, had demanded something new and flash from Bond Street.) Though a little tight, which was to be adjusted by the jeweller in Witney on the following day, to his surprise and delight it fitted Lara's finger. As a treat and by way of celebration, David produced a bottle of armagnac after supper, and together they started to work on his campaign.

Stan, as (political) agent for the party, would book the venues for David's meetings, which he hoped could be chaired by Perry; he would organise poster and leaflet distribution; he would feed the media with releases: and, most important of all, he would keep a tight control of the finances of the campaign to ensure that they stayed within the stipulated limit, explained David.

"Quite, Darling, and I am sure that he will do all of that foot-slogging bit really thoroughly," replied Lara. "But forgive me for having a couple of artistic suggestions. First, everything that emanates from your headquarters — and where are they, by the way — must have a picture of you and Kaid on it, and what is more Kaid must be with you wherever you go from now on.

55

Then art-work of an oak-leaf must somehow be worked around your party slogan. We joked about this over supper, but I still think that 'Country Folk Vote County Party' is the snappiest." David's suggestion of 'Farmers - Vote County Party before they "Gatt" you' was held to be too long. He also secretly dreaded the corruption of the adopted text by the graffiti artists when the posters appeared on the streets.

'I don't like one bit of what I am hearing at the moment,' pondered Kaid, half dozing by the fireplace, 'Who are they expected to vote for, me or him?' He gave a large sigh. and hoped that Sonny would not be involved.

"Second, party colours are a bit of a problem, since most of them have been grabbed years ago," Lara continued. "So I would suggest ordinary black type, Garamond perhaps, for the literature, and white rosettes with gold print for your party workers. Ivanhoe Publishing in Oxford put in a very competitive and successful bid for some work that Robert wanted doing in a hurry the other day, so would be worth talking to about the printing, while that firm near Bristol that always advertises in *Horse and Hound* should take care of the rosettes. Also, we could use the photograph taken by that freelance for the *Echo* after the river rescue. We can give him a credit, so he should be quite reasonable about money."

"Stan will be told to get on with all that in the morning," said David, his head beginning to spin. "We could use the farm office for our party HQ, but we'll need someone to staff it. My book-keeper only comes in on Fridays and is rather set in her ways, so she's no good. But let's work on the manifesto. The electorate is largely agricultural, so if we both write down all of the bull points which we can think of with that in mind, I'll knock it into shape tomorrow."

Lara left early on the following day, Wednesday, to wrap up the filming at Sunningdale, so David settled down to work in his own office, always referred to by Mrs Kerr as his study. Although his estate was large, with him being present for most of the time, he felt there was no way that he could justify a full-time secretary. The book-keeper managed the calculation of the weekly wages, prepared the pay-packets, the VAT returns and so forth, but she had little time, and limited ability, for coping with David's small, though constant, correspondence. As a result, he had learned how to work a word processor at Cirencester, and now had one of his own, and a fax machine, on his desk.

His first task was to send fax messages to both the *Times* and *The Daily Telegraph* instructing them to carry the announcement of his engagement to Lara on the following day. Then Stan, who was *incommunicado* but also of the fax generation at his cottage, was sent the instructions about printing and rosettes that he and Lara had discussed on the previous evening. David then settled down to the manifesto. Since it was Wednesday, he had the benefit of Auberon Waugh's mid-week column in his paper — always a source of inspiration in such matters.

Though David held some fairly firm views on law and order ('Bring back the village bobby and the birch'), defence, religion and, with Lara's notes to help, agriculture, he knew that taxation and finance were his weak suits. Thus his luckless accountant in Weybridge was pestered with calls way beyond his remit throughout the morning. He had to field such technicalities as to how many civil servants would need to be cut in order to de-amalgamate the regiments which suffered under the 'King Axe' of 1992, and still to balance the books.

Lara telephoned from her car in the early afternoon to say that she was on her way back, and had good news: Robert Summer, her employer, was so delighted with the news of her engagement to David, whom he had met, and so intrigued about the possible by-election, whatever that was, that he had given her extended leave. The period was turning out slacker than usual — even the film industry was not recession-proof — so he had volunteered, with her consent, the efficient Nikki from his Greek Street office to come down to work as campaign co-ordinator for the duration. That solved the problem of help in the office, thought David, as he walked out to ask Terri if she minded a visitor staying with her in her farm cottage for a week or so. The farm office, next to the tack-room in the stable block, already had extension telephone lines from his own office so, by moving across the fax machine and one of the spare hand-sets, was almost ready to go.

Lara arrived with a rather fractious Buraq in time for tea, with further news that Robert had also said that he would make a promotional video for David, for use on Central Television, if David could find a backer to pay for the advertising slot. This was kindly meant, but Robert was totally unaware of the very strict financial constraints placed on candidates outside his native USA. No way, said Stan later, could they afford it. Besides, he privately thought, there was no point in going over the top when his candidate was scheduled to lose.

David made it quite clear to Lara that he hoped that she would stay at the Hall for the duration, if not until their wedding. Now that they were engaged, she felt that her position at Windrush was less anomalous than hitherto, so was more than happy to concur. That, of course, did not stop Mrs Kerr from making up the best spare room for her, which Lara found quite useful for bringing over some of her clothes. That evening they drove over to her home for a celebratory dinner with her parents, Simon and Ilona. David had known them both, though not well, since they had moved to Oxfordshire nearly a score of years before. Simon was secretly relieved that his only child had finally opted for, as he regarded it, a white man: Ilona was also pleased, but a little disappointed that David was a divorced heretic.

On Thursday morning they both enjoyed what Stan called a good press. Their engagement, by virtue of Simon Graham's past military rank, put them at the top of the engagements' column in *The Daily Telegraph*; and Roy Large, purely fortuitously, had illustrated his article in the *Evenlode Echo* entitled 'Likely Candidates for Vale Seat' with a picture of David, Lara and Kaid which had been taken, amongst others, at the time of Cat's immersion. Since David, together with Dr Paul Enstone, the Labour candidate, had been the only two to nail their colours to the mast for the forthcoming struggle, they received equal billing.

Nikki had arrived early and, after a brief trip to Witney to stock up with stationary and office supplies, was already taking all the calls in her new office beside the tack-room. As different as chalk from cheese to Terri, they both appeared to get on, neither feeling their space threatened. When David checked with her in the afternoon, the dozen or so calls had either been press inquiries, or calls from friends offering congratulations on the engagement. Nikki had been told to answer calls with a standard 'County Party Headquarters, how can I help you?' This had initially confused some of his friends, she told him, and had totally bewildered a Lady d'Artois, who in the end had given up. David forced himself back to work on his manifesto, with which by now he was beginning to become a little bored.

Friday was to turn out to be a momentous day. Ostensibly it was only planned to be the day of Sir Reginald Token's funeral. Reggie had stipulated in his will that he wanted no memorial service, neither in London nor anywhere else, just a funeral in the country in, or near to, his constituency. This would be followed by a private interment in the family vault near Stratford. Being long since a widower, and having no children (David often wondered if the bamboo cane had anything to do with the latter) the local Conservative party office took charge of the arrangements. There was not really a convenient church of sufficient size for the anticipated crowd of mourners within the Vale, so the service was to be held at the church of St Mary the Virgin in Witney, which was in the neighbouring constituency.

When David, clad in the morning coat that he had worn, when required, since Eton, and Lara, in a navy blue linen suit, pill-box hat with her hair neatly put up, and no Gucci shirt in deference to the occasion, emerged from the house with the two dogs, both now sporting cap-badges on their collars, they were in for a surprise. Standing beside his pickup van, hair brushed, regimental tie neatly knotted and trousers pressed, was Tony Stark, his farrier. Behind him, also well turned out, was Jack Kestrel.

"Reporting for escort duty, Captain Vyvian, Sir!" announced the former King's Lancer, coming smartly to attention. Jack, who had never been a soldier, shuffled in the background.

"Stand at ease, Corporal Stark," replied David. He would far rather have called the blacksmith Tony, as did everyone else, but that would have meant deviating from the script. "What the Hell do I want an escort for?"

"Begging the Captain's pardon, Sir," insisted Tony, who must have been brushing up on his dialogue from Kipling. "You don't, but Miss Graham and Kaid perhaps may. Those Young Conservative yobs are the equal of Militant Tendency any day." As far as David knew, neither of the pair had the slightest interest in politics, but he was not going to spoil their fun.

"Thank you both," he said, then changing his voice from the conversational to the military, "Escort, 'Shun! Crew, Mount!" Their self-appointed bodyguards climbed into the van, while he, Lara and the dogs drove off in the Mercedes towards Witney. On arrival in the market town's centre, the Thames Valley policemen on duty directed all cars to park on the Leys to the south of the church as Church Green, it being a weekday, was already full. The 'escort commander', Tony, briefed Jack to stay with the cars (Buraq was left in the Mercedes, which was parked in the shade with a window half-open. The young dog was unreliable at formal public gatherings) He then marched three paces to the rear of David and Lara as they proceeded towards the church. A solitary bell tolled.

There were quite a few pressmen outside, and David recognised one or two photographers from the national papers. Several took his picture, but that, he thought, was probably as much to do with being a figure in a morning coat with a beautiful girl on his arm and a large dog at his heel, as with anything else.

'Of course it was me that they were interested in,' thought Kaid later as he sat, rather uncomfortably, on the stone floor behind the pews in the south transept. 'If only humans would give credit where it was due.' He pushed his head under the pew in front, but could not quite reach a shapely pair of ankles that he saw there.

They had met up, by arrangement, with Lara's parents outside the 12th Century porch, complete with grinning gargoyles, and had gone inside to take a pew near to the back of the Lady Chapel. The verger had initially demurred at Kaid's presence, but had no time to make an issue out of it, such was the weight of mourners pouring in. No sooner were they seated than a disembodied head with slicked back hair interposed itself between the heads of David and Lara from the pew behind.

"Full house today, David," said Stan. "Let me mark your card." This he started to do in a low whisper throughout the service. While Perry d'Artois gave the funeral oration, party colleagues read the two lessons (King James's version) and the Rural Dean conducted the service, so Stan kept up a non-stop monologue, jabbing with his forefinger as he identified the opposition.

The silver-haired Dr Paul Enstone, he began, the Labour candidate, was the first generation of his family for many years not to have been a Nottinghamshire miner. After passing his eleven plus examination, he had gone through the Mansfield Grammar School to Medical College, where he had qualified as a doctor. A pleasant and kindly man, he had joined a practice in the Vale soon afterwards. Elected more on his personality than on his Labour ticket to the local District Council a few years later, this was to be the third time that he was to stand for the Vale, a traditionally safe Tory constituency.

He had become a close friend of Reggie over the years, in fact they often dined together, both being rather lonely widowers. Though certainly no 'champagne Socialist', it was perhaps the thought of generations of Enstone miners, coupled with the disintegration of the industry under the Tories, that kept him true to the cause. Recognising David, whom he had met from time to time in the past, Paul had caught his eye on the way in, and had given him a friendly wink.

The Liberal Democrat candidate, though he, like the Conservative, had yet to throw his cap into the ring, was almost too good to be true. Roger Mileham had a beard which, together with his full head of hair, almost obscured his face. From somewhere inside his tweed jacket there clearly smouldered an incompletely extinguished pipe, tendrils of smoke from which trickled up into the hirsute mass above from time to time. Mileham, a university lecturer, was accompanied by his wife, a matronly soul in 'granny' glasses and wearing some sort of home-spun smock. They both looked incredibly worthy, thought David, and had been specially chosen in an effort to wrest the seat from the Tories.

The podgy man in the blue suit, who had early on to be evicted from the front pew to make room for Reggie's cousins, was the hot-shot lawyer and soon-to-be-announced Conservative candidate, Norman Livkin. His grandparents had fled from Smolensk just one jump ahead of the Tsarist Cossacks, and he was now a junior partner with Schuster and Schneider in Cheapside who, coincidentally, had handled the divorce for Veronica. His shrew-like wife, Esther, was with him. She was a trained counsellor and was wearing a red ribbon on her lapel, showing that she supported AIDS. (Surely Stan had got something wrong there, thought David.) Between them, they had made a formidable team in the 1992 election, slashing the Socialist majority in a north London constituency while all about them were increasing theirs.

They lived in Essex, Stan added, and both abhorred Field Sports. If true, David pondered, the Conservatives were starting off with one hand tied behind their backs, as they had done at Cheltenham in the last election. That, and more, Stan fed to him, while the Last Post and Reveille were played by a bugler from the Green Jackets, and the coffin was finally carried out to the waiting hearse. David had also spied a figure which, from behind, looked suspiciously like his former wife. Though Veronica would have met Reggie in the past, he couldn't think what she was now doing here, other than to try to embarrass him.

The mourners filed out into the sun and made their way back to the Leys and their cars. Tony, who had nipped down to the Angel at the other end of the Church Green while the service was in progress, rejoined them, staying behind Lara when Stan took David, together with Kaid off to press some flesh, as he put it. Lara went to the car and let out Buraq, who promptly shot off at speed for a lap of honour round the Leys.

"You must be little Lara Graham," sneered a voice behind her. Lara turned to find that she was being critically inspected by a large red-head, a few years older than herself, she thought, with bright red lips and clad in a diaphanous dress with a pleated skirt.

"I somehow doubt that David has kept any photographs of me around at Turnip Hall, but I was married to him for a while.

I'm Veronica. I must say, you are so brave to return to the sticks, and I do hope that you know what you are letting yourself in for, my dear." She glanced down theatrically at Lara's left hand.

"Oh God! I see that David has fobbed you off with that little ring that his mother wore. He gave me a new one when we were engaged," she went on. She clearly had more to say in the same vein but, as a flushed Lara was formulating a cutting rejoinder, and while Tony and Jack were diffidently moving forward, uncertain what to do next, Buraq, had completed his run. He was returning to his Mistress when he saw her confronted by someone who gave off bad vibrations. At sixteen months he was full grown, about the size of a Doberman, but with the exquisite long nose of the greyhound in Van Dyck's portrait of James Stuart. A beatific smile spread over Lara's face.

Though Buraq's nose went unnoticed under the back hem of Veronica's light skirt, it was certainly only too apparent when the cold and wet tip impinged with the top of her thighs. Thoroughly goosed, her red lips formed a perfect 'O' as she leaped a good foot into the air.

"I am so sorry," said Lara. "He has only just become interested in bitches."

Veronica flounced off in the direction of County Mowers where, having arrived late, she had left her car. Meanwhile David and Kaid arrived from Church Green, Stan having melted into the background. He found his smiling fiancée patting her dog while the self-appointed bodyguards had collapsed on the bonnet of Tony's van.

"Darling," Lara said, looking angelic, "I'll put the boys in the car and wait for you inside." This gave David an opportunity to find out for himself what had happened. He strode over to the van.

"What the fuck is going on?" he enquired of his new minders.

"It was Miss Graham and her dog, Sir," explained Tony eventually. "They've just seen off Mrs Vyvian that was, in double quick time too." David was enormously relieved that the first, and he hoped it was the last, round had gone to Lara.

On the One o'clock news it was announced that the government had set a date for the by-election four weeks hence, and that the Conservative Central Office had put out a release to the effect that Mr Norman Livkin was their official candidate. After a hurried lunch, David put the finishing touches to his manifesto and sent Nikki with the fair copy on disk down to Ivanhoe in Oxford. She had checked earlier that they had located the picture of David and Kaid, so the wet proofs should be ready by midday on the following day, Saturday.

Chapter 5

THE STARTER'S GUN

Carmen diaz Alberdi was bored, very bored indeed. The same age as Lara meant that, by Latin American standards, she was well and truly on the shelf, her undiminished beauty and wealth not withstanding. Her parents therefore raised no objection when she proposed that she move to Europe in the Spring. April in Paris was always great fun, even though many of her friends from her days at the Sorbonne were either heavily married (the girls) or lucratively tied to a desk during most of the week (the boys).

Towards the end of May she decided to go to London where she would be in easy reach of Smiths Lawn for the Queens Cup and Ascot for the June Royal Meeting. So Carmen was sitting in some comfort in the nearly empty Club Class of a Tri-Star jet that was taking her to Heathrow. Sipping a glass of champagne, she was idly flicking through the pages of her complimentary copy of *The Daily Telegraph* when a quarter-page picture caught her eye. The caption read: 'The Foreign Secretary and Mrs Hurd were among the mourners arriving at St Mary's, Witney, yesterday for the funeral of the late Sir Reginald Token, former Conservative member of parliament for the Vale of Evenlode'. Although the Hurds were in the centre of the frame, slightly to their right and in clear focus was her friend Lara. She was on the arm of an incredibly dishy man, she thought, while at their heels was a dog, half hairy wolf, half noble greyhound.

Later, once she was ensconced in the Dorchester, she put a call through to Robert Summer in an effort to trace Lara. He, of course, was away for the weekend, so she next tried Lara's parents. They in turn gave her the number of Windrush Hall where she finally tracked her old girlfriend down. They had quite a lot of news to catch up on, which tied up the main line to the house for about half an hour. David did not mind that at all, as Nikki had gone into Oxford to pick up the wet proofs, and he did not wish to take political calls himself at this stage.

"Shall I ask her to lunch tomorrow?" whispered Lara to David, placing her palm over the mouthpiece of the hand-set. David nodded: he had heard so much about Carmen that he quite looked forward to meeting her for the first time himself. Stan had threatened to look in before lunch on the following day as well, but there was plenty enough for all.

Nikki returned from Oxford later on and left the proofs, both of David's manifesto and the posters, for him to peruse over the remainder of the weekend. She then closed the office, leaving a suitable message on the answering machine — 'This is the Headquarters of the County Party. Thank you for calling. We are sorry that we are unable to take your call, but please leave your name and number, and we will call you back on Monday morning.' — which should keep callers at bay over the weekend. After lunch David and Lara and their Lurchers spent what was to be their last free afternoon for some weeks sunbathing in the walled garden.

Kaid collapsed gratefully by his apple-tree. Buraq had irritated him all morning with some far-fetched tale of nearly bringing down a roe-deer in Sunningdale, but now, thankfully, he had gone to sleep with his long nose still sticking into the marrow-bone that Mrs Kerr had given to him at lunch-time.

Caspar Vyvian telephoned from France before dinner to let David know that he was coming over , with Yvette, to stay for a couple of weeks in order to meet his prospective daughter-in-law, and to 'give him a hand' with the electorate. David was genuinely delighted that they were proposing to come to stay — Mrs Kerr's daughter always came in to help when there were guests staying for any length of time — but was ambivalent about his father's ability, in the last decade of this second millennium, to promote his campaign. Caspar could always keep Perry out of the limelight while they got quietly pissed together, he reasoned. He thought that he and Lara should give a dinner party at short notice during the coming week to bring together the principal players in his campaign and to entertain his father and, perhaps, Carmen.

They drove down to Oxford, though the city was out of his prospective constituency, on the Sunday morning to go to Mass at the church of St Mary Magdalen. Nominally Church of

England, the Anglo-Catholic service contained enough Marian worship to satisfy Lara's Roman beliefs, however Kaid was rudely roused from his slumbers at the back when sprinkled with Holy Water from the aspergillum, and shook himself vigorously. The priest had sought divine inspiration when he saw the dog being brought into his church for the first time, but was at ease with his conscience when he considered that dogs were, after all, God's animals: he just prayed that the rest of his flock did not copy the example.

Stan was waiting for them in the library when they returned, having only just arrived himself. He readily accepted an invitation to stay on for lunch, and indeed for dinner on the coming Friday, which was the day that David and Lara had decided to give their small dinner party. He gave David a list of the most likely questions that he was liable to be asked, either when canvassing or at his meetings. These questions varied from queries on Gatt, EU, Law and Order, the Health Service, New Age Travellers and Defence, down to his views on hunting.

"You are lucky in that you don't have any party line to follow," he advised. "But do try to be consistent with your manifesto. I had a talk to Perry last night and, hopefully, have persuaded him to keep his introductions fairly anodyne. Could I suggest that Lara's father acts as chairman at meetings in the northern end of the Vale? That is, if he agrees with you starting your own party," he added hastily. Lara wondered uneasily why he was being so pleasant towards her, for a change.

"I must also warn you," Stan went on, "that your audiences will be pitifully thin to start with. Most of the constituents probably don't know that their MP is dead, let alone that a by-election is coming up. You will also have to realise that, in the beginning and leaving aside the three main party candidates, you will have about five other fringe contenders, including various shades of Green and the Oxford One party."

"What on earth is that, and Oxford isn't in the constituency anyway?"

"A driver tried to park his Sierra on top of the Martyrs' Memorial opposite the Randolph in Oxford last Christmas. When arrested he was about ten times over the limit, so got six months in Oxford jail. He had always told his wife that he was a teetotaller, so she thinks that he was framed. Hence her party."

None of them had heard the arrival of her Alfa Romeo, borrowed at short notice from the First Secretary at her embassy, so the first that they knew of Carmen's presence was when the ubiquitous Mrs Kerr showed her into the library. She is certainly as stunning as Lara had always said, thought David, and equally she certainly knows how to make an entrance. Lara went forward to greet her and they kissed warmly. She then introduced her man, and Stan who seemed, for once, temporarily lost for words.

Carmen had dressed down for the country, which in her case meant carelessly mixing Versace with Ralph Lauren. Remembering vaguely that the British upper classes rather frowned on jewellery before the evening, she had limited herself to a diamond bracelet. She had wondered, facetiously, if she could buy any fashionable bullet-proof clothing, were she to witness at first-hand this by-election that Lara had told her about on the telephone: such events at home in the past had often been close-run contests between the ballot-box and the bullet as various military *juntas* strove for power. She had also determined to purchase some ultra-chic Barbour and Driza-Bone clothing while she was in England.

A perceptive girl, she had taken in the Italian giltwood console table in the hall. Pretty, she thought, with its shell, floral and acanthus carvings. A Louis XIV Boulle bracket clock rested on it, backed by the lower half of a Florentine gilded wall looking-glass. Carmen wondered idly as to which early forebears of Lara's man had plundered Europe in the 18th Century. She now observed the two men before her. David she liked immediately, though she never would try to steal a man from such a close friend as Lara; and Stan, with his sleeked-back hair, had a certain reptilian fascination. Undoubtedly a shit, she thought, though probably quite amusing with it.

She was genuinely interested in the British electoral system, (a new experience) so spent much of lunch quizzing Stan on the details. David was aware that Stan was making up the answers when his limited knowledge on the subject failed him, but let it pass. Carmen had to leave soon afterwards — a friend of her father had brought over a polo team for the season, and they were due to play in the second match of the afternoon at Windsor in the first round of the Queens Cup — but not before she had accepted an invitation to the dinner party.

Lara then took the dogs for a walk up to the hill above the Hall, while David and Stan continued their plan of campaign. Stan was shown the copies of both the manifesto and the posters, which were temporarily stored in a loose-box next to 'Party HQ'. (The special rosettes would be with them by the end of the week.) David then asked Stan what he had planned for the coming week.

"I think Carmen really fancies me," mused Stan, the eternal optimist, his mind elsewhere. David was non-committal: he doubted whether Stan, for all his skills at estate, and now political, management and his Winchester education, was any match for the toast of the jet-set on both sides of the Atlantic. His agent had obviously mistaken Carmen's genuine interest in the local political scene with lust for him. "I am glad that you asked her for me on Friday. Always engage an opportunity target, as my father used to say."

"She has been asked as Lara's friend, not for you," answered David, vaguely irritated. He knew full well that Stan's father had been in a reserved occupation during the War, so had not 'engaged any targets'. "Can we get back to business?"

"There is no point in peaking too early, even in a four-week campaign," replied Stan, coming back from the world of fantasy with a bump. "Starting tomorrow, I will be spending much of my time in your farm office with Nikki setting up visits to as many local firms, organisations and bigwigs as we can get hold of. I'll get your nomination papers in to the returning officer once I've got the necessary ten electors from the Vale to sign them, and I'll need a cheque for £500 as a deposit. Don't fill in the payee line, as I'm not entirely certain who you should pay. Just keep your diary free for the next four weeks."

"I'm tied up for the Fourth of June already." said David.

"No problem," replied Stan, consulting his diary. "It's a Saturday."

"'Fraid not. It's on Wednesday week this year."

The penny dropped. Stan sighed wearily. Those bloody Etonians! It was bad enough that they chose to write off a day in memory of one of the Georges, but then to state without a trace of humour that, for the current year, the fourth of June was, in fact, on the first, defied logic. He knew when he was beaten.

"Okay, David, we'll leave the first free, but no more engagements please. I'm naturally looking forward to Friday, but we need to keep clear heads if we can, as I've pencilled you in for a little doorstep canvassing in Hampton village on Saturday morning."

Lara returned with two panting dogs soon after Stan had left. Over tea on the terrace, David outlined his proposed guest list for the coming Friday. As well as themselves, Carmen and Stan, and Caspar and Yvette, he proposed Lara's parents, old friends of Caspar, as were the d'Artoises and John Crispin and his wife. It was clearly too late to write at this short notice, so Lara telephoned her parents, who accepted with alacrity. Dinner parties were all too few these days, thought Simon Graham as he put the receiver down: besides, they hadn't been to Windrush Hall since Caspar moved to France about six years previously.

David had one refusal: John Crispin's wife would be away at a conference at Stoneleigh for Pony Club District Commissioners which involved an evening reception, though he would certainly come. With a flash of inspiration, David dialled Mirza Sind, who was at home in his London flat. They lapsed into their familiar banter.

"And what can I be doing for the honourable burra sahib?" asked Mirza in his best Peter Seller's spoof Indian accent.

"The broadcaster sahib can get his arse down here for dinner on Friday, juldi, juldi!" replied David. "Eight o'clock, Black tie or the ethnic equivalent."

Mirza accepted. His colour rode easily with him, helped by the fact that he looked like a mixture between the Pakistani cricketer, Imran Khan, and the Indian-born actor, Art Malik. Historically, he regarded the British as having been short-term visitors to his country, who had done much that was good

71

during their sojourn, but who had the good sense to get out when in danger of outstaying their welcome.

David's last call was to Ivor Digney, another staunch member of the Evenlode Brigade, who had served for a full twenty-two years with the Welsh Guards, of which most of his time was in the officers' mess. On retirement, he and his wife had bought a small tobacconist's shop in the village where it was said that if you could not obtain an item from the Digneys, then it did not exist. More importantly, Ivor Digney was a freelance, though unlisted, butler. He was fairly choosy for whom he buttled, indeed this would be the first time that David had asked him. He was also a man of few words.

"Right, Sir, this Friday that ever is, twelve for dinner at Windrush Hall. Please tell your cook that I will be over at 1700 hours to do the silver. Good evening, Sir." Nothing as common as money was discussed, though he was known not to be unreasonable, For tax purposes, he would expect a settlement in cash in due course. He would wear a tail-coat, expect to be called 'Digney' by his temporary employer and would provide immaculate service. By virtue of his presence at most of the dinner parties, luncheons and weddings that took place in the Vale, he was indubitably the best informed man in the area.

There was a certain amount of comment about the by-election in the nationals on Monday, and rather more in the local evening paper. However, they all took much the same line, namely could the Tories, from their rock-bottom position in recent polls, hold the hitherto safe, but now critical, seat against the upsurge of support for the Liberal Democrats? The Tory press made much of Livkin's proven ability during the last election, but the local *Evening News* was more realistic. Sir Reginald Token, stated its leader, had been very popular, whereas Livkin was neither local nor known. Moreover, the signing of the Gatt deal by the present government in the previous December was seen as the final betrayal for the predominant farming community in the constituency.

The one point on which all the papers seemed to agree was that it would be a two-horse race. Paul Enstone, the Labour candidate, received the odd mention, and the others who,

David apart, had yet to make their participation known, were discounted. David was not altogether surprised, as that was largely what Stan had led him to expect. Stan himself was busy in Party HQ. He needed to speak to Perry about establishing a network of volunteers across the constituency, hopefully from the Evenlode Brigade. These would eventually distribute copies of the manifesto to households, and later on put up posters in the run-up to polling day. But it seemed that every time he tried to telephone the baronet, he was put on to his lady who, convinced that someone was trying to sell double-glazing, promptly put the receiver down.

That would have to wait, he thought, so he concentrated instead in mapping out David's programme for the following week. Providing that he could let the *Echo* have a copy by Wednesday morning, it would appear in Friday's edition, together with those of such other candidates as had submitted theirs. He then settled down to fill in David's nomination papers. Terri and Jack had both volunteered, as had Mrs Kerr. Lara, whose parents had kept her on the local voting register since she had left home, was the first to sign, and Stan was certain that he could pick up the remainder in the d'Artois Arms at lunch-time. By signing the forms, there was obviously no commitment to vote for the candidate, but it ensured, Stan supposed, that the contestant was a bona fide person.

Caspar Vyvian and Yvette appeared, as planned, in time for tea on Tuesday. Caspar was at the wheel of his faithful 'R' type Bentley which pre-dated David by a year or so, and would, with continuing careful maintenance and a low annual mileage, probably see him out. Both Stan and Mrs Kerr, the latter visibly moved, were on hand to greet him, as was Jack Kestrel who had been an under-keeper on the estate in Caspar's day. David kissed Yvette and introduced Lara to her and to his father.

"You're the image of your mother when you all first moved down here," said Caspar, hanging onto her hand rather longer than was absolutely necessary. "How are your parents anyway?"

"They are dining here on Friday," Lara replied, gently retrieving her hand. "They're both well and looking forward to seeing you." She was at a slight disadvantage in not knowing who, amongst the local people, Yvette had met on their rare and brief visits to the Hall in Veronica's day. Her father had always referred to her, a touch enviously she thought, as 'Caspar's French bit of fluff' which did not really help her.

She was soon to learn that Caspar, finding that the English in the Alpes Maritimes were either dying, or rather common, had made the effort, with Yvette's help, to update his French from the schoolboy to the colloquial. This enabled them both to socialise freely with the natives, as Caspar jokingly described his neighbours, but also meant that she was a bit hesitant with her English. Lara put her at her ease straight away by reverting to French while Yvette found her feet. Caspar, of course, wanted to see everywhere and find out about everything after tea, but David dissuaded him.

"I'm not that busy for the rest of the week," he told his impatient parent. "Nothing is going to change overnight, and you've both had a tiring drive, so I suggest an early supper and bed."

"You're the boss now," said Caspar, secretly relieved that his son had not rushed to fetch the Land Rover. "I've a bit of legal stuff that I want to talk to you about before supper, but the sight-seeing can wait, I suppose."

In the meantime Jack Kestrel had been tasked by Mrs Kerr to take all the luggage from the Bentley up to Caspar's former bedroom. Yvette was just in time to rescue a wooden pannier from the boot which she handed to Lara. From both the smell, and the subsequent inspection, it contained a mouth-watering selection of various cheeses that they had collected during their leisurely trip across France. Lara accepted the gift gracefully: Friday's cheese course was now in hand, so to speak, but she must pick Yvette's brains over the rest of the menu.

Kaid had smelled the cheese soon after the Bentley had arrived. A fastidious eater, he would not eat any that had been pasteurised, and whatever was in the boot definitely had not. Stupid Sonny hadn't cottoned on to the treat in store and was still trying to ingratiate himself with these new humans.

"Yvette and I have discussed marriage from time to time," Caspar said later over a drink in the library. "But basically she doesn't want to. We have been together now for around six very happy years, and she is content with the way things are. She is known locally, both in the village and with our friends as 'Madame Vyvian' and I suggest we stick to that while we are here." David was relieved. He had intended to raise the matter himself, but his father had saved him the trouble.

"She will almost certainly outlive me," continued Caspar. "So she'll have the villa for the rest of her life, and income from a lump sum in the bank to live comfortably on. Then it will all revert to the family trust for your sons." He grinned wolfishly. "Simon Graham's girl has turned out to be a right little cracker. Hang on to her, boy!"

David winced at his father's last remark, which was the sort of thing that he might have said twenty years ago when he brought a pretty girl home for the weekend. He was to wince again on the following morning at the start of their tour of the estate. Their first port of call was the farm office where Stan and Nikki were dealing with the morning's mail. Stan, reverting to his role as the estate agent, gave Caspar a brief run-down on the various enterprises and diversifications which they had adopted since his day. He then started to brief David about the proposed canvassing on Saturday, when they were interrupted by a shriek of rage.

"You randy old goat!" exclaimed Nikki, rubbing her posterior. She had been bending over the fax machine to insert a new roll of paper and Caspar had succumbed to temptation and pinched her bottom.

"Sorry, my dear girl," said Caspar, not sounding sorry at all. "Just keeping my balance." Nikki snorted, and David thought it best to remove his rejuvenated parent before his behaviour deteriorated further. They climbed into the Land Rover with Kaid and spent the rest of the morning on the estate.

Neither his father, nor his step-mother, made any demands on them for the next couple of days. Caspar took himself off to see the Bladon hounds in kennels, lunching with Major John Crispin in the local pub; he consumed more than he should have with Perry d'Artois as they talked of old times; and he laid some flowers on Mary's grave in the little churchyard in the village and shed some tears.

Lara and Yvette were getting on famously. Though Lara had been hostess at dinner parties before, either for Luigi's Roman friends or for Robert Summer's occasional 'bash' at the end of a big filming job, those had always been in restaurants: now she had to plan the catering as well, so was heartily glad of Yvette's expertise.

Jack Kestrel had promised her some plovers' eggs — apparently some neighbour was due to plough a set-aside field early; there was a saddle of home-bred lamb in the 'fridge; the part-time gardener had come up with some asparagus and broad beans from the kitchen garden; and the wine cellar was well stocked. The rest they needed to buy. Fortunately, Mrs Kerr had never regarded the kitchen as her private domain, so did not resent what others in her position might have regarded as interference. Lara tactfully sought her advice over the amount of vegetables and fruit that they needed to buy, all of which they obtained from the local greengrocer on Friday morning.

Ivor Digney arrived at five to five in the evening, and after being told by Mrs Kerr what the menu was to be and being shown by David where the wine, removed from the cellar that morning, and other drinks were kept, set to work on the silver. It was perfectly clean anyway, but the former Colour Sergeant required it to be up to Household Brigade standards. He wore a yellow and black horizontally striped waistcoat for this task, and would change into his evening-wear once he had laid the table.

David and his father were first down in the evening, Caspar in some old ruby-coloured smoking jacket and bow tie to match. Yvette was close behind them, wearing the 'little black dress' which French women have got down to a fine art. The Grahams were the earliest to arrive, having given a lift to John Crispin, whose house was on their route anyway. Digney greeted the arrivals at the door and offered them a choice of a vodka martini, or sparkling mineral water that came from an artesian well on the estate which Caspar's father had drilled in the Twenties.

Perry d'Artois, however, was handed a crystal tumbler half full of malt whiskey, with a little ice on his arrival. But he insisting that Maris be content with a glass of the well water. He did not want a repeat performance of her inebriation that had followed her overindulgence with the Lurchers' Revenge earlier in the year. David was wondering what had happened to the girls; Carmen, having driven down after tea, would be staying for the night, and as yet neither of them had appeared downstairs. Stan eased in next, shortly to be followed by Mirza Sind.

The Indian was dressed in a three-quarter length jacket of midnight blue which was buttoned to the neck, with skin-tight black trousers beneath. He stopped on entering the drawing room door, gave a half bow with his hands pressed together before his chest, before advancing towards his host. David returned the namasti and grinned at Mirza.

"Come and meet the others," he said. "I'm sorry you won't stay the night, but if the Beeb are sending you down to Harwich tomorrow morning, I suppose it makes sense to get back to London tonight." He introduced him to the other guests, with whom he shook hands. Perry, when they came to him, immediately noticed the light coffee-colour of Mirza's skin and his blue eyes. Touch of the Pathan there, he thought. A combination of the name and Mirza's appearance rang a bell in the far recesses of his brain.

"Any relation to Randy Sind?" he asked.

"My father, Sir." replied Mirza. Perry's eyes misted over, as his mind went back fifty years. He had then been a Brigade Major to an Indian brigade in the 7th Indian Division at Kohima. Together with other troops, they had been surrounded by the Japanese who threatened to over-run their position. He remembered so well the Indians' steadfastness under fire, in particular that of a young Sandhurst-trained captain, Ranjit Sind. Perry had taken over a bren-gun, the crew having been killed, and, with Sind as his number two, they had done their bit to hold the perimeter. He had seen him again during the storming of Mandalay, but after VJ Day they had lost touch. He blew his nose loudly into a large bandanna handkerchief.

"And he is well, I trust?"

"Indeed Sir. He is now Rajah of our tiny state, not that anyone pays much attention to that sort of thing any more. He often talks of the war."

Further conversation in the room came to an abrupt halt with the entry of Lara and Carmen, followed by the two dogs who had been sulking in the library. Though both individually beautiful, as a pair they were truly stunning. Lara's fair hair caught the rays of the sinking sun which shone through the bay window as it fell shimmering over her pale aquamarine brocade bodice, embroidered with gold. She wore a full skirt of the same colour with a heavy golden fringe. Her only jewellery, apart from her engagement ring, was a plain gold crucifix.

Carmen's dark hair was swept back to show off her shoulders to their best advantage. Her strapless silk top was studded with seed pearls and it revealed enough breast to cause Stan to choke on his martini. Her simple full-length black taffeta skirt emphasised her height, and she, too, wore a crucifix, though in her case it was studded with diamonds and rubies. They both accepted martinis from Digney, who then proceeded to hand around the shelled plovers' eggs, still warm from cooking.

"By God, I wish that I was a young man again," thought Caspar as he ogled the girls with unconcealed admiration.

"What a pair," thought Stan as he gazed at Carmen's cleavage with unconcealed lust.

"Oooh goodie, I love gulls eggs!" cooed 'Stella' d'Artois, who had managed to get hold of a martini when Perry was talking to Mirza.

Further introductions were made and general small-talk followed. Yvette nipped out to the kitchen shortly before they moved into the dining room to give Mrs Kerr a hand, as promised, with the Hollandaise sauce which was to go with the asparagus. When she returned, on cue Digney announced dinner to Lara.

The seating had been a bit of a headache to work out, especially as they were unbalanced, there being two more men than women. In the event, David had put Caspar in his old place at the head of the table with the Grahams on either side of him, while he took the foot with Maris, by precedence the senior female guest, on his right, and, by custom, his fiancée on his left. Once Lara had seated them all, Digney served the asparagus. It is not ever the easiest of things to eat, but with finger-bowls, damask linen napkins and caution, it can be done quite tidily by using one's fingers. Maris was never totally at ease with that most delicious of vegetables, but could not put her finger, either literally, or metaphorically, on the reason. She watched with silent disapproval as Lara and Carmen, both sitting on the other side of the table, dipped the shoots into the sauce on their plates before putting the tips between their lips. Maris preferred to use a knife and fork.

Stan, however, found the whole performance wildly exciting. Though seated between John Crispin, whose main conversation was either about hound breeding or scenting conditions, and Yvette, who was amusing enough, he was nevertheless opposite Carmen! He felt a light sweat on his brow which started to mingle with the oil on his sleeked back hair. With an effort he averted his gaze from the diamonds on the cross around her neck.

"Is there much bullfighting in Ecuador?" he asked, watching a plump asparagus tip, coated with sauce, hovering an inch away from her mouth.

"*La corrida*? A certain amount," Carmen replied, feeling for what was coming next. "My brother tries his hand from time to time."

"So he's a toreador then?"

"No way!" Carmen wondered what her brother, who ran the family's varied enterprises in the frequent absences of their diplomat-father, would think of the question. Professional bullfighters came from the ranks of the *campesinos*, but it was considered obligatory, for *machismo* reasons, for young men from the ruling families to wear the 'suit of lights' from time to time.

"I'm glad to hear it. It's fairly barbarous, isn't it." Stan had misread her denial as dislike for what is, in many Latin countries, a national sport.

"Stan, you really mustn't say things like that." Lara quickly stepped in to defuse a potential explosion of Latin temper.

79

"You take no risks whatsoever with your shooting; I take a few when I go hunting; but it must take skill and bravery to face a bull one to one. You'll be saying that hunting is cruel next!"

"Good girl!" cried John Crispin, in a Pavlovian response to the word 'hunting'. "Hike on forrard!" He then resumed his monologue to Maris on out-crossing with border packs. Stan turned back to Carmen, but found that she was deep in conversation with Mirza about pig-sticking. Well, good luck, Gunga Din, he thought sulkily. Digney, with the saddle of lamb which had been carved in the kitchen, having been cooked anointed with rosemary and garlic, and Mrs Kerr's silent daughter bearing broad beans and Jersey royals, brought a halt to the discussion on field sports

Kaid was in a bad mood. When the humans had removed themselves from the drawing room, he had noticed that two plovers' eggs had been left on the serving dish on an occasional table. When he went to liberate them, he found Sonny licking his lips, having got there first. He cheered up a lot when he overheard Lady d'Artois remarking to the Boss that she thought that the French parsley, which dressed the new potatoes, was always so delicately flavoured at Windrush Hall. Grinning, the dog sauntered into the kitchen and lay down on his blanket by the Aga, awaiting for a bit of lamb.

While Digney served the claret, Caspar was quizzing Ilona about her Bazadais cattle. Though, like his son, he had employed an efficient cowman for the day to day running of the Windrush Charolais herd, he was interested in exotic breeds. Meanwhile Simon Graham, with his background which included a spell as military attaché, found no trouble in having an amusing talk with Yvette about the Côte D'Azur that he had known as a child in the summer holidays. This left Stan with only Perry opposite to talk to. The baronet, it transpired, didn't want to talk to anyone at that moment. A known great trencherman, he was intent on demolishing the pile of warm, pink, lamb to which he had helped himself earlier. He quaffed heavy draughts of claret from a glass that Digney was hard pushed to keep filled.

'The bugger is gaining on me,' thought the temporary butler as he fetched yet another bottle from the sideboard. At that moment Lara gave him an imperceptible nod to signify that it was time for the next course. Perry had to sulk with an empty glass while they were all offered strawberries coated in fresh raspberry sauce. Only then did Digney return with a bottle, this time Tokay, which was served in a smaller glass, to Perry's chagrin. He only hoped that David had not finished the last of Caspar's excellent cellar of port.

His wife, Maris, was by now in fine form. Turning the tables on the Master of the Bladon, she was berating John Crispin for not catching the fox, or foxes, that had been killing her hens during the winter; at the same time she was taking David to task for not allowing hounds to draw his coverts on the days immediately prior to his shooting dates.

"Between the two of you," she ended triumphantly, "there soon won't be an egg to be had in the county." She turned to Lara. "And you, my dear, had better try to knock some sense into these men if you don't want to end up eating foreign muck from across the Channel!" In the circumstances, Lara thought that Stella's last remark was particularly stupid, even for her. She smiled sweetly and remembered the oft-repeated classic English newspaper headline: 'Fog in Channel: Europe isolated'.

Perry, having demolished his strawberries and two glasses of Tokay, turned his attention to Carmen. She was still deep in conversation with Mirza, so he decided on the tactile approach and edged his right knee towards where he imagined her left thigh to be under the table. He made contact. His *frisson* of excitement was followed within a second by a gasp as Carmen, without altering the flow of her discussion on suttee with Mirza, removed the gilded dessert fork from her plate to beneath the table and gave him a quick jab.

Caspar, in the meantime, was in high good humour. He would liked to have been seated nearer to Carmen, although whatever she had just done to Perry had made him jerk like a shot rabbit. He cast an anxious glance down the table towards Maris — he knew that they all called her 'Stella' behind her back, after the Belgian beer — who was advocating the shooting of foxes if the 'Bloody Bladon' wouldn't catch them.

The strawberries were followed by cheese and, for the topers present, to whit the baronet and the master of hounds, port. Lara, who knew the tastes of senior establishment figures fairly well, had added a large slice of Cheddar to Yvette's French selection. She also put out some warm *petit pain*, for those with continental tastes, with the peculiarly English collection of cheese biscuits. Mindful of doctor's orders, Caspar proposed to limit himself to one glass of port and passed the decanter on to Simon Graham on his left. By the time that the depleted vessel reached John Crispin, his place setting could best be described as a disaster area.

Predictably disdaining the peppery goats cheeses in olive oil from the Alpes Maritimes, the Roquefort from the Massif Centrale and the Camembert *au lait cru* from Normandy, he had cut himself a large slice of the Cheddar. He had already broken up several cream crackers on and around his plate, which also held a couple of sticks of celery. Together with some butter he was trying to cement haphazardly cut pieces of cheese to the flakes of the biscuits to make, as he saw it, mouth-sized portions. Greedily, he filled his glass to the brim and settled down. 'How sad,' thought Major Crispin, 'that it was the wrong time of the year for nuts: a few walnuts would really round this lot off.'

"My goodness gracious me!" whispered Mirza to Lara. "Is the Hunting-Sahib preparing tiffin for his hounds?" Lara giggled immoderately, and Maris d'Artois wondered if the Indian chap had just propositioned her. East is East and West is West, she thought, which was her stock-in-trade mantra to any question which involved race. It was a pity, those around her sometimes said, that she had never read the full text of Kipling's *Ballad of East and West*.

After allowing John Crispin a decent interval in which to reduce the pile of edible rubble before him, Lara caught Maris's and Yvette's eyes and they rose, followed by her mother and Carmen, to have coffee in the drawing room. This would be preceded by a lengthy spell upstairs during which they could hold a post mortem on the behaviour of the males whom they had just left behind. The men, having risen briefly to their feet as the girls departed, now closed around Caspar, who was delighted to see Digney produce his father's old humidor. The older men lit up, and soon there was a blue haze of Havana smoke above the table.

"David, I want you to know that you can count on all my members and supporters who are, on the voters' roll to turn out for you next month," pronounced John Crispin, belching somewhat. "Livkin is on record as being against hunting, and we don't propose to vote ourselves out of existence."

"You can count on the Evenlode Brigade to a man," added Perry. "The old soldiers will never forgive the government for the drastic Options for Change cuts in 1992, and others later on. I also think that you'll be able to count on the farmers," he turned to Simon Graham. "Correct me if I'm wrong, Simon, but the signing of Gatt equals no confidence in the Tories." Simon nodded in agreement.

"Your main problem, David," his father chipped in. "Is that, to use a military analogy, you may have got the support of both the Officers' and Sergeants' messes, but without the support of the NAAFI, you are wasting your time. Perhaps Stan here can let us know how he proposes that you get to the rank and file." Stan could not.

He had not expected to be quizzed by the Old Guard on his non-existent plans to make David the People's Favourite. True, the *Echo* had carried an outline of all the candidates' schedules for the coming week, including David's walk-about on the morrow in Hampton, but he had not gone into any details. He therefore floundered, very much on the defensive. Mirza unexpectedly came to his rescue.

"I've covered two general elections in this country, and several by-elections," said the television news reporter. "The action really all takes place in the last two weeks, whatever the party managers may say. That should give you all a further week's grace to get David's act together."

"Could I just suggest that Kaid has a shampoo? Those of us, myself included, who like dogs, know that they smell, well, doggie. Your non-owner may warm to him more if he smells a bit like the shampoos that they see advertised on television." he added.

Kaid, only recently back from the kitchen, rose to his feet and stalked majestically from the room. He had thought up until now that Mirza had been his friend. The Boss brushed him fairly regularly and, when the need became apparent, sprayed him to kill the fleas that he picked up from hares. He liked water and was prone to wallow in the pond after a good walk, which kept his coat silky. But he was damned if he was going to be dragged around the county smelling of Wash and Go. He would never live it down!

The port circulated twice more before David stood up and suggested that they should join the ladies in the drawing room for coffee. Perry led those guests who felt the need for a pee into the garden to relieve themselves, which they did, copiously, on the roses. 'Keeps Charlie away from the hen-house,' thought John Crispin. Meanwhile Ivor Digney, his duties over, was chatting to Mrs Kerr at the kitchen table as they finished the last of the claret. Mrs Kerr's daughter and Terri, who always liked to be involved, were loading the dish-washing machine and polishing the steel blades of the heavy pistol-handled Georgian silver knives.

"That Sir Peregrine must have hollow legs," Digney mused. "And his good lady runs him a close second. I wish your Captain Vyvian luck with his politics, but I can't see him getting through to the man in the street, or, around here to the man on the tractor, shaggy dog or no shaggy dog."

"People round here don't have much time for papers or the news programmes on the telly," he continued. "It's more the case of a cooked meal when they come home from work, a pint or so down the pub and home to bed. If there's a Fair or a rock concert not to far away during the summer, the younger ones will probably go, but only once in a while." Terri had been listening to every word; now she had an idea. She must have a word with Nikki in the morning.

Meanwhile the party in the drawing room was beginning to break up. They had all been chatting for about three quarters of an hour, when Perry suddenly stood up, thanked Lara and David for a great evening and marched out, dragging his twittering wife behind him. The Grahams were next, after slight trouble in moving John Crispin, who kept on insisting that he could 'go another brandy'. Then Stan, looking pointedly at his watch, suggested that they should all have a reasonably early night and left as well. Mirza, who had only had a couple of glasses of wine and some water throughout the whole evening, was also on the point of leaving, when David stopped him briefly.

"Lara and I are planning to have a picnic for the Fourth of June holiday at Eton next Wednesday." he explained. "Carmen has agreed to come, and we will be meeting up with my sister and brother-in-law. Can you get away and join us?"

Mirza quickly replied that he could, and they agreed to tie up the details over the next few days. He then left for London. Carmen had been thoroughly amused by the whole performance of the 'Landed Gentry at Play'. But it was to Mirza that her thoughts kept returning as she climbed the stairs to her bedroom. David and Lara took the dogs out into the walled garden.

"At last," he murmured, taking Lara in his arms and kissing her hair. "That was a wonderful evening. Thank you."

"I thought Daddy and Caspar behaved quite well," Lara smiled, sleepily "But darling, do the locals around here always revert to the nursery in the evening?"

"'Fraid so," sighed David.

Too damned right,' thought Kaid from his stand over his parsley.

Chapter 6

THE HUSTINGS

Feeling slightly foolish, David pinned the white party rosette onto the left lapel of his tweed jacket and handed another to Lara. It was Saturday morning and they were parked beside the war memorial in Hampton village at ten o'clock, awaiting Stan who was late. Behind them, in the farrier's van, sat Tony Stark, together with Jack Kestrel, the pair both wearing their rosettes with considerably less embarrassment than did the candidate himself.

Showing the initiative for which Robert Summer, the film producer, paid her a generous salary, Nikki had obtained for David a copy of Ivor Stanbrook's helpful book, *How to be an MP*. David was rereading the section on personal canvassing in which the former Conservative member for Orpington stressed the importance of it. So, when Stan arrived ten minutes later, full of excuses, David asked him if he had the relevant copy of the electoral roll. Stan had not. Muttering something about it being Nikki's fault, he suggested that they press ahead regardless.

"Fine," said David. "How?" It now transpired that his agent, though clear on when and where, was short on how. His experience at helping with parish and district elections, where most of the electorate can be reached by the candidate, or at least by his supporters, before polling day was unequal to the task. David realised that he would have to take charge himself. He summoned his minders.

"Slight change of plan," he told them. "Farrier Corporal, we will advance in slow time down this street," he looked up at the street sign, "Acre Bottom, in an inverted 'V' formation. You will take the left side, and Jack the right. Miss Graham with both dogs, Mr Harcourt and I will be on the centre-line, traffic permitting, twenty paces in rear." Knowing their somewhat rough and ready tactics when dealing with hunt saboteurs, he stressed the importance of good manners, whatever the

provocation. He added that all adults should be addressed as 'Sir' or 'Madam' and invited to 'come out to meet David (not Captain) Vyvian, the candidate for the new County party'.

David thought afterwards that it was Lara and the dogs that saved the day. The householders of Hampton were, if anything, rather deterred by the burly appearances of his blacksmith and of his tractor driver-cum-keeper. But when their women and children spied the two dogs, and indeed when the men focused on Lara, they left their terraced houses and came out onto the street. Both dogs were friendly enough, though Kaid fastidiously declined any of the crisps and sweets that he was offered. Not so Buraq, the greedier of the two, who took whatever was on offer. As a result he was copiously and noisily sick in the gutter before they had covered half of Acre Bottom. Not that the bucolic locals minded at all, but the few 'weekenders' who had recently arrived in the village were seen to beat a retreat to behind their varnished front doors.

Kaid had always thought that his son's greed was disgusting, inherited from his mother, Flicka. He was rather enjoying the attention he was receiving, but hoped that nobody thought that he and Buraq were in any way related.

Although Stanbrook had specifically advised against entering private houses on such occasions, David went into the village store, ostensible to buy some matches. Then, taking over the dogs from Lara for a moment, he sent her into the Chemists for some toothpaste. He hesitated when they came to the local picture gallery, with the Union Flag flying proudly above it. However, his arrival had been observed by the proprietor who, it turned out, had done some picture framing for Caspar in the past. Yes, said Mr Marley, of course David could have his vote, providing he would ensure that Great Britain would not be ruled by Europe. David told Stan to note that here was one window, at least, where his poster would be welcome.

The presence of strangers in Acre Bottom, even on a Saturday, was enough to arouse curiosity in the sleepy little Cotswold village. The last time that anything interesting had happened was when the vicar's false teeth fell out in the pulpit during a coughing fit, and that was two years ago. 'Out of the mouths of babes and sucklings' was the theme for his unfinished sermon, which the villagers had found most appropriate.

By the time that they had reached the Red Lion at the end of the street, David felt like the Pied Piper. The men were delighted for an excuse to get away from the odd jobs around the house that needed fixing, and down to the pub early; the women were delighted for any excuse to get out of the house; and the children, who could not vote anyway, made up the numbers into a good-sized crowd for a village.

Jack and Tony slipped into the pub with practised ease and, knowing that any expenses would be reimbursed by David, bought the odd pint here and there, eventually emerging with half a pint for David and a glass of lager for Lara. David, spying a television crew from Central approaching, made a great show of asking the landlord for a bowl of water for the dogs that, needless to say, neither of them wanted. The interviewer asked David one or two banal questions to which he gave well rehearsed replies. The cameraman focused on Lara and the dogs.

Not so bad, thought David as they drove home to lunch. He had made one or two mental notes about improving the act for future occasions, the main one being that older men would be more suitable for the door-stepping than the likes of Jack and Tony. He must speak to Perry about mobilising some of the more senior members of the Evenlode Brigade. Also, if Stan was going to be unreliable about getting the copies of the relevant electoral rolls at this stage, he would put Nikki on to it on Monday.

Nikki had spent a busy morning. Terri, once she had checked all the horses out at grass, came into Party HQ, as they now all called the farm office, and told her about Ivor Digney's remarks in the kitchen on the previous evening. Not that she wanted Captain Vyvian to become Prime Minister, she explained, but if only they could take up Lance Thrust's offer to do anything for her employer.

"What has Lance Thrust to do with this anyway?" demanded Nikki. "He's a pop star, not a politician." She had not yet made the connection between Windrush Hall and the news of the great rescue that she had heard about a couple of months before.

"The Captain told me that Lance — he came here by the way — was so grateful to him after he and Kaid saved Cat from drowning, that he said he'd do anything for him in return," Terri told her. "A pity that we can't ask him for a few votes."

Nikki liked nothing better than rock concerts, having graduated from illegal raves in her 'teens. After being volunteered by Robert to spend four weeks in the outback, she had made it her business to find out where the local action was. So she knew that Lance Thrust and his group, Rock and the Hard Place, were starring at a huge charity gig at the disused RAF base at Lower Norton in a fortnight's time. Lower Norton, previous base for the RAF's VC10 fleet before privatisation, had been sold by the Ministry of Defence to a property developer. He, while awaiting approval of his plans, was happy to let out various facilities at the former base in order to service his huge bank borrowings. The base was also right in the middle of the Vale of Evenlode.

She called Tracy, who was not best pleased at having to work on Saturday mornings to cover for her absence, and told her what she wanted. Tracy tapped into the Clyne Films' database and gave her Lance Thrust's unlisted home telephone number. That is how it was that Nikki spent Saturday afternoon at Lance's Thames-side home, well chaperoned by Mandy Thrust, discussing David's problem.

David in the meanwhile was attending the Evenlode Show. When he and Lara had returned home for lunch they found that Carmen, a habitual late riser, had just got up, while Caspar and a reluctant Yvette had gone to watch cricket at the University Parks in Oxford. Carmen wanted to go back to London after tea, so David and Kaid, leaving the two girls together, went to the show on their own. He was on the committee anyhow and, knowing many of those watching and competing, it was not a great hardship.

He watched with amusement as Norman and Esther Livkin, both in their blue Tory rosettes, were firmly stopped when they tried to push their way into the members' enclosure. Both of them were reeking of scent, he of Brut and she of Fantasme, to block out the horsey smells that they were likely to encounter.

"Can't have any old riffraff in here!" said a voice in his ear. It was the silver-haired Paul Enstone, the Labour candidate, complete with red rosette. He had been on the committee of the show for longer than had David. They both grinned at each other before moving off in different directions. From the *Evenlode Echo* David had gleaned that the Liberal Democrat candidate, Roger Mileham, and his worthy wife should now be at the local cottage hospital. There, no accusations could be made against them by the Green candidates that they were condoning the exploitation of animals, even though their exposure at the show would have been far greater.

David had also read that the Oxford One party had not come under starter's orders. The aggrieved woman, whose jailed husband was the cause of her crusade, had bullied ten of the warders of Oxford jail to sign her nomination papers. Since they all lived in or around Oxford, in other words well outside the Vale's constituency boundaries, her nomination was invalidated: she gave up the unequal struggle.

As committee members, both Paul Enstone and David had to take their turn at presenting some of the prizes, and both refused to remove their party rosettes when invited into the main ring. David was caught for the Hunter Championship, while Paul presented the trophies in the class for the Best Trade Turn-out. Norman Livkin, penned in on the far side of the ring, snarled with anger and turned on his agent, a man who had served Sir Reginald Token well in the past.

"You stupid old git!" raged the Tory candidate. "How the hell do you expect me to win this fucking by-election for you if you let that Socialist pox-doctor and that fringe party public school snob steal all the limelight?" His wife mouthed vigorous agreement.

"If I hadn't devoted the best part of my life in working for the Conservatives," retorted the agent, himself an Old Marlburian, with some heat. "I'd tell you to run your own bloody campaign, Livkin."

"I'd run it a hundred times better," screamed Livkin, furious that the older man should have answered him back. "At least I wouldn't end up in the oiks' enclosure ankle-deep in horse-shit!"

Their altercation, taking place as it did outside the ever popular beer-tent, had attracted quite a few spectators by this stage. Keep on like that, gentlemen, thought Ivor Digney, who had been watching his daughter in a showjumping class, and the Captain may have a sporting chance yet. Unfortunately the protagonists suddenly became aware of their audience and fell silent. A wag at the back made some crack about the fine example being set by the party of law and order, while odds were being laid on the agent in the event of a punch-up.

David was back at the Hall in time to see the Central News. The by-election coverage contained clips of both the Livkins and Paul Enstone separate arrivals at the horse show; of Roger Mileham being greeted by the Matron at the hospital; and of himself, Lara and the two dogs outside the Red Lion in Hampton. The other candidates had not announced their plans, so consequently received no publicity.

After supper Lara had work to do, and that was to sell to David the Cunning Plan. Terri had sown the idea, Nikki and Lance had nurtured it and now the product was ready for the customer. The rock concert that was due to be held at Lower Norton in two weeks time had been set up by Lance's organisation, Rock Hard Music, some months ago. The original idea had been to stage it for the charity Bear Aid, which tried to prevent appalling cruelty to the animals in China; but soon after Cat Thrust had been rescued from the river by Kaid, Lance had decided that Greyhound Rescue, a locally based organisation devoted to finding good homes for abandoned greyhounds and Lurchers, should be co-beneficiaries.

After around thirty years as lead guitarist with his group, and as a composer, lyricist and publisher of most of their work as well, Lance had amassed such riches that he even ran a polo team at the Royal Berkshire Club during the summer. He did not need to work again in his life so, apart from indulging Cat, his only child, and Mandy, his third wife, most of the group's public appearances were now for charity.

Nikki had suggested to him over tea that perhaps, in view of the canine charity, Kaid might be allowed a guest appearance or something, to help David with his County Party. Lance went one better: yes, Kaid could put in an appearance with Dave, but for the night he would adapt the lyrics of his current hit, *Party Time*. The oft-repeated chorus of 'Come to me Party, Come to me Party' would now read 'County Party! County Party!'. Lara had one or two ideas of her own to add to the Cunning Plan in due course, but at this stage she contented herself with merely giving David the general outline.

"Darling Lara, you've got to be joking," David laughed dismissively. "I'm prepared to make a moderate fool of myself to go along with Stan's plans to get me elected, but you can't seriously expect me and Kaid to parade in front of a crowd of screaming teenagers. I'd lose whatever little cred that I may have in the constituency!"

"God, you make me so cross at times!" Lara cried, repressing an overwhelming desire to stamp her foot, her colour rising as the hot central European half of her approached melt-down. "Is it just because the girls have come up with an idea, for a change, that makes you so amused? Or are you too stupid to recognise a vote-catching opportunity when it stares you in the face?"

Ho Ho! thought Caspar, this one has a bit of spirit to go with the looks. He remembered how his dear Mary had reacted when an over-familiar policeman had addressed her as 'Luv' many years ago.

"Come on, David," he intervened. "Even I have heard of Rock and the Hard Place. They were just making the big time when you were in your last year at Eton. Like the Moody Blues, the reason that they've stayed near the top over the years is because they've held their old audiences at the same time as attracting new ones. I'd think that around half the locals will go to their gig."

Kaid had never been to a rock concert, nor a gig, whatever that was. He was not at all certain that he wanted to change the habits of a lifetime, but realised that, come the event, he probably would not be given much choice.

Only Yvette, who would have preferred a good Gérard Depardieu film to a modern band concert, and most certainly to the afternoon's cricket match, kept out of it, remaining neutral. David, out-gunned, conceded that it might not be such

93

a bad idea after all. Lara snorted, but peace was restored. for the remainder of the evening.

"Only one thing to do when girls act up like that," Caspar said, confidentially, when the girls had gone upstairs and his son and he were locking up and turning off the lights. "Take 'em straight up to bed. Works every time!" Once again, David winced.

Although David was to take Wednesday off for the picnic at Eton, he was up early on Monday morning to continue with Stan's now fairly punishing schedule, unseasonable rain not withstanding. Banbury, though well outside his boundaries, was the location of the Midland Mart's weekly sheep and pig sale. So he and Kaid went over; he knew that it would be well attended by farmers from the Vale. Cattle and cereals were the main enterprises with which he was involved at Windrush, but he knew enough from both his *Farmers' Weekly* and his Cirencester days to make intelligent talk about livestock in general, including the current prices.

Then it was on to Midland Mills, the giant farmers' co-operative that served most of the farms in three counties. He met up with Stan, punctual for a change, who briefed him with the names of the various managers he was, by prior appointment, to meet on his tour. In view of the heavy machinery in the factory, there was a strict ban on dogs, so Kaid had to be left in the car with the rain hammering on the roof for the short visit, though with all the windows down by a couple of inches for fresh air. This was certainly not the first time that this had happened to the dog, and he really did not mind. It did not stop him, however, from whining piteously whenever anyone came near.

After a snatched lunch back at the Hall, and receiving some incomprehensible message from his sister, Georgina, via Nikki about meeting up on Wednesday at Eton, he drove with Lara over to her parents' farm at the other end of the Vale. Simon Graham had agreed to introduce him to some of the farmers in his area, which he now did. Although the hay was yet to be cut (a deep low was sitting over the British Isles) David was all too well aware that neither farmers, nor farm workers, liked to have their routines interrupted. Thus he limited himself, after every introduction, to a few remarks germane to the individual's stock or crops, and parted, unless pressed to stay to discuss his views on a particular subject, with the hope that he might be remembered come polling day. Consequently they spent most of the afternoon on the muddy roads between farms, but Lara's father seemed to think that David had gone down quite well with his neighbours.

A quick bath and a quick drink (vodka, with its lack of odour, was almost *de rigeur* in the circumstances) and they were off once more, picking up Perry on the way, for the first public meeting of the County Party's campaign. Stan met them outside the modest village hall, carrying a huge golfing umbrella, ten minutes before the advertised time of the meeting and led them into a room behind the small raised platform that served as a stage when required. David adjusted his rosette. White had not been that good a choice, he thought, noting that the tails were already looking a little grubby. He also noticed Jack and Tony sitting at the back of the hall. He hoped that they had limited their liquor intake for the meeting.

At the appointed hour they entered the main body of the hall, the three men taking their seats behind the trestle table on the platform, together with Kaid, while Lara took hers in the front row facing them. Stan then rose to his feet to address the audience of around three dozen.

"Ladies and gentlemen, thank you for coming to our meeting tonight. As agent for the newly formed County Party, I would like to remind you that all of the public appearances of your candidate, Mr David Vyvian, are listed for this week in the *Evenlode Echo*." He indicated David, who was sitting at the other end of the table. "I'm sure that some of you will have met our chairman, Sir Peregrine d'Artois, before, but I now would like to ask him to say a few words before we hear from the candidate himself." He sat down.

Perry, though he had not stuck rigidly to the 'vodka only before the meeting' protocol, rose magnificently to the occasion. He started off by saying how both his family and David's had known each other for generations, both being

95

near-neighbours in the Vale. He then came up with some fairly anodyne platitudes before concluding.

"Before I ask the candidate himself to explain where he stands on issues that affect us all," he finished, briskly. "I must say this. Like some of you, I have been a Tory voter for all of my life and was a close friend of Sir Reginald. But, in my view, all of our interests now will best be served by giving our support to the County Party, and in particular to Mr Vyvian, a man born and bred in the Vale who shares many of your views." He sat down to a smattering of light applause, and it was David's turn.

Mindful of Stan's advice to keep it simple, he ran lightly over his position on matters of national interest, as stated in his manifesto, then spoke at greater length on issues closer to home. Unless natives of the Vale themselves, all home buyers of properties valued at less than £150,000 in the Vale, for instance, should pay a twenty-five percent surcharge. The money so raised would underwrite a Co-operative County Bank that in turn would lend money at a low rate of interest to farmers and small businesses alike. This could eventually be applied nation-wide to give greater stability to rural communities.

He would like to see an Evenlode official seal on some of their finer produce, such as Evenlode lamb, Blue Wyncham cheese and Oathurst apples, scarcely known outside the Vale, with a view to them reaching a wider, indeed a European, market. He also proposed that around 100 acres of the Lower Norton former RAF base be set aside for the so-called 'New Age' travellers, and also for the few genuine gypsies. Both groups, the former in particular, tended to be an expensive nuisance during the summer months. Another point on which he felt strongly was the continued building of super-stores on green-field sites outside small towns, to the detriment of local traders. He would advocate a freeze on all planning applications for such developments.

After about twenty minutes, he had come to the end of his scripted speech so, to polite applause from a slightly enlarged, if damp, audience, sat down. Stan rose and asked for questions. He had warned David to expect to be asked literally anything and to avoid, if possible, too much shooting from the hip. His first was from a member of the Evenlode Brigade, doubtless primed by Perry. How. the questioner asked, could the state afford to pay for the increase in the armed forces that David was proposing?

"Great Britain and France were the only Western European countries in Nato with any stomach for fighting," argued David. "The two, as the Sword-arm of Europe, would therefore undertake any reasonable out of area commitments, for which the United Nations might require assistance, in return for a steady subsidy from the less bellicose Nato members to support their extra forces ."

"What were his views on the disestablishment of the Church of England?" asked another.

"I believe that it would stand a better chance were it to be disestablished," answered David. "But I regard this as a Christian country, if somewhat lapsed, so I believe that there should be a Christian act of worship daily at assembly at all secular schools, and regular religious instruction." He was, predictably, clapped for his last answer. He personally thought that the denial of the Virgin Birth, the Nativity and the Magi, the Resurrection and the Second Coming by a senior bishop was on a par with utterances of the jeweller, Gerald Ratner, who had described the items on sale in his chain of stores as 'crap'.

"What did he think about sex before marriage?" This was from one of a small group who had just wandered in. From the slurred tones, it was probable that they had just left the pub, a few doors down.

"And in particular are you having it off with Miss Graham?" hiccuped another. David was saved the necessity of a reply, though both he and Lara had been expecting something like this at some stage. Jack and Tony were more than a match for the inebriated yobs who found themselves out on the wet street and propelled on their way before they could draw breath.

David was in the meantime listening to some endless and boring question about drains which was a matter firmly within the jurisdiction of the local council. Kaid intervened at that point. He stood up from his position beside David, stretched out as dogs do when they rise, and, firmly facing the audience, gave an enormous yawn. That brought the house down. When the laughter subsided, Perry was quickly onto his feet to thank everyone for attending and to close the meeting.

What a load of old bollocks, thought Kaid, who did not appreciate the bare boards, the slight draught and the speeches. Enough to make a saint yawn.

"Not bad, not bad at all," said the baronet as they drove him back to d'Artois Court. "You want to keep those minders of yours on a fairly tight leash though. 'County Party Stewards on Assault Charges' is the sort of headline that we could do without."

Back at the Hall, David and Lara had a little cold meat with some of Mrs Kerr's special chutney that she had left for them, Caspar and Yvette having eaten earlier. Later, over a drink in the library, David told his father what had happened, and gave Lara a run-down of the programme for the following Day. He also made a note to telephone Georgie at some stage to tie up a rendezvous for their picnic on Wednesday.

Tuesday followed a similar format to that of the previous day, though the rain had stopped. The personal canvassing, with additional help from the Evenlode Brigade, was that much slicker, the audience at the evening meeting was slightly larger and he was pleased to see his poster appearing in various windows.

He was also pleased to hear that Norman Livkin's Tory meetings were being regularly picketed by supporters of the Bladon, some shooting syndicate members and fishermen. They would infiltrate the audience and all want to ask the same question, namely what were the candidate's views on Field Sports. The candidate could only reply that, although he naturally abhorred the violence associated with the saboteurs, he was personally against hunting, shooting and fishing, as was his wife. At that point all the hunters, shooters and fishermen would silently depart from the meeting, leaving a much depleted hall.

Livkin, in all fairness, was good at handling barracking from hostile audiences as he was with dealing with the cut and thrust of his legal work. But this silent contempt was beyond his experience. Over the weekend, so Stan told David, he had lost his cool and had called the departing sportsmen a bunch of stupid peasants, to the despair of his long-suffering agent.

On BBC 2's *Newsnight* that evening, the results of the first set of opinion polls were announced. As always at such times, with over two weeks to go before polling day, the results would have been only of passing interest and given without comment. But these were exceptional and surprised them all. Roger Mileham, the Liberal Democrat who had yet to make a controversial speech, led with twenty-seven percent, while Livkin trailed two points behind. Paul Enstone, for Labour, was on eighteen percent, about the figure that he had achieved in 1992, while David, to his immense surprise, was on fourteen. The 'don't knows', and to a lesser extent the Green fringe parties, accounted for the remainder.

"David, is there any of the Dom Perignon left in the cellar, or have you drunk the lot?" Caspar enquired. "This calls for a celebration."

"We'll celebrate when I've won the seat, not before," David replied soberly. "Anyway, you'll be getting quite enough to drink tomorrow at the Fourth of June. Talking of which, if you have arranged to have something to eat with the Heneages, we had better take separate cars. Besides, we'll have the dogs."

Stan, too, had been watching the poll results on his television. His boy was doing nicely, thank you, and just needed to take a few more off the Tories to achieve Stan's hidden agenda plan of a win for Mileham and the Liberal Democrats. He had a sudden and unexpected twinge of lust as he thought of Mrs Mileham, granny glasses, shapeless dress and all. Perhaps, were he to just hint to her that he could help her husband . . . ?

Chapter 7

AN INTERLUDE AT ETON

The telephone conversation that David had held with his sister, Georgina, on the previous morning before he went out, had proved less than satisfactory. Her husband Dougal, Master of Ardkinglas, had himself been to Ampleforth, thus had required some persuading to let their youngest child and only son, Hamish, to be put down at birth for Eton. Now that their boy was in his final summer, he had allowed himself to be dragged south of the border to attend the Fourth of June festivities.

David had been trying to pin Georgina down over a time and a place to meet up among the thousand-odd other cars that would be jostling for a place in the shade around the perimeter of Agar's Plough. The ideal places were to be found along the tree-lined avenue that separated the field from its neighbour, Dutchman's.

"I thought we might try to get a position by that tree that I was under two years ago," said Georgie helpfully. No good, David had not attended the event two years ago.

"Well, half way along the avenue, on the right."

"The right coming from which direction down the avenue?"

"David, don't be so tiresome and military about all this. You can't miss us: the vehicle will have our usual silver capercaillie mascot on the front." A lot of other cars would have silver mascots on the bonnet, thought David, but his sister's use of the word 'vehicle' rang alarm bells.

"What make of car will you be travelling in?" he asked, fearing the worst.

"We won't actually be travelling anywhere tomorrow," said Georgie, brightly. "Dougal has decided to bring down the VW Camper so that we can stay the night *in situ*, so to speak. He doesn't want to be 'rripped offf' by any Sassenach inn-keepers, so he says."

Dear God, thought David, thank goodness that his nephew was now a senior boy, so should be able to handle something as ghastly as this. His brother-in-law, a tall, raw-boned, ginger-haired heir to a large slice of Scotland, member of the Royal Company of Archers and a title to come, was rich by any standards. David had stayed at Ardkinglas Castle from time to time and, depending on the season, there was never any shortage of gillies, loaders, stalkers, horses or servants. Dougal even had his own piper, for Heaven's sake! His father, the 10th Baron, conveniently lived on his own island in the West Indies.

With five children all born within a seven year span, he had told his factor to buy a suitable vehicle in order to transport the family as one to witness such important events as the first day of grouse-shooting, or the caber-tossing at the Ardkinglas Games. The luckless man was sacked on the spot when the Master learned that the Camper was German but, being reluctant to lose money by sending it back, Dougal had kept it for the last fifteen years. It had not, as David remembered, grown old gracefully.

David had sighed, and they had decided to meet at midday, the onus being on him to locate the Camper when they arrived on Agar's Plough. Now, on this lovely June morning and still elated from the opinion poll of the previous evening (it was repeated in the morning papers) they all prepared to set forth. Mrs Kerr had packed a picnic hamper with enough food for Georgie and her family, Carmen, who was giving a lift to Mirza, and themselves. There was a last minute hitch as Buraq had elected, once his smart collar had been put on, to roll in something that was very old, very dead and very smelly. He was consequently left in Terri's care for the day.

Kaid shed no tears for Sonny as they motored down the drive. He had not wanted him to come in the first place and indeed had urged him to 'freshen up' for the outing, so justice had been done. He stretched out voluptuously to his full length on his rug on the back seat.

They arrived a good ten minutes before the appointed hour and found the Camper without difficulty. Not only was it the sole Camper present, especially one with a sort of silver puffed-up cockerel on the roof, but parking next to it was quite easy as most others had given it a wide berth. Of Dougal and Georgina there was no sign, but Hamish emerged with a grin from nearby. David introduced the handsome lad to Lara, and indeed to Kaid.

"Mum's dragged Dad off for a glass of sherry in the house with m'tutor,' he explained easily and with a charming smile. " I'm afraid they're a bit fraught, as Dad wanted to camp here for the night, but Security moved them on pretty sharpish and they ended up shelling out to stay the night at the Monkey Island Hotel at Bray."

Details emerged later. Dougal had parked the Camper at dusk on Eton's playing fields and had got as far as lighting an old Primus stove on which to heat some Barley broth. A man from the school security, not best pleased to be turned out so late, had driven up in his little white van and had ordered them away.

"I don't think you realise who I am," Dougal had said with his clipped Scots accent. "I am the Master of Ardkinglas!"

"And I'm Flora MacDonald," replied the testy guard. "Do you move on, or do I radio for the police?" They had moved on, though with bad grace.

Carmen, to whom Lara had explained roughly where they would be, and Mirza arrived shortly afterwards. What an attractive couple they made, thought Lara. Her friend, if anything the darker of the pair, was clad in a stunning Armani trouser-suit, her diamond bracelet, and a bird of paradise broach that must have cost a King's ransom. Mirza was in western dress. When conducting interviews for the BBC, he wore the off-the-peg suits and the garish ties that the job almost demanded; but today he was wearing a well-cut navy-blue jacket with brass buttons, cream wild-silk trousers, an Hermès tie and Lobb crocodile-skin shoes.

David was amused to see his nephew's eyes start from their sockets like organ-stops when he realised that Carmen was joining them. Hamish quickly recovered in time to be introduced to her. They all started to unload the rugs and the picnic from the Mercedes, while Kaid pee-ed on a wheel of the Camper. David devoted his energies to the cool-box, and soon they were all seated on the ground sipping either Pimms or champagne. David reflected that unless Caspar and Yvette joined them for a pre-lunch drink fairly soon, there may well be none of the precious Dom Perignon left.

They heard, rather than saw, the approach of the Ardkinglases. They were bickering, as usual. Dougal was dressed for June in the Highlands rather than in the Thames Valley, while Georgina, with her wonderful figure, oozed effortless elegance. After being patronised by Hamish's housemaster, while being offered a choice between beer and sweet sherry to drink, and pondering on the amount of money that he paid for the doubtful privilege, Dougal was not a happy man. David dug into the back of the drink basket (he knew better than to offer Pimms or champagne to his brother-in-law) and came up with some malt whiskey. He half filled a tumbler which he pressed into Dougal's hand as the pair reached the car. The Scot drank it straight down, belched gently and smiled.

His ancestors had come to Scotland from Norway with Eric the Red on a raping and pillaging mid-summer break. Having, through overindulgence, missed the last longboat home, they had, perforce, no option but to stay where they were. Consequently, when Dougal espied, and indeed was introduced to, Lara and Carmen, some latent Viking blood stirred, deep down. He cuffed his son out of the way and sat next to Carmen.

"Hello Veronica," Georgina, maliciously, greeted Lara, whom she had never met before. She rather resented that she had stuck it out with Dougal for the best part of a quarter of a century, while her brother had called time on his marriage after only three years. "Oops, there I go again. I'll be muddling up my own name next!"

"Bloody Mary or Marguerita for anybody?" interjected Mirza, who had produced the ingredients for both. These they enjoyed with Caspar and Yvette, when they briefly wandered in before lunching with their friends elsewhere. Georgie hadn't seen Caspar for about a year, so their greeting was an especially warm one and they promised to meet up during the afternoon as they left. It was now lunch time, almost the *raison d'être* of the whole day.

Carmen had brought a huge jar of Beluga caviar from Fortnum's, but had deliberately only ordered five horn spoons to go with it. So, while Georgie, Lara, David and Hamish were allowed one each, both Mirza and Dougal needed to be hand-fed by Carmen, which amused them all except Georgie. The Ardkinglases, having been forced to spend the money that they had brought for the trip on overnight accommodation, and Dougal not believing in plastic cards, were strapped for cash. Georgie had hoped to do some last minute shopping for comestibles at Sainsbury's in Windsor, but that was not to be. Neither David nor Lara had expected what they regarded as their guests to bring anything anyway, and Mrs Kerr had packed more than enough for those assembled.

His housekeeper had outdone herself. David was not a great one for picnics, confining himself usually to one at the Bladon point-to-point on Easter Monday and another on the International Polo Day at Windsor in late July. For him to require one in early June was an ideal time for Mrs Kerr to clear out the freezer of surplus game-birds, which she had converted into one of her famous game pies. Poussins, roast the night before and now split in half, her Cumberland sauce, buttered baguettes and cherry tomatoes made up, with trimmings, the bulk of what was on offer. For those who still felt hungry after that, there was fresh fruit and Häagen-Dazs ice-cream to follow. She had even baked a Swiss Roll, filled with raspberry jam, for Hamish to take back to school.

Mirza had been having an interesting time talking about polo to Hamish , who had recently captained the school team in their victory over Harrow. He was also trying to ignore the increasingly blatant attempts by Georgina, who seemed to be casting aside garments like Salome, to attract his attention. A keen observer of human life, he had been noticing during their meal that, by and large, the smarter the car and the picnic arrangements, such as a Company Rolls Royce, snowy white table cloths, garden chairs and even the odd Persian carpet, the less smart the occupants, and vice versa.

"Who's for the Art Exhibition?" asked Georgina, suddenly standing up, cross that she hadn't had her fair share of the tomatoes. She announced that they were off to the Drawing Schools, a tidy hack from Agar's Plough, to see one of Hamish's paintings that was hung there. Hamish heartily wished that he had never mentioned that his picture was on show; he would have far rather have stayed around these two gorgeous women that his Uncle David had produced. However, he had no option but to tag along behind his determined mother and his truculent father. The rest of them packed up the car, feeding Kaid, who had been asleep in the shade, the last of the game pie. Then they sauntered, four abreast round the cricket pitch where the School XI were under pressure from the Eton Ramblers.

Not bad, that pie, thought Kaid. It had gone rather well with the cold beef sausage that he had scrounged, by putting on his pathetic act, from the BMW party two cars away. He could do with a drink now, to be honest. He trotted along behind the Boss and Lara, the polished cap-badge gleaming on his collar.

There were inevitably photographers about and weeks later *Harpers and Queen* ran a pictorial page on 'The Fourth of June at Eton'. Among others, there was a particularly good photograph of the four, with Kaid, captioned 'Miss Lara Graham, her fiancé Captain David Vyvian, Señorita Carmen diaz Alberdi and Rao Rajah Mirza Sind, accompanied by Captain Vyvian's saluki, Kaid'. Mounted policemen from the Thames Valley force were in the background.

David was amused by the reaction of his contemporaries and friends on their promenade. Some cut him dead, especially those with (Tory) political ambitions: however most seemed to think that his candidature as an Independent, for want of a better word, was a capital prank. Among the latter was Brigadier 'Buff' Mainwaring. He made no pretence of being an Old Etonian — indeed he was defiantly wearing an Old Harrovian tie. He had tried to persuade his landlady, Lara's Aunt Virginia, to come down with him for a couple of hours, but when she had declined, and after a good lunch, he had asked Pearl instead. Wednesdays were half days for her so, intrigued, she had accepted.

She was in her late twenties and looked rather like an older version of the model, Naomi Campbell. She was now so smart (and, it was rumoured, so expensive) that she could afford to pick and choose her clients. But she always retained special rates, Buff later told David, for old friends. The Brigadier was completely unfazed by running into friends with Pearl on his arm. She was very discreet, and it was doubtful whether any of her Old Etonian clients would recognise her in her day, rather than night, attire. Introductions were in order.

"And I don't think that any of you have met my niece, Pearl — uh — Martinique," said Buff, improvising without blinking an eyelid. "I must say, David, you've got yourself in a pretty pickle. Hope you beat that bastard Livkin though. Fellow ought to be strung up!"

Pearl coolly shook hands with them all, and recognising Kaid from their brief meeting in Shepherd Market well over two years ago, without thinking gave him a friendly pat. Kaid wagged his tail. He recognised her, too. David did not know if he had been remembered, as her face was inscrutable. In his case, the acquaintance dated back to a brief encounter after a regimental dinner some six years ago.

"Probyn's Horse?" enquired Buff, peering at the brass buttons on Mirza's jacket and guessing wildly.

"Pierre Cardin, I am afraid," replied Mirza Sind.

After further talk, they moved on, Carmen to show the 15th Century College Chapel to Mirza, and David with Lara to complete the circuit of the cricket pitch.

" David, that can't have been Buff's niece," said Lara, frowning. "And how on earth did she recognise Kaid?"

How indeed, thought the dog, the Boss needs some nifty foot-work here!

"I think the Americans would call her a high-class hooker," David answered lightly. "Buff had arranged to meet her behind the Club that time when Kaid got lost in Mayfair."

"Did you ever — "

"Once, in my bachelor days."

"Lucky David!" said Lara, mockingly. '*Et ne nos inducas in tentationem*,' she thought. She would have to watch out in the years to come.

Further discussion on David's past was interrupted by the arrival of a tall woman of about Lara's height and David's age. His brain raced for a second until he recognised Joanna. He could not have seen her for over twenty years.

"Joanna!" he kissed her chastely on the cheek, "What a nice surprise. I don't think that you've met Lara Graham, my fiancée. Darling, this is Joanna — ?" he looked at her enquiringly.

"Matheson. Hello." she seemed rather flustered, while David now recalled seeing in his paper that she had married Leo Matheson, a prominent member of the Tory back-bench 1922 Committee, some years ago.

"Leo and the others would shoot me on sight if they saw me talking to you," she added. "But listen, they're out to get you. When you were just a name as a loony fringe candidate, they didn't mind. But now that the polls show that you are attracting support, which they think will split the Tory vote, you're hurting them. They fight dirty. Bye." She was gone.

"Can we go to see the Procession of Boats or something," laughed Lara. "All of this is becoming a bit heady for a country girl!"

They wandered down towards the College buildings, past Upper Club where some lesser game of cricket was taking place, past College Field, site of the legendary Wall Game in winter, and branched off down to Fellows' Eyot on the banks of the Thames. Quite a few people had gathered there already, but they soon spotted Carmen and Mirza and joined them on the bank. Hardly had they sat down on the grass than some highly genteel shrieks rent the air. Kaid had assuaged his thirst in a tributary of the Willow Brook that ran behind them. Because it was so hot, he wallowed in the none too clean water before emerging. He then shook himself vigorously.

The fathers did not mind the odd drop or two of water on the backs of their jackets. The teenage sisters and mothers, many of whom were exposing a fair amount of pink flesh, objected vigorously. "You little bugger!" yelled a Duchess at Kaid, as David rescued his Lurcher from the vicinity of the outraged dowager. Lara hoped that she did not live in the Vale of Evenlode.

On cue, the Eights, together with the ten-man *Monarch*, came into sight from around the upstream bend in the Thames. The boys, who were all in uniform of a style worn by Nelson's sailors, raised their oars to the vertical; then they individually rose to their feet until the whole crew, including the cox, resplendent in Admiral's uniform, were standing as they passed the crowd. The coxes threw bouquets into the river as they passed a certain point; the crews, whose straw hats were bedecked with flowers, shook them, first to port, then to starboard, then to port again; so, with ensigns flying from the stern, the boats disappeared downstream on a carpet of petals. The occasional grandfathers present snorted into large handkerchiefs: for them, perhaps, their school-days had really been the happiest days of their lives.

Oh Lord Krishna! thought Mirza, thoroughly impressed. He supposed it was arcane traditions such as the one he had just witnessed that had enabled such a tiny country to win not only the battle of Waterloo, but also to subjugate such an enormous subcontinent as India.

The party over, adults made their way back to their cars, while boys repaired to their houses to pick up their luggage for Long Leave. Once back at the Mercedes, Mirza retrieved what was left of his vodka and tequila, and he and Carmen prepared to go back to London in her borrowed Alfa Romeo.

"Mirza," said David. "You're a media man. Apparently the Tories are out to get me, so if you hear anything, you'll let me know, won't you."

"Of course I will, David," replied the Indian. "All I know is that, at the moment and on past form, the three main parties will try to set up a debate in order to try to score off each other. Usually, they freeze out the minority parties, so as not to give them free publicity."

As they left, the Ardkinglases returned with Hamish dragging an enormous suitcase. Georgina was in high good humour, having met up with various admirers from her past. The same could not be said for Dougal, who was dreading the ten-hour drive in the Camper that lay before them. So when Lara suggested in all kindness that they should stay the night at the Hall he, mindful of the generous dram of the malt that David had dispensed all too long ago, accepted almost before Lara had finished speaking. David gave Mrs Kerr a call from his car to warn her of the extra guests before they left Agar's Plough. Caspar and Yvette were dropping in for drinks with an old friend of his near Henley and would rejoin them for supper.

Mrs Kerr was delighted to see Georgina again, and also Hamish who had spent the odd Sunday at the Hall on days out from Eton. He thanked her nicely for the Swiss Roll, and confessed that he and his parents had devoured it for tea in his room. Georgina, who had taken up three-day eventing again after a lay-off of some twenty-five years, wanted to see the horses before supper, so Lara took her out to where they were grazing. Kaid and Buraq, sweet-smelling once more, came too.

"I hadn't really taken in that David had bred from Kaid," said Georgie, rather regretting her stress-related rudeness to her future sister-in-law before lunch. "We've got a wonderful deerhound bitch of about the right age, who has already had bred some lovely puppies, that would do him quite nicely, if you want another litter."

"That's very kind of you," Lara replied cautiously. "But quite honestly, the trouble that both Kaid and the bitch gave David last time has rather put him off further plans on those lines for the moment, but I know he'd like a long-haired litter at some stage."

There they go again, thought Kaid. I wasn't consulted last time and it doesn't look as though I will be this time either. He mellowed slightly when he thought of dear old Uncle. He had been a deerhound. There might be some advantage in making it with an experienced bitch.

Supper was a quiet affair, since they were all quite tired, and anyway the Ardkinglases planned to leave at first light. Afterwards, as they sat in the drawing room having a night-cap; as Dougal sunk in a form of catatonic state with a large balloon glass of brandy in a deep armchair; and as Yvette was telling Lara and Georgie how they must all come over to stay in France with them in the autumn, the telephone rang.

David, not wishing to break the party up prematurely, switched the machine over to his office and went across the hall to take the call. It was from a staff reporter on the *Morning Chronicle*, a tabloid that followed a rather populist Tory line. The man apologised, rather insincerely David thought, for calling so late, but was doing an up-date on the main parties in the by-election for the following day. How, he asked was the County Party doing?

"Very well," David replied, flattered to be thought of as a main party, but suspicious nonetheless. "We seem to be attracting more support all of the time."

"Captain, we gather you went down to Eton today," stated the hack. "Was that a part of your canvassing, being as how it was some sixty miles away from the Vale of Evenlode?"

"No, I took a day off. And it's Mister, not Captain."

"And did you give your farm workers a day off too?"

"No. If they want a day off at any time, with pay, they clear it with my farm manager and it counts against their annual entitlement."

"Thank you Captain," said the reporter, well satisfied with the exchange. "Good night to you!"

David decided against telling the others when he returned to the drawing room, but later, in bed, he told Lara about it.

"Don't worry about it, Darling," she murmured, when he had snuggled up to her beneath the large duvet. She was stroking his head which was resting on her breasts. "Don't worry at all."

Chapter 8

A MILE TO RUN

The national papers largely ignored the by-election in their issues on the following day, with the exception of the *Morning Chronicle*. Jack Kestrel had bought a copy in the village and, after reading the relevant pages, passed it to Mrs Kerr in the kitchen. By the time that she and Terri, who had dropped in for an early cup of coffee and a gossip, had also perused it, it was a well-worn tabloid when it reached the dining room table. David and Lara were breakfasting alone, the Ardkinglases having been waved off by David at six o'clock. Caspar and Yvette were being indulged by Mrs Kerr, thus were allowed breakfast in bed.

It was obvious from the contents of page two that the paper had assigned a photographer to David on the preceding day at Eton. The top left quarter of the page was devoted to the Livkins, who were seen peering at a rather moribund hedgehog at a wildlife sanctuary in the Vale. Apart from the printed copy on the page, the rest was devoted to David. He was shown with Lara and Carmen on each arm, with Kaid behind them (Mirza had apparently been air-brushed out); he was seen with Pearl, Buff Mainwaring having been removed in a similar fashion; he was pictured with Joanna, luckily for her, a branch partially obscured her face; and the paper had dug out an old picture, taken about four years previously, of him and Veronica at a polo match.

The copy beneath was headed 'The Captain's Rainbow Alliance'. Underneath the story read: 'Old Etonian and former Lancer Captain David Vyvian, 39, certainly covers the field on his days off. Brunette, blonde or redhead, white or black, the Captain, a divorcee, always has time for the girls *(see pictures)*.

The Captain, a wealthy landowner, has decided on a whim to enter politics. He is standing as an independent in the forthcoming by-election for the Vale of Evenlode, where the Conservative majority is already under threat from the Liberal Democrats.

Mr Norman Livkin, the official Tory candidate, told us yesterday evening that he deplored the Captain's candidature. "The serious contenders from the major parties shouldn't have to be distracted by these lunatic fringe people," he stated. "Let the squirarchy stick to parish councils, village fêtes and bossing their yokels around, while we get on with running the country."

When asked if he had allowed his farm workers the day off also, the Captain told our reporter that they should have asked his manager first. Cap in hand, no doubt!'

There was more in the same, snide, vein, all implying that he was playing at politics and thus damaging the serious Conservative efforts to hold the seat. He was also rather uncomfortably aware that he had some degree of carnal relations with four out of the five girls pictured in the paper in the past. His lawyers in Gresham Street would have to tell him if there was anything he could do.

Lara was hardly thrilled by the coverage of their day at Eton; Pearl, when she was shown the paper that evening by an admirer, was quite pleased; Joanna thanked her lucky stars that she was unrecognisable; Veronica hoped that it would do her ex-husband harm; and Carmen went ballistic.

It was not that she would not have minded, in different circumstances, being 'covered' (as the paper had put it) by David, but rather that she objected to being lumped, together with the *puta negra*, as part of a harem. She telephoned the First Secretary at her Embassy (he was still hoping for the return of his car) and made her feelings plain. He in turn told the Ambassador that the daughter of their Ambassador to the United Nations, still in the running for the Secretary Generalship when the ageing Egyptian incumbent retired, had been insulted in an English tabloid newspaper. A flurry of diplomatic activity followed during the morning. Finally the Ambassador of the Republic of Ecuador to the Court of St James cut through the niceties. He told the Foreign Secretary that, unless a retraction was published on the following day, he would feel compelled to advise Señor diaz Alberdi to regard Great Britain as an unfriendly power.

The open-mouthed Foreign and Commonwealth Office men were appalled. They all knew roughly whom the Ambassador was talking about, of course. Why, the way some of these Latin-American countries worked, it could well be *El Presidente* diaz Alberdi next. There was also the not completely unconnected fact that Ecuador had placed a provisional order for fifty Scorpion light reconnaissance tanks and a squadron of Harrier jets with the Ministry of Defence, to the fury of the Americans, only weeks earlier.

David, while all this was going on, was having less luck with his lawyers. They would, they said, serve a writ on the *Morning Chronicle* for defamation, if those were to be his instructions; it would undoubtedly be vigorously defended by the paper, and would not, in any event, come to court until long after the by-election. Dispirited, David told them to await further instructions. He called Kaid and they wandered over to Party HQ where Stan and Nikki were hard at work up-dating what David called his battle map.

Having no party ward infrastructure of their own, Stan had marked the various boundaries on the wall map. In conjunction with the address list of members of the Evenlode Brigade which Perry had thoughtfully provided, he and Nikki were trying to identify at least one member per ward who would be capable of acting as ward boss for the next vital two weeks. The criteria were fairly demanding in that the chosen individuals had to be somewhere between retirement and senility, sometimes a rather narrow gap, be capable of limited organising abilities and be on reasonably friendly terms with their neighbours.

Stan was, in fact, in high good humour. While he had been firmly rebuffed by Nikki, whom he had propositioned on the previous morning, he had managed more success with Mrs Mileham, granny glasses and all. A swift glance in the local paper had informed him that the Liberal Democrat would be attending a school sports day nearby; so he had attended the function and had cornered the good lady behind the tea-tent while her whiskered husband was presenting the prizes for the egg-and-spoon race.

"Mrs Mileham, please spare me a moment," he had started off in a beseeching voice that he hoped would appeal to her maternal instinct. "Unlikely as it may seem, I'm in a position to

113

help your husband win this seat, though he must never know of my involvement. Can we meet to discuss it further when he is tied up somewhere else on the stump?"

Intrigued, Teresa Mileham had asked him to drop in that evening when her husband would be taking the Chief Whip around the constituency. She was sure that she had seen this smooth chap with the sleeked-back hair somewhere before and, at any rate, she would do anything to get Roger into parliament. A child of the flower-power generation of the Sixties and Liberal both by name and nature, she was more intent, when Stan insinuated himself into her house later, on deeds rather than words. There had been a lot of her beneath the home-spun caftan, Stan had reflected wearily as he eventually made his way home. He was surprised that the candidate was able to stand up by day, let alone to rush about the constituency being nice to people.

Now, he was not in the least bothered by David's exposure in the *Chronicle*. The Vale contained no nests of chattering classes to feign outrage at the suggestion that the County Party candidate might be a womaniser. Indeed, the men would be likely to chuckle over the paper in the pubs that evening on the lines of 'Good on the Captain', while their women would probably think that David was better looking than any of the other candidates. All that the paper had really achieved was to give David a higher profile. He made sure that photo-copies of the relevant page were faxed to the local media, together with a brief statement to the effect that Mr David Vyvian, candidate for the County Party at the forthcoming by-election, had visited his old school on the previous day, together with his fiancée Miss Lara Graham, where they had met some old friends.

That night they had their first taste of trouble. David and Stan had spent most of the day in what was by now becoming a familiar routine of canvassing, with the help of appropriate members of the Evenlode Brigade. They were both encouraged by a trickle of invitations from new supporters to look in on coffee mornings and wine and cheese parties during the coming fortnight of the campaign. "Never go into a house on your own," Stan had warned him. "Always have me, or Lara, or both: otherwise the next thing that you know will be someone shouting 'Rape!' which won't do your cause much good."

When David left the Hall later in the evening with Kaid, Lara having gone over to see her parents for supper, his purpose was to go straight to the village hall in Lower Norton where he was due to speak. Both Perry and Simon Graham, his co-chairmen, were otherwise engaged, so Stan would introduce him to his audience. He was about to climb into his Mercedes when there was a discreet cough behind him. It was Jack Kestrel.

"'Scuse me, Cap'n, but Tony thinks you should go with him tonight." he was informed by his keeper-cum-bodyguard, who indicated the farrier's pickup truck parked further down the drive. "Feeling is, there'll be trouble tonight."

These humans really are so stupid,' thought Kaid. He had sensed a troubled night ahead since midday, but these two-legged idiots had only just realised it. For the first time in his life, he rather wished that Buraq, with his Doberman physique, was coming too. Sonny could be a bit of a pain for most of the time, but he felt that tonight he would have welcomed some filial support.

"Okay," said David easily. He knew better than to argue with country people when they had a feeling about something. Anyway, he always suspected Jack, with his dark complexion, of having a touch of Gypsy blood. He saw a minibus parked further on, and raised his eyes in unspoken question.

"Stewards, Sir," said Tony, who had joined them. "We'd best be on our way if we aren't going to be late."

Some twenty minutes later they arrived at the back of the hall to find a nervous looking Stan awaiting them. About thirty assorted yobs, many of whom appeared to be 'new age travellers', had apparently been bussed in earlier. They were already rowdy, in some cases, drunk and all very dirty, with long matted hair. Stan looked relieved at the sight of the Stewards, all of whom were wearing not only the party rosettes, but also smart red arm-bands embroidered with the word 'Marshal' and supplied, on Jack's suggestion, by Nikki.

Leaving the marshals in the back room under Tony's control, David strode onto the stage with Stan, Jack, who was ostensibly in charge of Kaid and the dog himself. Stan, clearly unhappy, gave a terse introduction before David rose to his feet. He was greeted by a storm of abuse and the odd tomato from the rent-a-mob element, some of whom, he noted with unease, had dogs with them. He managed to get through most of his standard prepared speech until he came to his eminently sensible suggestion about setting aside 100 acres of the disused air-base three miles outside the village for the travellers.

"So you want to stick us behind bars like animals in the zoo, do you?" yelled one androgynous youth. "Well, I've got news for you, you big ponce, next time we get together, it'll be on your fucking farm!"

"To put you in a zoo wouldn't be fair on the other animals," retorted David, stung. At that point the troublemakers rushed the stage, hurling eggs and assorted vegetables and fruit as they came. Kaid was magnificent. While David kicked over the table onto its side to form some sort of a protective barrier, he faced the mob with hackles raised and teeth bared, alternately snarling and barking. Two of the travellers dogs, braver than their human owners, came at him, one rangy mongrel going for his throat. The thick leather collar with the large King's Lancers cap-badge saved him from injury from that attacker, while the other dog came away choking from a large mouthful of the long, silky, coat.

It was really all over in seconds, as Tony with his marshals ran into the hall and formed an unbroken line between the stage and the audience. A few blows were exchanged, but, though numerically superior, the travellers were no match for Tony Stark's hand-picked squad of former soldiers. As they slunk out of the door at the far end of the hall, David was slightly shocked to see his groom, Terri, land a blow on one of them that would have felled an ox. Thank goodness he had firmly vetoed her request to join his personal retinue!

David made a huge fuss of Kaid, who by now thought that he had done enough. So he thanked those villagers who had remained in the hall — most had left at the first signs of trouble — and apologised for having to cut short his visit on account of the mercifully slight injuries suffered by his dog. He also commiserated with Stan, who had sustained a direct hit from what he hoped was only a rotten apple.

Tony drove him home in the pick-up, but not before he had dismissed his marshals with some gratitude. "That's all right Sir," said one ex-corporal. "Reminded us all of clearing out the NAAFI on pay nights."

Sergeant Hill of the local police, whose Panda car was parked outside the Hall, was in the kitchen drinking Irish coffee with Mrs Kerr when David arrived back. He took a last swig from his mug and rose to his feet as David came into the kitchen.

"Sorry to trouble you so late, Sir," explained the policeman. "But we've received a complaint from a member of the public who claims that he was assaulted by your people at the meeting at Lower Norton earlier this evening. Seems as how he's got three broken ribs." he added.

"My marshals, who were under the control of Tony Stark, whom you know, had to intervene at one stage when some yobs tried to rush the platform," said David, choosing his words carefully. "But most of the blows came from them. They also set their dogs on my Lurcher." He indicated Kaid, who was being comforted by Mrs Kerr. She had given the dog the steak, having sliced it up, that she had been due to serve up to her employer for his supper.

"Completely understood, Sir," replied the Sergeant. He would not have minded some of that steak himself, especially as Thursdays were whist nights for Mrs Hill. Cold meat and salad was all that he had to look forward to. "He was way over the limit, according to the hospital, so he probably fell over and did himself a nasty." He rose to go. The complainant had certainly been one of the new-age yobs, the bane of the police across the country during the summer. The only name that he would give to the hospital had been 'Spring Ur'.

Lara came back at around eleven and was predictably cross at having missed all of the action. Buraq was misguided enough to try to grab his father's ruff, and received a sharp nip for his pains.

Friday's *Morning Chronicle* contained two items of interest to the inhabitants of the Hall. For on the back page and under a single column heading 'Miss Carmen Alberdi' was an apology. 'It has been suggested,' it read. 'That our page two article in yesterday's edition implied that there was a relationship between Miss Alberdi and Captain Vyvian. That was not our intention, and we apologise unreservedly for any misunderstanding that may have occurred.' (The Prime Minister had practically to offer the proprietor a peerage to get even that!)

On page two of the later editions (again) was a lurid account of Mr Spring Ur's brutal treatment by Nazi-style storm-troopers at David's meeting on the previous evening. There was a picture of Ur, clutching his side as if in pain. He was also sporting both a CND badge and one from the Animal Liberation Front, neither of which got him much sympathy in the Vale. For good measure the hippie, who had dropped out from Worcester College a year earlier, also spoke about some animal being present that must have been a cross between Cerberus and the Hound of the Baskervilles. 'Never have I seen a man run as Ur ran that night', thought David inconsequentially.

He took Lara and Kaid (Terri had polished his smart collar) to a school for crippled children in the morning. Luckily, Kaid was good with the young, so the visit was a great success, with happy little faces waving good-bye to the dog as they left.

"A pity that they're too young to vote," commented David, as they drove to a nearby pub for a sandwich and a glass of beer. There, he found himself very embarrassed when the landlord refused to accept any payment when they wanted to leave.

"I heard on Fox FM about the trouble that you had at Lower Norton last night," he explained (which was more than David and Lara had). "It isn't right, what they did. Lock the lot of 'em up like you said, and good luck to you!" David felt that perhaps his message had not come across precisely as he had intended, but let it pass.

They spent the afternoon walking around the grounds of an old people's home and chatting to the residents. David listened with genuine interest to the war-stories from some of the old boys, while Lara tried to draw the old ladies out on tales of their youth. A few of them expressed a wish to vote for David, but pointed out that they had no transport. He made a note for Stan to speak to the matron in due course when they made their plans for getting potential voters to the polling stations.

When they arrived back at the Hall, Nikki gave Lara a message to call Carmen. Lara called the Dorchester, and soon the two girls were chattering away in French, the language that they always used between themselves. David left her to it as he went to have a bath. Tonight it was wine and cheese with the vicar of Much Binding 'just to meet some of the parishioners, you understand'. Lara was excused duty after her sterling work with both the young and the old during the day, so Stan would be his chaperone.

Lara came up later and sat on the side of the bath. Idly, she picked a lump of ice from her drink and dropped it into David's navel. He made a grab for her, but she was too quick for him and retreated to the bathroom stool .

Kaid , lying between the laundry basket and the towel-rail, reflected that humans, rather like Lurchers, liked a good wallow in water. But he could never understand why the Boss always had to spoil his with Badedas. The smell reminded him vaguely of the shampoos to which he had been subjected when, as a puppy, he had rolled in something particularly choice.

"I thought that Carmen would never stop talking,' she told him. "Apparently the Ecuadorian polo team won their semi-final of the Queens Cup at Windsor this afternoon and so are due to play against Lance Thrust's team on Sunday in the final. Her Ambassador is taking it all fearfully seriously and has prevailed on the Guards Polo Club, through the office of the Marshal of the Diplomatic Corps, to let his people erect a tent next to the Royal Box. We've been asked to lunch, as has Mirza."

"In fact it was Mirza this and Mirza that for most of the time," she continued. "Anyway, I checked with your campaign diary, and we can fit it in between Matins in St Cuthbert's and drinks that evening with Perry and Stella. Carmen has also been asked to the Presentation of Standards to the Household Cavalry tomorrow, and wanted to know if it was something to do with the government's 'Back to Basics' campaign. I told her that it was all about regimental flags, although Daddy always said that his Green Jackets didn't go in for that sort of thing."

David winced at the mention of consecrated standards being described as 'regimental flags', just as he had winced when the ice-cube came into contact with his anatomy earlier. However, he was pleased that they were going to the Queens Cup, which he had not witnessed since his brief membership of the Guards Polo club over ten years before. He asked Lara to pass him a towel and continued to get ready for the wine and cheese that Much Binding had prepared. For choice, he would far rather leave Kaid behind to have a good walk with Lara and Buraq, especially as he suspected that the dog's boredom threshold was fast approaching, but found that the fickle electorate felt short-changed if Kaid was not instantly available.

Come Sunday, the vicar of St Cuthbert's was getting increasingly fed up with the by-election. David had taken the trouble to warn him that he would like to bring one of God's Creation, to whit his Lurcher, to Matins, and that they would sit at the back, as they did in his own parish church, and would give no trouble. Now, just as the vicar was settling down after Holy Communion to his boiled egg and the News of the World, Norman Livkin's agent had rung to say that his candidate's wife, Esther, would be bringing a cat to Evensong. He hated to think what the Green candidates could bring if this sort of thing caught on.

Livkin himself was in his normal foul temper. He had hoped to show his party's commitment to a multi-racial society by attending a synagogue, mosque or temple on the appropriate days leading up to Sunday, but apparently there were none within the Vale. The Roman Catholics he considered far too elitist, especially now that the Duchess of Kent had joined them. He would therefore go that evening to St Cuthbert's, plonk himself in the front row with Esther and her damned cat, and rely on his agent to tell him what posture to adopt at the appropriate times.

Roger and Teresa Mileham were on a day-long hike with the Ramblers Association across a large chunk of the Cotswolds; Paul Enstone planned two rounds of golf on the municipal course near Windrush; and the Green candidates, in an unexpected display of unity, sat on a hilltop where two ley-lines met and celebrated some festival to summer.

Chapter 9

THE QUEEN'S CUP

David, Lara and Kaid went straight from church to Smiths Lawn in Windsor Great Park, a journey of about an hour and a quarter. Entering the Park through Blacknest Gate, Lara was struck by the beauty of both the Virginia Water, and the Valley Gardens with their late-flowering Rhododendrons and Azaleas in full bloom, the trickling water-courses and the carefully recreated flower-bedecked meadows.

Polo she had seen before, of course, during what she thought of as her Italian days, but never at Windsor. Having no tickets of any sort caused certain problems as flustered officials tried first to turn them away, then to send them to the public, as opposed to the members', side of the main ground; eventually Mr Saunders, resplendent in his bowler hat, recognised David from the old days and found his name on the right VIP list for the Ecuadorian Ambassador's party.

David parked in the shade of some trees, then they walked over to the open-fronted tent beside the Royal Box. He noticed sniffer dogs with their handlers giving the white-painted wooden building, a gift from a German industrialist some years earlier, a check over. There were also two members of the Diplomatic Protection Branch (SO 16), both with the characteristic bulge on their left breasts that denotes a shoulder-holster, on duty outside the Ambassador's tent. Inside, after giving their names at the entrance, they were taken over to meet the Ambassador and his wife.

"Any friend of Carmen is surely a friend of ours ," purred His Excellency as he bent over Lara's hand. Although highly regarded in his country's diplomatic circles, he was not quite in the same league as Carmen's father. "I am glad that you have brought your dog also. We will need all the support that we can get this afternoon against Señor Thrust and his *pistoleros*." David looked across the tent and noted with amusement that Lance Thrust's two foreign professional players on the Rock

Hard team were Argentines, as was the top player with Los Andes, the Ecuadorian team.

Carmen, together with Mirza, came over to greet them. She was still breathless with excitement from the previous day. She had gone to Horse Guards Parade as planned to see, as Lara had put it, a distribution of regimental flags. As a frequent visitor to London, she was used to the sight of the Household Cavalry as they trotted between Horse Guards and their barracks in Hyde Park, but had no reason to know that they had an armoured role as well. Consequently, when two squadrons of tracked reconnaissance vehicles, or tanks as Carmen described them, suddenly clanked towards what is after all the back of Downing Street, she naturally assumed that she was witnessing a coup at first hand. She ascribed the subsequent lack of gun-fire to the fortuitous arrival of The Queen, who clearly still commanded the loyalty of her Guard Regiments.

David left the two girls and made his way over to where Lance was holding court, a cigar firmly clamped between his teeth, regardless of the fact that he was due to play six hard chukkas in just over two hours time. He recognised Lance's son, Cat, who rushed over to welcome Kaid, his erstwhile saviour.

"Hi, Dave," Lance Thrust, captain of the Rock Hard team, greeted David with both arms outstretched. "Hi, Kide. I gather that we are doing a double act on Saturday." He turned to introduce his team, which enabled David to gather his wits. Of course! Saturday was the rock concert at Lower Norton at which Nikki had arranged for his and Kaid's guest appearance. The local papers and the tabloids had been carrying advertisements for tickets for the last three weeks.

David failed to notice Lance's agent steering Cat, followed by the trusting Kaid, out of the tent and into the fenced off grass enclosure in front of it. Although the Ambassador would never have allowed press photographers onto his patch, he was in no position to prevent them from leaning over the picket fence. This they were now doing, using up rolls of film, as the publicity man explained that the two had featured in the rescue drama earlier in the year, and were to appear together at the group's concert on Saturday. The photographers were delighted, as Cat's indisposition after the affair meant that this was the first opportunity that they had had to picture the victim and his rescuer together. When David heard the whir of the motors on the cameras, coupled with cries of 'Kiss the mutt, Cat!' he realised what was going on and, with a fixed smile. led the pair back to the tent.

'Honestly! There I was, being appreciated for once, when the Boss drags me back into the tent!' Kaid went into his pathetic routine, and, sure enough, was soon rewarded with a smoked salmon canapé.

Meanwhile, it had been Lara's turn for a surprise. She was chatting to Carmen, Mirza and the First Secretary (he had been forced to hire a car since Carmen showed no signs of returning his Alfa Romeo) when, on a cloud of after-shave and like a Genie out of the proverbial bottle, there appeared Luigi. His political career had never really taken off; he was now a sort of super-salesman for his Milanese father-in-law, and was currently trying to sell domestic appliances to Ecuador. He had recently suffered the mortification of overhearing his fleshy-faced mother-in-law describe him as 'my son-in-law, the Count'. But, suave as ever, though a trifle more podgy around the jowls and waist, he was immediately all over Lara.

"*Carissima, bella carissima,*" he murmured as he showered her with kisses. Lara broke away just as David and Kaid returned, and tried to defuse the situation.

"David, you won't have met Luigi Montecuccoli from Rome. Luigi, this is my fiancé, David Vyvian." Luigi nodded briefly at David before ostentatiously focusing his attention on Carmen.

"What did the ice-cream salesman want?" David asked crossly, once they were alone.

"Darling, don't be so silly!" Lara prodded him in the ribs. "I had to meet a positive harem of your women on Wednesday at Eton, so allow me just one old Italian boy-friend." David smiled ruefully: she had a point.

Lunch was then announced, so around fifty people sat down at tables of eight according to an elaborate seating plan. David found himself between the Argentine Ambassador's wife, fortunately fluent in English, and the wife of a committee member of the club, delighted for an excuse to escape lunch with the day's tobacco sponsors. He glanced over to Lara at a nearby table: she had the Los Andes Argentine 'ringer', Hector something-or-other, and the local (Tory) MP as her companions.

Lunch was a very relaxed affair. Although the Argentines had been banned from playing polo in England for a few years immediately after their unsuccessful invasion of the Falkland Islands in 1982, and indeed a handful of members of the polo club had been members of the Task Force that recaptured them, there was no lasting bitterness. Indeed, the Ambassador's wife raised the subject herself over the Lobster Mousseline, diplomatically referring to the Islands as 'Les Malouines'.

Cold slices of filets of beef, roast and stuffed with pâté de fois gras, followed, during which David gently teased the committee member's wife over the internal politics within the club. Founded in the Fifties as a mainly military organisation, their obsession with secrecy over the most trivial of matters was a constant source of amusement to all and sundry. No, she giggled, there was nothing behind the rumour (that David had just invented) about Colonel Smallpiece's wife going off with Major Strongi'th'arm; but surely he had heard about the assistant chairman and the girl groom at the barbecue?

Passion-fruit sorbet was the final course and general conversation ensued. Someone from the other side of the table asked David if he was not the 'chap in the coming by-election'. David, who obviously was not wearing his by now rather grubby rosette, no more than he had done at the Fourth of June, said that he hoped that he was 'that chap'. The Ambassador's wife promptly assumed that he was England's answer to the former populist dictator, Juan Perón, whom she had always secretly admired. However, the committee member's wife, a true blue Tory, felt that she had been nurturing a viper to her (ample) bosom, so gave a small shudder of horrified fascination.

After coffee and some bitter, black, Ecuadorian chocolates had been served, the Ambassador made a short speech in which he thanked them for coming, hoped that they would enjoy the afternoon and cheer for Los Andes. "Not me, mate," laughed Lance. He had sent his professionals to prepare themselves for the game about twenty minutes before, and the Los Andes team had also left. The Ambassador added, once the laughter had died down, that he hoped to see them back in his tent for tea after the match.

With time in hand, David and Lara wandered past the clubhouse (No Dogs Allowed, read the sign on the door) and down to the pony lines, where David knew that Kaid could get a drink from the horse-trough. (Kaid, on form, declined the heavily chlorinated product of the Water Board, and pee-ed contemptuously on the side of the trough.) The Ecuadorian team had brought their own ponies, and grooms, over for the season, so Lara was fascinated by the Gauchos, with their baggy black pantaloons, silver coins on their belts and berets on their heads.

The ponies, too, were nearly all from South America and to the uninitiated all looked the same, mainly bays or chestnuts with hogged manes, plaited and bound up tails and without an ounce of spare fat on them. The exception, of course had to be Lance. His favourite pony was an Appaloosa mare of uncertain age but with a wonderful temperament. Her owner, for whom much of what happened beneath the saddle was a closed secret, always referred to her as 'Spotted Dick'.

The five-minute warning bell was rung by Jock Gunn, for many years the chief time-keeper at the club, so David and Lara made their way back to that section of the stand that had been reserved for the Ambassador's guests. Kaid's presence inevitably meant that they would have to sit on the lower seats near the front, as he always feigned vertigo if invited to go any higher. The Queen's arrival was marked by the playing of the National Anthem by the band of the Grenadier Guards, resplendent in their bear-skin caps and red tunics, The band then moved to the goal area nearest to the pony lines prior to leading the two teams onto the ground in a formal parade. Cat Thrust, whose mother's place he was taking for the day (Mandy was indisposed, Lance explained), was a bit at a loose end while his father was out on the ground, came and sat next to Kaid.

'*If I have to watch this stupid game,*' thought the dog. '*It will make the time pass quicker with this nice little boy stroking my silky coat. I suppose that my picture will be in all the papers tomorrow . . .*'

The teams duly paraded with the band, coming to a halt in front of the Royal Box. While the band marched off, the commentator called out the players individually, who removed their assorted head-gear and cantered around to rejoin their teams. Once that was completed, the two mounted umpires moved with the teams to the centre of the ten-acre ground and one of them threw the small white ball down between the two lined-up teams.

Both Carmen, who was sitting behind them with Mirza, and Lara had seen enough polo in the past to preclude the need for constant explanations from Mirza and David as to what was going on — indeed, with the blaring commentary over the loudspeaker system, it would have been doubtful if they could have made themselves heard anyway. so they all settled down to watch two of the strongest teams of the season playing off the maximum allowed handicap of twenty-two goals fight it out on one of the finest polo grounds in the country.

Los Andes, the Ecuadorian team, was most probably the better balanced team of the two, though all bar their Argentine 'hired assassin' were strictly amateur players. That is not to say that they did not take the game seriously: for had they not left lunch early, having eaten little and drunk only soft drinks? Machismo demanded that they should be lean, fit and win. The 'patron' of the team, Carmen's father's friend, was in his fifties, but was still well worth his four-goal rating.

The strategy in Lance's Rock Hard team was totally different. The veteran star had worked hard for all of his life, only started riding, let alone hunting and polo, in middle-age, and was damned if he was going to deny himself the pleasures that money could buy once he could afford them. Squash kept him physically fit for his now rare appearances on stage, which often involved a three-hour performance.

But cigars, the odd glass of *fine champagne*, and a modest two-goal handicap meant that he was obliged not only to hire, but also to provide ponies for, three (two Argentine and one

British) professionals. Though he was more than capable of giving the ball a smart smack with his polo-stick if it came within range of Spotted Dick, or any of the other ponies in his string, the bumping and the rough stuff, often against players of half his age, he left to the hired help: that is what he paid them for.

By half-time at the end of the third chukka the score was three goals apiece, with both sides having concentrated much of their efforts in trying to trick the weakest members of the opposition into involuntary fouls. When this ploy succeeded, a penalty hit would be awarded to the aggrieved team which, with the legendary big hits of the Argentines, often resulted in a goal. During the break the spectators followed the polo tradition of walking onto the ground, ostensibly to tread back the divots cut by the ponies' hooves during play from the pristine billiard table-like surface of the mown grass.

In practice, those on the members' side treated it as an opportunity to socialise with each other, hard to do when cooped up on the stands; while those on the visitors' side rushed like a thundering herd of Bison across the ground to the front of the Royal Box. Her Majesty retired on such occasions to the upstairs balcony, though Prince Philip 'trod in' with the crowd. David pointed out various individuals of interest to Lara as they wandered towards the centre of the ground.

"Mirza is at present talking to the Rajmata of Jaipur," he indicated a serene Indian lady in a sari walking with their friend. "She was, apparently, one of the most beautiful women in the world when her late husband, 'Jai', used to play here in the Sixties. Behind them, and walking towards the stands, are Jilly and Leo Cooper."

"And there are rock stars Kenny Jones, Mike Rutherford and Stewart Copeland, together with Ginger Baker, who is based in the States nowadays. They've obviously come to support Lance. And, unless I am mistaken," he added. "Here is Buff with your Aunt Virginia. Let's have a little fun!" They walked over to the pair.

It was unfortunate that Virginia Graham had tried to adjust her make-up by using the tiny driving-mirror in Buff's car. The result was not an outstanding success, to put it mildly. Poor Buff was soundly berated when the pair were back in London for not pointing out the error to her earlier, but, being short-sighted, he had noticed nothing amiss. They chatted for a few moments. As they moved on David, by way of a Parthian shot, asked after Buff's 'niece'.

"But you told me that you were both a bachelor and an only child," Virginia was saying accusingly to Buff as they moved out of earshot and back towards their seats.

The tension between the two teams increased during the final three chukkas. To win the Queen's Cup was the proudest feather in any team's cap. Luckily, the two umpires, the Hipwood brothers, were both firm and impartial, so Latin histrionics were kept to a minimum and fouls were comparatively few. The score stood at five-all at the start of the final period, which is where it remained for most of the chukka. But, in the closing seconds, Hector, the Los Andes Argentine, picked up the ball from a hit-in by his own team and, after a run down the length of the ground, drove it firmly through the opposition's goal. A bell signified the end of the match.

Her Majesty presented Her cup to the winning Los Andes team and small gifts, provided by the sponsors, to all of the players. There were also prizes for the best player of the match, the best pony, the best turned-out team and so on. The Ecuadorian Ambassador's guests moved back into his tent for tea. All the tables had been moved to the sides and there was plenty of tea, China or Indian, little cress and cucumber sandwiches and small cakes. The reason for the rearrangement of the tables became obvious when the Ambassador announced quietly, '*Señoras y Señores, Su Majestad La Reina!*', He went forward to meet Her Majesty and Prince Philip as they arrived at the entrance of the tent.

It was obvious to David that the visit had been prearranged, even at such short notice, right down to the detail of briefing the Royal couple as to whom they would meet. The Embassy staff would take couples, or indeed individuals, to either the Ambassador, who stayed with The Queen, or to his wife, who accompanied Prince Philip. They in turn would present the guests who would be quietly disengaged after a minute or so as another guest would be produced.

Thus Mirza, having exchanged namastis with Prince Philip, had a chat with him about polo in India, where the Prince had played on many occasions in his polo-playing days. David and Lara were presented to The Queen, which involved token obeisances on their behalves.

"They tell me, Captain Vyvian, that you plan to enter politics," said Her Majesty, absentmindedly patting Kaid on the head and examining the shiny cap-badge on his leather collar. "I see that we have a King' Lancer here!" She turned to Lara. "And you must keep your fiancé from doing anything foolish. One should never sever one's roots from the land." After further chat about Kaid, it was time to move on.

Kaid, who had sensed the respect that the Boss had for this gracious Lady, had sat firmly down at her approach. His detractors had held that his tail-carriage, a little too curly perhaps, was a trifle common, and he wasn't going to let the side down in front of The Queen.

They went to commiserate with Lance, who was very philosophic about his narrow defeat, and promised to be in touch before Saturday's concert. The Queen having already departed, they thanked their hosts effusively for their hospitality, said good-bye to Carmen and Mirza and made their way back to the car. They wondered how Buff had talked himself out of the slight corner in which they had left him concerning his non-existent niece.

"Is polo always as glamorous as that at Windsor," asked Lara, as they drove back towards the M40 along the Drift Road.

"'Fraid not," David replied. "If it was, I just might take it up again. It beats canvassing any time!"

Chapter 10

THE FINAL FURLONG

A drink that evening with the d'Artoises was a necessary, if irksome, chore: for he had gathered together a group of influential and disaffected local Tories, all of whom would be prepared to speak on David's behalf at meetings over the next vital eleven days. David was quite relieved, as, Perry and Simon Graham apart, he had no local 'senior figures' to back him up. True, both Buff Mainwaring and Dougal Ardkinglas had offered to help, but he had politely turned them down. The former was quite capable of turning up with Pearl, as living proof of his commitment to a multi-racial society; while the latter's clipped and slightly dour tones were hardly a vote-catcher. He had also heard from Stan that Livkin was due to receive support from at least one cabinet minister.

Monday's tabloids produced a crop of photographs taken the day before of Kaid and Cat, together with some of The Queen commiserating with Lance Thrust at the prize-giving ceremony after the Queen's Cup final. The papers also produced the results of the latest poll, taken over the weekend. Roger Mileham, the Liberal Democrat who still had yet to say anything remotely controversial, remained on twenty-seven percent, now three points ahead of the Tory, Norman Livkin. Dr Paul Enstone, for Labour, had increased his share to twenty percent, while David had risen to seventeen, both largely due to 'don't knows' starting to make up their minds. The odd-ball fringe parties seemed to have made no effort whatsoever, and were only there, David suspected, to gain their deposit-worth of publicity by being on stage when the final results were announced.

"Isn't our boy doing well!" chuckled Stan to Nikki as he strode into Party HQ prompt on the dot of nine o'clock. Not half as well, thought Nikki, as he will be doing by this time next week, if Lance's plans for Saturday come off.

"We've had a bid for more posters from our man in the Oathurst ward," she said aloud. "And David has left a list of local big-wigs who he wants involved in appropriate meetings, if possible. I've dug out their addresses to show which wards they live in."

"David also says that he is going to show his face at the rock concert on Saturday evening, which seems clear in the diary," she added. "He dreads it, and certainly doesn't expect you to go along as well." Here Nikki was being economical with the truth. David had expressed no feelings either way about the concert, apart from agreeing to attend, but Nikki, during her short time at the Hall, had developed the same distrust of Stan as had Lara.

That suited Stan very well. He had better things to do on Saturday nights at the moment, Tessa Mileham being one of them. He knew that he was neglecting Veronica somewhat, but felt sure that she was finding solace elsewhere. Meanwhile, 'Party Time', the single performed by Rock and the Hard Place, has reached number two in the charts of the New Musical Express.

The week passed quickly, and to give Stan his due, his arrangements worked like clockwork. With the help of the Evenlode Brigade, and an increasing amount of local volunteers, all households in the Vale received a visit by some reasonably articulate supporter of the County Party, who left a copy of the manifesto if there was no-one in. The posters of David with Kaid were seen in most villages, though local wags had taken to the habit of adding graffiti on the lines of 'What's your pedigree, Chum' and bubbles coming from David's mouth containing the words 'Woof! Woof!'

Lara came with him to most meetings, as did of course Kaid, but there was no repetition of the rowdy night that they had experienced at Lower Norton. Caspar often threatened to join them, but was diverted by the four-day Royal Meeting at Ascot. He and Yvette would leave the Hall at about eleven in the conventional finery — which entailed Caspar complaining every morning that his morning coat and trousers had shrunk considerably since he last wore them — and return, he slightly the worse for wear, at some time during the evening.

David had gone so far as to volunteer Jack Kestrel as a chauffeur for the Bentley, but Caspar would have none of it.

"Damned good chap to have around," was his only comment. "Not needed on the voyage, though. The car practically drives itself to Ascot and back."

Saturday was on them all too quickly and David suddenly realised that he had given no thought to the concert that evening. He voiced his misgivings to Lara at breakfast, but she hastened to assure him that everything was in hand.

"Don't worry, Darling, everything is tied up. with Lance. Just make sure that you're back by six after your jumble sale, or whatever you've got on this afternoon, and I'll brush Kaid while you have a bath before we leave."

'I don't think that the Boss quite realises how very important I am these days,' the dog thought. 'So who had his picture all over the papers on Monday? Him or me? I am really not sold on this concert idea at all.'

So David went about his duties with Stan during the day. At one point, in Evenlode itself, he came face to face with Roger and Teresa Mileham, owing to a change of plan in the Liberal Democrat's itinerary. Mileham, wreathed in pipe-smoke and bonhomie, gave David a smile as they passed, and Stan gave Tessa a little flick on the rump with his clip-board; something on account, he thought.

They both lunched with one of the local Scout Groups before going on to a Morris dancing festival, held in honour of some visiting Austrian folk dancers. David dredged from his memory such German as he had picked up during his Army days and made an effort to talk to the visitors, but it was doubtful if they understood much of his badly accented *Hochdeutsch*. Then, at last, it was time for home; time, too, to prepare for a novel experience, the gig at Lower Norton.

Lara had been giving some thought as to what her man should wear for the event, and had discussed it with Terri, Nikki and Jack Kestrel in the yard. There was no point, they all agreed, in David appearing in leather and the sort of gear sported by Rock and the Hard Place, even if they were much of an age. In any case, it would be right out of character, and possibly alienate some of his older supporters, many of whom, as life-long supporters of the group, were expected to be present.

"And you can't put the Captain in a suit and tie, like when he goes to London," Terri added. "The kids'd die laughing." Finally is was decided that David, who had a reasonable tan anyway from constant exposure to the elements in the Vale over the past three weeks, should wear 501s, his thick leather belt and his cream silk New and Lingwood shirt, open at the neck. A new party rosette would be fixed to his belt on the hip, and another rosette, less tails, would be fixed to Kaid's thick leather collar next to the King's Lancers cap-badge.

Kaid listened with increasing disgust to these plans, He had put up earlier with being brushed by Lara — usually the Boss's prerogative — and it now looked as though he was going to be dressed up like a clown as well!

At half past six, two minibuses appeared in front of the Hall. The first, driven by Jack, was for David, Lara, Kaid and also for Terri and Nikki who apparently had some task to perform connected with David's appearance. Tony Stark was driving the second vehicle, which appeared to contain some of the younger elements of the Evenlode Brigade. David, slightly dismayed, turned to his employee.

"Jack, what on earth do we want with a bodyguard of that size? Has Tony gone mad, or something? Am I going to be lynched by the Teeny-boppers or what?"

"Question of status. If you turn up on your Todd at these things, then you're a nobody," Jack replied. "You've got to be like those generals on the telly in the Gulf war."

In for a penny, in for a pound, thought David, recalling the images of General Sir Peter de la Billière arriving for briefings in Saudi Arabia surrounded by SAS and Saudi Special Forces. Not quite the same thing, perhaps. They all climbed in and Jack drove off in the general direction of Lower Norton. Unbeknown to David, one of the road managers from Rock Hard Music had been over to the Hall earlier in the week to supply all the necessary passes and detailed instructions about timings and vehicle parking. Lara had taken in precisely what was expected of both David and Kaid, and had also made sure that Jack and Tony knew exactly where they were going.

This turned out to be one of the more obscure back gates to the now obsolete airfield, the chain-link fence of which was still intact. There were about five private security guards and a couple of alsations at the gate which was, Jack explained, the entrance for the VIPs. They drove to the back of the huge stage, which had been put up beside one of the old hangars. Jack parked among some very expensive looking cars and they all got out of the minibuses. Feeling slightly ridiculous, the bodyguard of six escorted them to a large trailer-caravan which was Lance's base for the night. Other, slightly smaller, trailers were parked nearby, presumable for the rest of the group, and indeed for the support band which would start the concert.

Lance and Cat were sitting in armchairs while watching television and drinking what looked like Orangina. He waved at them as they came in. motioning them to other chairs in what was, presumably, the living area.

"Sorry to get you here so early," he explained. "We've sold out at 15,000 tickets for this gig, and all the roads in the area will be jammed solid in about half an hour. Help yourself to drinks from the cupboard if you want. We tend to lay off the hard until after the show, but feel free. Smokes are in there also, but go outside if you use them, and don't leave the butts lying around where some nosy parker might pick them up."

"I'll have to go and get hyped up with the boys when the support band starts up, which'll be in about an hour, then I reckon that you all want to be in the wings at half nine," he added. "And whatever you do, don't leave this compound. You'll never get back!" He grinned wolfishly.

David had not anticipated a two and a half hour wait, but since there was nothing that he could do about it anyway, he helped Lara and himself to a weak whiskey-and-soda each and chatted lightly to Lance. He was not altogether surprised to learn that life backstage was not one long orgy, and that, although pot-smoking was almost mandatory to relax before around three hours on stage, alcohol was taboo.

"At our age," Lance explained. "All we need is some little under-age cracker screwing us all stupid, and then crying 'Rape!' to the tabloids. That's why security is so tight in our compound. There are enough groupies of all ages out there as it is."

"Drink used to be fine when we were working the clubs up north in the early days," he went on. "The audiences were all half pissed anyway, and expected you to be the same, but it won't work in the big-time, especially when we're on world TV. We drink a lot of fluid before we go on, because, on a warm night like now, and with the lights, we'll all lose a few pounds in weight before we finish." David was reminded that Yvette had spotted that some of the concert was due to be shown on Central television that night. She had promised to make Caspar watch at least some of the coverage.

Lance left at about eight and they heard dimly in the background the noise from the Drongoes, an Australian support band who were very much the warm-up before the real thing. Cat stayed with them, being considerably keener on watching television in the comfort of the trailer than on seeing the preliminaries to his father's performance. They went out at about nine, and were in time to hear the roar from the crowd as Lance and his group took over from the Drongoes. David's minders appeared out of the dusk and escorted them to the back of the stage, where they were taken in hand by one of Lance's men.

As David looked out from the wings, there seemed to be a crowd for as far as he could see. A limited amount of stands had been erected for some of the group's older supporters, who nevertheless had to pay rather more than the standard £25 a head for the privilege of a seat for the duration. Giant closed circuit screens relayed a blown-up image of what was going on, for the benefit of those near the back, and the noise backstage was a mere fraction of what he supposed it was in front of the numerous amplifiers. There was a slight smell of frying from the numerous burger bars on the fringes.

While Rock and the Hard Place played on, seemingly unconcerned by what went on around them, the floor of the stage positively slithered with electricians, sound men, and television men with hand-held cameras and microphones. The stage was a good six feet off the ground, and if that was not enough, there was a cordon of yet more security men between the stage and the audience. Lance, the sweat already running off him in rivulets, was totally master of proceedings, and appeared to have complete control.

At around the appointed hour, David was asked to bring Kaid and Cat to the wings, from where Lance would lead them on for their, presumably brief, appearance. He beckoned to Lara, who had borrowed some Versace palazzo pants with a vivid Aztec motif from Carmen. With a flash of inspiration, she had dug out a garish old Pop waistcoat that David had worn at Eton which she now wore over her silk shirt. On her feet, David having refused to let her go bare-footed, she wore a pair of exotic sandals from her Italian days, and had her blonde hair down. Anyway, it had been to an extent her idea, David thought, so she could share the experience with him. As the number (a revival from the Sixties) ended, Lance moved upstage and held out his hands, palms down, for silence. You could have heard a pin drop within seconds.

"God," whispered David to Lara. "He's the one who should be running for parliament, not me. He'd be Prime Minister inside a week!"

"Friends," intoned Lance, deliberately stressing his Scouse accent. " We're all here tonight to have a ball and raise some money for two good causes. First, we want to stop the Chinks from being cruel to Teddy bears. Second, we want to support Greyhound Rescue who're local, just across the border in Gloucestershire. They look after greyhounds and Lurchers which people abandon when they get bored with them." A lone spot opened on Kaid, waiting in the wings, his lead being held by Cat.

"This Lurcher, Kaid, saved my son Cat from drowning in the Thames this Spring, something that I can never repay him for. He is the sort of dog that we don't want to see abandoned!" Further spots opened on Cat, David and Lara as Lance strode across to the wings and led them back to centre stage, where they halted and faced the audience. The applause was deafening. Kaid was a little unsure what was going on, but gave his tail a small wag. Further applause and cheers. Lance motioned for silence once again.

"His owner, Dave Vyvian, is also here with his girlfriend Lara. Don't ask me why, but Dave wants to be an MP and is standing for the County Party in the by-election on Friday. We're going to play you a number in a moment, and I want you all to join in the chorus which I've changed a bit for tonight. Remember to vote for Dave on Friday! Good luck to you, and thanks a million, Kaid!" At that point Terri, Nikki, Tony and Jack entered left, and showered the front of the audience with County Party rosettes as Kaid and his group exited right to yet further tumultuous applause. Lance strode back to the group, picked up his guitar and led in with the opening bars of his top hit, Party Time.

Cat was left in the wings as the Windrush Hall group, complete with bodyguards, returned to their transport. As they all piled in, the air was rent as 15,000 voices all screamed 'County Party! County Party!' into the night air. Popular rumour had it later that the noise registered on the seismograph in Oxford.

Caspar, with Buraq asleep at his feet, was still watching the concert on television when they came in. He told them that the commentator, who usually did not have much to say during this sort of thing, had been completely wrong-footed (Caspar used the word 'gob-smacked' which he had recently picked up from the Sun) over the guest appearance. It was, at any rate as far as the media were concerned, unscheduled, so they had no chance of hiding the party political element of the concert behind a commercial break.

Roger Mileham missed the programme: for he was involved in an all-night caring vigil to highlight the plight of the homeless, in the porch of the Evenlode parish church. His wife, Teresa, missed it also, as she was involved in an all-night carnal vigil with Stanton Harcourt. Oh! The sacrifices that must be made for husbands, she thought as she goaded him into a further engagement. Dr Paul Enstone missed it because he was playing bridge with friends of his own age-group. The Livkins did not.

They had been watching a programme on female circumcision in the Third World, Esther's choice as it would give her further background information for a tract that she was preparing on the plight of feminism in the post-Thatcher Tory Party. When the programme had ended, somewhat, it must be said, to Norman's relief, she was flicking through the channels with the remote control and stopped on Central. For there was that bloody man Vyvian, complete with his equally bloody dog and blonde bimbo, hogging centre stage with an ageing pop-star that even they had heard of!

Incandescent with rage, Norman was on the telephone to his agent even before David had left the stage. Had the agent been watching television? No, the agent had just returned from an early supper with friends.

"Well, get a tape from Central first thing on Monday morning," instructed the irate Tory candidate. "If we can prove that he paid that pop star for the appearance on his show, we can get him for overspending."

"That won't help you win the seat," replied the agent wearily. God, how he hated this man. "You still have to beat Mileham, who is ahead in the polls."

"And I am prepared, in the circumstances," continued Livkin, as though the agent had not even uttered. "To agree to a four-way television debate where I can use my court-room skills to demolish the others once and for all. Kindly arrange it. Good night."

David's appearance at the concert had been too late for the Sunday papers, and although Kaid, Lance and Cat received a certain amount of column inches, and the occasional photograph, in Monday's tabloids, the broadsheets tended to be a bit dismissive. The *Morning Chronicle* even ran a third leader implying that David was bringing politics into disrepute by resorting to such gimmicks. However Roy Large in the *Evenlode Echo*, the local weekly paper, later went so far as to suggest that perhaps politicians of whatever hue could learn from the example of the new boy. His paper also carried the results of a telephone poll conducted locally on the previous evening which put David on level terms with Norman Livkin, but still behind Roger Mileham.

Stan felt the first cold fingers of worry gripping his guts. Up until now, everything had been going according to plan; his runner had neatly split the Tory vote, but now there was a slight chance, after the stunt at the concert, that he might overdo things and win the by-election. Time for contingency plans, he thought. He was alone in the Party HQ office, so he risked a quick call to Veronica in London. Veronica answered.

140

"Veronica, my gorgeous butterfly, I'm in what could be a slight spot. Yes, I know I've not been in touch for a bit, but I've been busy here in the sticks. Yes, busy, like work. I tried to explain to you when I last came up to London that, for reasons that we needn't go over again, I needed David to do quite well in this by-election, no more. Well, there is an outside chance that we've overdone things and he might win." He paused as Veronica's idiotic prattle came back down the line.

"At worst, if things go that way, I'll have to play my Joker," he added. "So what I want from you is any form of shit that we can dish up on him at short notice — small boys, whips or whores, fiddling his taxes, anything like that." At that point Nikki came back into the office, so he said that he would call back and rang off.

The BBC called shortly afterwards and wanted to know if Stan's candidate would be prepared to take part in a four-cornered discussion during the week for one of their current affairs programmes. Stan said that he was sure that he would, but would call back to confirm. This could suit him quite well as David, with scarcely any party infrastructure or researchers apart from himself, would surely be chewed up by the three candidates from the main parties, who would come fully briefed by their Central Offices.

David was a little offhand when Stan brought the matter up. He realised, of course, that it was unusual for the major parties on such occasions even to acknowledge the existence of fringe parties: for them to do so now must mean that he was making some impression. He also knew that the others were, to a greater or lesser degree, fairly experienced performers on television, so he would make his own terms.

"Agreed," he told his agent. "Subject to me being allowed Kaid on camera, to Mirza conducting the discussion and to it taking place in the new studio at BBC Oxford." Stan spluttered a bit, but said that he would see what he could do. It was, after all, in his interest that it went ahead.

David was facing a punishing final four days of campaigning, all of them weekdays when most adults, apart from young mothers, pensioners and the unemployed, were out at work by day. And they were not, by and large, all that eager to be solicited on their doorsteps when they were home in the evening. He now tended to take Lara, armed with the appropriate register of voters for the particular ward which Nikki would supply, with him by day. Stan would deal with Press enquiries and forward planning at Party HQ, but would come with David for the evening meetings.

Since he was finding that his (and Kaid's) faces by now had quite a high degree of public recognition, he often tended to go for the High Streets, rather than the largely empty housing estates, in the mornings. The village post offices, those that had not been closed down, tended to be especially profitable or, failing them, village general stores. Inevitably there would be small queues, and invariably someone would recognise Kaid, with his smart collar and party badge, and the ice would be broken without David having to accost people. To his surprise, he found that his local butcher, much frequented by Mrs Kerr because he hung his beef for at least three weeks, pledged his support because of David's stand on hunting.

"Could I have seen you out with the Bladon?" David enquired.

" I'm afraid not, Sir," replied the modern equivalent of a Surtees character. "I'm strictly a Heythrop man." A slightly chastened David moved on.

'The butcher is a great chum of mine, Bladon or no Bladon.' Kaid licked his lips, for Jack Kestrel was wont to take the butcher the odd hare that the dog caught in excess of the requirements of the Hall. In return, the butcher would often bring the dog marrow-bones when he delivered an order to Mrs Kerr.

He would be quite glad when the whole thing was over, David thought. It was not that he minded going around and talking to local people, but it was taking up almost every day to the detriment of all else. Luckily, his farm manager was a capable man, but this year it had been he, not David, who had taken the decision that morning to make a start on cutting the hay. He also felt for Kaid a great deal. Neither of them had had a good walk around the farm for the last three weeks, very much to his regret.

When they returned that Monday afternoon to the Hall, Stan was waiting for them in the yard wearing a large smirk below the sleeked-back hair.

"*Peccavi!*" he announced, with the air of a conjuror pulling the proverbial rabbit out of the hat.

"No need to unburden yourself," commented Lara sarcastically. "I know it was Latin, but what did it mean?"

"Brilliant," said David. "Just hang on a moment, and I'll be right back." He went into the house with Lara and Kaid.

"It meant that Stan was doing the normal Wykehamist trick of assuming that they, alone, are educated," David answered a trifle testily. "'Peccavi' means 'I have sinned' and was the code-word sent to Dalhousie in Delhi by, I think, General Napier when he had captured Sind in 1843, or thereabouts."

"Didn't they teach you that at the Lycée?" he added teasingly. "I think that Stan was trying to tell me that the BBC has agreed to get Mirza Sind to be anchor-man for this by-election special that they want to do. Why don't you have some tea with Caspar and Yvette and I'll join you after I've checked with him." He went out to Party HQ.

"They agreed to Mirza without a murmur. He's only a freelance, so they don't have to pay him a fortune to move off the Green in Old Palace Yard," Stan told him. "Apparently all the others were more than happy with Oxford, now that they've done away with that silly booth with the back-drop of the spires and have got a proper studio. They kicked up a bit about the dog, but gave way in the end when I said that he didn't bark."

"And it's Wednesday night at seven o'clock," he added. "You've probably noticed the studio in Summertown, opposite the BMW garage. There's a good-sized car park behind it."

David spent a further half hour in the office, checking, among other matters, that the transport plans for getting house-bound voters to the polling booths on Friday were in hand. He was mindful of Stanbrook's advice on not stirring up the voters too much in wards where the inhabitants tended to be strongly polarised towards any of the other parties. So he tried to ensure that all of the smaller villages, where there was no, or little, public transport, were covered by volunteers from the Evenlode Brigade.

The next two days passed in a blur. He knew that he could never hope to match the facts and figures that the other candidates would have at their disposal, but thanked his lucky stars that they could not, on television, have them all laid out in front of them during the programme. He just hoped for some breaks, come the night.

On Wednesday, David was back from canvassing with Lara early enough to relax for a moment before setting off for Oxford. Since he regarded the programme as a short affair, he set off alone with Kaid — besides, Caspar was incapable of setting the video to take a copy of the proceedings. On arrival he was met by Mirza as he climbed out of his car.

"David, a quick word if I may. As you probably realise, it has to be 'Mr Vyvian' and 'Mr Sind' tonight," his friend explained." I'll do my best for you, of course, but I have to be seen to be impartial."

"I'm using quite a bit of recent film footage to lead in with," he went on. "So the actual discussion won't be that long. By the way, Livkin has brought a cat!" He vanished back into the studio.

'This just could be a night to remember,' thought Kaid. I am bored to tears with this election thing anyway, but at last we may have some fun!'

David took Kaid for a turn round the near-empty car park and, ten minutes before seven o'clock, went in with him. After a perfunctory couple of minutes with a make-up girl, some chap who seemed to be the floor manager as well as the director introduced himself. He apologised for the lack of a hospitality room and invited David, and the other candidates who had arrived earlier, to take a seat at a table in front of the cameras. David went to a chair at the right end, and had the silver-haired Paul Enstone between himself and Mirza in the middle. Norman Livkin went and sat at the other end, clutching a cat basket, while the hirsute Roger Mileham, reeking somewhat of the herbal shag which he had been smoking only moments before, sat on his right.

"Gentlemen," explained Mirza. "This will be a recording that will close a programme that we have put together for broadcasting later tonight. Once we are live, I will be introducing you one by one and starting with you Mr Livkin, then Dr Enstone, followed by Mr Mileham and ending with Mr Vyvian." he gave David a brief nod.

"Please keep your opening addresses to half a minute at the most, or I will have to cut you off. We will then, I hope, have a few minutes for question and answer between the four of you. You all know the form, but I must remind you not to interrupt another speaker or drown him out when he is speaking. No one hears anything that way."

The floor manager looked up to the small gallery, received a nod, and started counting down from five on his outstretched hand. Livkin in the meanwhile extracted a large furry marmalade cat from the basket and placed the animal on his lap where, because of the table, it could not be seen. The red light came on and Mirza looked straight into camera and spoke.

"We have all four of the main candidates in the studio tonight." (David tried not to smirk as a second camera panned down the table.) "First, Norman Livkin who is seeking to hold the seat for the Conservatives despite some local opposition. Mr Livkin."

"Thank you Mizra," replied the Tory. "We'll hold this seat come Friday, mark my words. None of the other parties have any positive policies anyway." He then continued in a flat monotone about how Gatt, Back to Basics, Cuts in the Armed Forces and increased taxation had all been misrepresented by the media, and how the National Health Service and the education system were the envy of the world. Mirza, irritated at having his name used incorrectly, tapped the glass of his watch at twenty-five seconds, and five seconds later cut him off with a firm ' Thank you, we will try to get back to you later on'.

By contrast the Labour candidate, Dr Paul Enstone, was crisp, concise and to the point. He also knew that this was probably the last time that he would face the electorate: there were enough Young Turks around who would ensure his deselection on the grounds of age next time. Labour may not win the seat, he said, but he hoped to attract enough votes to show that working class solidarity was far from dead in the Vale of Evenlode.

Roger Mileham served up his normal platitudes, many of which he appeared to have lifted from the no-hoper Greens. If you turned him round, thought David irreverently, no one would really know the difference. His floppy grey jersey would look the same from either side and he had, if anything, more hair on the front of his head than on the back. Mileham was under orders not to get involved in any verbal fisticuffs: the voters across the country, with their disenchantment with the present government and their distrust of the Left, seemed to like the Liberal Democrats' mixture of whimsy and froth.

Then it was David's turn. Remembering to sit up straight, to appear relaxed and to look at the interviewer rather than at the cameras, he launched into an abridged version of his standard spiel that he had been using for the last few weeks. Kaid rested his head on the table, never taking his eyes from David's face. Scarcely had he finished than Livkin, the terror of the law courts, was off.

"Is Captain Vyvian not aware that, in his haste to return to the Colours, the IMF would not allow any increase in the amount of the GNP allocated to defence, even when allowing for the tranche set aside for out-of-area commitments, excluding Nato and the UN?" he asked. He plonked Edwina, the marmalade cat, onto the table for better exposure. The cat belonged to Esther, who had persuaded him to bring the spayed feline along 'to show his care for animals, too'.

Kaid had been well aware of the presence of some hostile living animal in his proximity. Now, for the first time, he could see it. He gave a low growl, at which the cat turned towards him, back arching. David had the dog in check with a coursing lead, a present from his sister, Georgina, who had bought it in Paris. Now he involuntarily, as he told himself afterwards, flicked the quick release catch and Kaid was gone. The dog had no particular intention of catching the cat — indeed it reminded him rather strongly of a mink that he had once treed by the Thames, all snarling and spitting. But it ran, so he chased.

"Oi Weh!" wailed Livkin, flinging back his chair and bounding after the animals. Esther would kill him if anything happened to blasted Edwina.

"I am afraid that my questioner appears to have left us," said David to Mirza, thankful for the diversion and confident that the animals would come to no great harm. "Had he still been with us, I could have explained how massive savings could be made within the Royal Air Force to finance the return to the status quo ante of the Army."

Mirza had covered Afghanistan for Indian television in his younger days, so was not to be put off by the departure of a guest at short notice, nor by the occasional 'Tom and Jerry' reappearances of the cat. the dog and the lawyer. Likewise the camera crews carried on as normal, though one of them was directed by the gallery to focus on the chase, whenever the participants came into vision. Since Roger Mileham was still intent on saying nothing, apart from nodding sagely from time to time, David and the doctor spent the last few minutes of the recording by feigning sparring together over well-worn topics such as nationalisation and private health insurance.

Mirza then wrapped the interview up, apologising for the lack of the Conservative, and they all prepared to go home. Mileham went out by the front to catch a bus, while Enstone headed out of the back entrance to the car park. David called Kaid, who was by now rather bored with the cat chase, the quarry having 'gone to ground' in the control gallery. He waited while Livkin retrieved Edwina to check that she had come to no harm. "No thanks to you that it hasn't," said Livkin bitterly, putting the ruffled cat back into her basket.

David shrugged and went out into the car park to see a fight in progress near his car. He ran over, with Kaid bounding ahead, to find Paul Enstone, a useful amateur boxer in his youth, putting up a brave but unequal fight against three youths, one of whom was black and was wielding a baseball bat. David went to the older man's help, receiving a split lip for his pains, but the arrival of reinforcements, one of which was a snarling dog, dampened the attackers' enthusiasm. One dropped a wallet, presumably what they had been after, while the one with the bat gave the victim a passing swipe to the head as they ran off. David knelt to check on the doctor, who had been rendered unconscious by the final blow.

It was at this point that Norman Livkin came out of the building with his cat basket. He had heard a commotion, emerged to see David kneeling beside the prone figure on the ground, and had drawn his own conclusions. He rushed back into the building. "Help!" he shouted, "Police!"

Chapter 11

THE FINISHING POST

David took off his jacket to make a pillow for the injured man who, though unconscious, seemed to be breathing normally. In the meanwhile Kaid had come limping back, whining slightly with his tail well down. Though by no stretch of the imagination a war dog (apart from where hares were concerned) he had given chase, snarling furiously, until a sharp kick on the shoulder had made him desist. David quickly ran his fingers up the dog's foreleg: there appeared to be nothing broken, but it would be as well to have him checked out by the vet.

'I was really sorting them out before that brute kicked me so hard,' complained Kaid to himself. 'That man should be locked up for a long time for attacking a dog who has been presented to The Queen.'

Norman Livkin meanwhile had been skulking by the entrance to the studio. Somewhere in the back of his mind was the realisation that there could have been some other people involved in the attack, but this was too good an opportunity to miss. If he could keep David out of circulation for the next forty-eight hours, the one-man County Party would loose all credibility and, more importantly to him, all votes. He would fix the sod yet! When he heard the siren, and once he had ensured that the police car was actually turning in to the studios' car park, he rushed over to David and started to cavort in what he thought was a threatening posture, fists raised.

"You rotten ponce! Beating up a man old enough to be your father! I'll see that you're well punished for this." A further prance brought him within range of David, who gave him a firm push in the middle of his chest. Livkin collapsed with a scream.

"Help, officers, over here! He's trying to kill me too."

The sergeant was approaching retirement age and nearing the end of his shift. The Oxford police were well accustomed to near-riots down in Blackbird Leys, to the south of the city, but Summertown, to the north, was meant to be respectable. Yet here were three grown men, give or take, who appeared to have been brawling in the car park of the BBC studios. He radioed for an ambulance and for back-up and approached the group on the ground, taking out his notebook at the same time.

David had to admit afterwards that his appearance was against him. He was well smeared by both his own and Enstone's blood, had no jacket on and his tie was askew. Livkin, by contrast, was unmarked and still smartly clad in his pinstripe suit. He had quickly recovered his composure and was telling the sergeant how he had come upon Mr Vyvian, whom he recognised, beating up Dr Enstone, whom he also recognised. Mr Vyvian had been involved in a bitter argument with the doctor only moments before in an interview in the studios, and had then clearly gone on to attack him afterwards, so he maintained.

It all seemed cut and dried to the sergeant. Providing the old one on the deck did not croak overnight, he thought, he would have enough to get the other charged before the beaks in the morning. The ambulance had arrived and the paramedics were efficiently loading the still unconscious doctor into the vehicle prior to taking him to the John Radcliffe hospital.

"Thank you, Sir, you have been most helpful." he said to Livkin. "Could I trouble you to follow us down to our station in St Aldgate's and to provide us with a written statement?" The sergeant turned to David. "As for you, Sunshine, you're nicked. Get in the car!"

"Officer, my dog needs veterinary attention rather badly." Even as David was saying it, he felt that his plea would fall of deaf ears.

"So does that poor bugger in the ambulance, no doubt." answered the officer. He was beginning to enjoy himself. Let the toff squirm. "The other car will call for a van to take the dog to the pound, same as any other stray. Oh, and don't leave it there for too long, as they put down the unclaimed ones."

"You bastard!" shouted David, goaded beyond endurance.

The sergeant made a note of the time, and entered 'You barstard' (sic) in his notebook. "Another crack like that, mate, and I'll have the 'cuffs on you." He pushed David into the back of the car, climbed in beside him and told the driver to move off. At that point Mirza appeared by his window.

"One moment please, Inspector, I know this man." Mirza, as ever the chameleon, had adopted what he called his senior officer's accent. "David, What's up?"

"I've been set up by Livkin," David groped in his pocket and handed his keys to Mirza. "Please get Kaid into my car before he is run over, telephone Lara to let her know the form and drive back to the Hall. They're taking me to St Aldgate's police station."

"That's enough!" The sergeant felt that he was beginning to lose full control of the situation. "Constable Dixon, drive on now as I told you to a minute ago."

On arrival at St Aldgate's police station, David was booked in by the desk sergeant, taken into a cell and left there. It smelled vaguely of carbolic soap and urine. In the distance he could faintly hear Livkin talking to the police as he made his statement. After a time, he was taken into an interview room, formally cautioned, and then charged with inflicting grievous bodily harm that evening on Dr Paul Enstone in the BBC car park. He made no answer to the charge. David was then grudgingly allowed to make his one telephone call.

He had given the matter some thought while waiting in his cell. Mirza would by now have spoken to Lara — indeed, he should have arrived at the Hall some time ago. Knowing Lara, when she saw Kaid in distress, she would have immediately called out their no-nonsense vet, Mr Alderman, or one of his partners, to give the dog the once-over and a shot of an analgesic if required. Likewise Caspar, though good for moral support, was a bit out of touch with local politics; and Stan was, on past form, rutting around in London. He therefore dialled Perry d'Artois's number. Stella answered.

"Good Evening, Maris, it's David here. I'm sorry to telephone so late, but I need to talk to Perry rather urgently. Is he there, by any chance?"

"I don't know who you are, but you are certainly not David Vyvian," said Lady d'Artois reasonably. "He's on telly at the moment, and he isn't speaking to me on the telephone."

"It's a recording, Maris," said David wearily. God give me strength, he thought. "Please get me Perry." Puzzled, she nevertheless tossed the cordless receiver to the baronet, who was weeping with laughter at the sight of his usurper, bloody Livkin, chasing animals around the television studio.

David briefly outlined the situation to Perry and asked him to reassure Lara, and for that matter his father, that he was all right. He further tasked him with contacting his lawyers in Gresham Street as soon as they opened in the morning and to instruct them to get him out. Perry's nostrils flared, rather like those of an old war-horse which hears, at a distance, the trumpet call for the charge. As soon as David had finished his call, he gave Lara David's brief message, then laid siege to the Chief Constable.

They were out to dinner, said the Chief Constable's housekeeper with satisfaction. In that case, Perry had boomed at her, in the name of the Queen whom he had the honour to represent in the County (stretching a point), kindly page him and have him call Sir Peregrine d'Artois straight away. The baronet did not fully understand how pagers worked. But, from his time as Lord Lieutenant, he remembered that important policemen carried pocket-sized devices that bleeped when contact was necessary. And so, deflated, the housekeeper concurred. Ten minutes later, the policeman called Perry back. He did so with a sense of foreboding, as Sir Peregrine had never bothered him, nor his predecessor, without good reason.

"Listen, Plod, (he always called senior policemen 'Plod', a term of affection, as he, if not the addressees, saw it) your boys have gone mad and locked up David Vyvian in Oxford on some trumped up charges, including GBH, earlier this evening. Very much not on, I'm afraid. Be a good chap and sort it out, will you?"

The Chief Constable sighed. He had met David only the week before when the latter had paid a visit to his Headquarters in Kidlington, and hardly thought that he was the homicidal type. He now dialled the Headquarters and asked to be put through to the Duty Superintendent (Crime). It looked like being another of those evenings, and just when his host

had been on the point of dispensing some rather fine old brandy.

Once Mr Alderman had been to see Kaid and pronounced him no more than badly bruised (his injection of Buscopan seemed to give the dog more grief than had the actual kick) Lara went into action. She realised that stamping her foot with rage and demanding the release of her man instantly from whichever luckless police officer would be on duty in the front office when she arrived there (her first impulse), would not get her far. So she went out to the tack room, emptied and rinsed out a suitable dark-coloured medicine bottle, and refilled it with whiskey in the library. Then, taking care not to exceed the speed limits, she drove to St Aldgate's and presented herself at the desk. The young duty sergeant looked up with approval as this beautiful blonde smiled at him.

"I gather that Mr Vyvian is here, due to some misunderstanding," said the apparition. "He needs his medicine every night, so I have brought it in for him." She handed the officer the bottle. Being an observant man, he knew exactly who David, and indeed who his fiancée, were. He unscrewed the top and sniffed the contents.

"Don't worry, Madam," he said with a wink. "He is due for a cuppa in a moment, so I'll mix some of the medicine in with it." He lent towards her and lowered his tone.

"If we were alone, I might've been able to arrange a quick visit, but we've got company from the press." Lara looked along the desk to where a drab looking man, probably a stringer for one of the nationals, was surreptitiously perusing the incident book. She gave the officer another smile, asked him to let David know that his dog was fully recovered and left.

David, with the aid of his 'gunfire' laced tea, managed to get a reasonable night's sleep. His solid bunk compared not unfavourably with his bed during basic training, he thought. Then, after some breakfast, he was taken back to the interview room and, having been reminded of his caution of the previous evening, arraigned on two further charges: namely assault and battery against the person of Mr Norman Livkin and using abusive language to a police officer during the execution of his duties. David was also warned that he would be appearing before the Magistrates later that morning.

Perry d'Artois was having a most frustrating time with David's lawyers in Gresham Street. Hardly surprisingly, he had not achieved much before about quarter past nine (the Oxford Magistrates were due to sit at ten) and then only that they would instruct a local firm to apply for an adjournment and for bail. Meanwhile the papers, or at any rate those later editions which came to the Vale, were full of the incident of the previous evening. 'Labour Candidate Attacked — Man Charged' was the tenor of most of them, however the *Morning Chronicle* had managed to interview Livkin.

"Although I witnessed a *prima facie* case of grievous bodily harm, and was, in fact, myself also assaulted when I went to the aid of the victim, matters are still *sub judice*," he was quoted as saying. "But I think that we can say with some confidence that we have heard the last of the County Party."

Stanton Harcourt also had his problems. He had managed a quick assignation with Teresa Mileham while her husband was giving the 'silent movie' impersonation during the television interview, and had then crept home to bed. Thank God, he thought as he collapsed, fully clothed, into deep repose, that there were only two days to go. A call from Lara at half past seven awoke him.

"Stan, we're in trouble. Livkin swears that David beat up Enstone last night, so David is in police custody awaiting the Magistrates' Court later this morning. Perry and the rest of us are doing what we can, but I thought that you should know what's going on." Stan thanked her and rang off. He wondered if a bull-shot would make him feel better, or worse. Before he could make up his mind, the telephone rang again. It was Veronica.

"Listen, Love-chops, the only shit that I can serve you up at this moment about my ex is that at some stage he had a black tart," she gabbled. "Any good? Exploiting our coloured brothers, sort of thing?" Coloured sisters more like, thought Stan. He thanked Veronica and told her to hold everything for the moment. His plans were going fast awry.

The Chief Constable was having a bewildering time. On the one hand was a clear statement from Livkin, a member of the legal profession (even if his party had produced that dreadful Sheehy report) stating unequivocally that Vyvian had beaten up Dr Enstone and assaulted Livkin to boot; and there was a further statement from one of the Oxford-based sergeants that Vyvian had sworn at him. The last two charges he regarded as trivial, but a custodial sentence was the usual outcome of a guilty finding on a charge of GBH.

On the other hand, several things did not match the first scenario. In the circumstances he had felt it necessary to leave the dinner party of the previous evening early and return home to await developments. When he and his wife came into their house, their housekeeper was still up. She, a chatty soul, had told them what a pity it was that they had missed the by-election special on the television — it had been so funny. When, later, he had heard from his Headquarters the gist of Livkin's statement, he had quizzed the good woman further. No, she had told him, there was certainly no argument between Mr Vyvian and the doctor. "They seemed ever so friendly and chatty," she had told him.

Then there was the wallet on the tarmac towards the exit of the car park. If Vyvian, by all accounts a rich landowner, had attacked the doctor in a fit of political rage, why bother with the wallet? Taken together, these facts sent sufficient alarm bells going as to cause him to dig out his police doctor in the middle of the night. He asked him to do basic tests on both David's jacket, which was being held as material evidence at St Aldgate's, and on Paul Enstone's, from the unconscious doctor's bedside locker in the John Radcliffe. Patrol cars picked up the clothing and rushed it to Kidlington.

Now, as the Chief Constable was shaving before grabbing an early breakfast, his office called.

"Sorry to call so early, Sir, but I thought you would like to know the findings of the forensic report which you ordered as a rush job last night," his PA, a woman Inspector with a face and figure that, to an extent, explained why some men have uniform fetishes, told him. "They found out the doctor's blood group from the hospital, and most of the blood on both garments is his."

"A large amount of the remainder, again on both items, matches the group shown on a blood donor card in the prisoner's wallet," she continued. "But there are significant traces of other types, one of which tends to come mainly from the — ah — Negroid population."

"Thank you, Inspector," said her superior formally, mainly for the benefit of his wife, who, suspicious woman, sometimes eavesdropped. "I'll be in after I've grabbed a cup of coffee."

He glanced at the papers and noted with incredulity Livkin's outburst that, although not naming David directly, certainly did by implication. Indeed, the *Morning Chronicle* had headlined the item 'County Party out of the Race?'. If this case ever got to the Crown Court (God forbid!) then the CPS would have an uphill task in rebutting a defence claim that the jury would have been influenced by earlier media coverage.

He was now in a quandary. In the light of Livkin's statement, he had to proceed, if only to ask for an adjournment so that both sides could prepare their cases. He clearly would instruct his people not to oppose bail, but that would still mean that a prospective candidate for a by-election two days hence would be awaiting trial on a serious criminal offence. He had long learned to subordinate any political feelings that he might hold where police matters were concerned, but he knew that something was wrong somewhere. If only Dr Enstone would recover consciousness!

Tony Stark heard the news on Fox FM. Although David was not named, Nikki had warned them all to watch the previous night's programme, so the news on the radio seemed a bit close to home. He telephoned Terri who, disturbed during the previous night by the unusual amount of traffic on the drive, had already found out the form from Mrs Kerr.

"That's a bloody disgrace. They've stitched the Captain up properly," the farrier said furiously. "Ask Nikki to meet me in the farm office, or Party HQ as you now call it, in twenty minutes and see if you can get hold of that idle sod, Jack Kestrel."

Meanwhile Paul Enstone was dozing quietly in a private room in the John Radcliffe hospital. Had he been consulted over the matter, the life-long Socialist would have opted for a public ward, but such was the press interest over their patient, that it was as well to keep him as secluded as possible. He had been X-rayed as a matter of course on admission and had been found to be suffering from mild concussion. Two tablets of valium had ensured him a good ten hours of slumber, but now he was awake.

Dozily, he watched the sun play on a vase of flowers that some thoughtful person had brought in. Nearer to hand was the back view of a pretty staff nurse who was fussing over the corners at the end of his bed. He cleared his throat.

"Ah, we are awake, Paul, I see!" said the nurse, straightening up. Had she been any less pretty, then he would have been tempted to make some remark such as 'Speak for yourself'. When he had run his own practice, his receptionists had always used the second person when talking to patients, and would address them as Mr or Mrs, rather than the modern habit of always using Christian names from the start.

"We would quite like a cup of tea, please, and a local telephone book," said the patient evenly. "And we would like to see the doctor in charge of our case." The nurse gave a tinkling laugh at the ready wit of one so old, and went out.

"Ah, we are awake, Paul, I see!" repeated the hearty young house doctor, who followed the nurse bearing tea back into the ward. Paul Enstone raised his eyes heavenwards. "No telephoning this morning for you, Uncle. Just take things nice and easy, Eh."

"Point one, I am not your uncle. Point two, I qualified before you were even a twinkle in the milkman's eye and point three, I have dealt with more concussion cases than you have had hot dinners, All right!" the patient became so cross that the memories of the previous evening came flooding back to him. "Get me a directory before I have you struck off!"

Once, moments later, that he had the directory, he looked up David's number at Windrush Hall and dialled it. Some girl answered. Could he speak to David Vyvian? He was unavailable at the moment, but could Major Vyvian help? Doctor Enstone had met Caspar before the latter had moved to France, so asked to be put through.

"Paul, my dear chap, we all thought that you were out cold," Caspar boomed down the line. "How are you, and what's all this business about David attacking you?"

"Attacking me! I know that I've been concussed, but what the hell are you talking about? He and that dog of his practically saved my life last night after three thugs tried to rob me in the car park." An uneasy thought crossed the doctor's mind. "But what do you mean about him attacking me?"

"Livkin has sworn that it was my son who beat you up, so David is in the slammer at the moment before going before the beaks," Caspar explained. "If you feel up to it, I'd be most grateful if you could set the record straight with the powers that be, otherwise he'll really be in the shit."

"Consider it done," replied Enstone, whose next call was to Police Headquarters. After some delay he was put through to the Chief Constable to whom he explained what had happened. Although he could not remember the final blow to the head, he was absolutely clear about the moments preceding it, even to the extent of remembering that David at one point was bleeding from the lips.

The Chief Constable then called the Superintendent at St Aldgate's with some unequivocal instructions. Not the least of these concerned the sergeant who had arrested David, and then had charged him without questioning him first of all.

David was by now awaiting the hearing down below the dock. The local lawyer, appointed at short notice by his people in Gresham Street, had popped in earlier, told him not to worry, and popped out again. Unbeknown to David, he had then been asked to spend a useful five minutes with the Prosecutor from the Crown Prosecution Service.

Now, the sergeant, whose fate was being decided elsewhere, was trying to rile David again. "The lads reckon on eighteen months, but I've put my money on two years," he taunted. "And don't think that you'll be spending it playing croquet at Ford Open with your fancy public school chums. Ford doesn't touch GBH cases." Another officer then came to tell the sergeant that the 'Super' wanted him, so he went away, and David was never to see him again.

Speedwell Street, outside the court, was beginning to fill up with respectable looking men of various ages, all wearing white rosettes. There was no chanting, there were no placards, but the traffic was beginning to grind to a halt. In fact the last car to enter the street, before the police were forced to close it, was Caspar at the wheel of his Bentley. With total disdain for the various No Parking signs, he stopped the car outside the main entrance to the Court and he, Yvette, Lara and a limping Kaid all dismounted. Jack Kestrel appeared from nowhere, and was invited to keep an eye on the car.

When an official put out an arm to prevent them from taking a dog into the building, Caspar just thought how good the service appeared to be. "Thank you, my good man," he said, handing the man his light covert coat and hat. They swept past the speechless (or 'gob-smacked', as Caspar would have put it) man and up into the crowded public gallery.

"The court will rise!" intoned the usher as three lay magistrates appeared from the room behind the bench. David was then escorted from the holding cell up to the dock, where he faced his judges. The Clerk to the Magistrates then established David's identity, read out the three charges, and asked David whether he pleaded innocent or guilty to the charges as stated. Quick as a flash, up jumped David's lawyer.

"My client submits that there are no cases to answer, your Worships!"

This resulted in some frantic whispering between the magistrates and their (professional) clerk. Eventually the senior magistrate cleared his throat.

"Although a case such as this would be referred automatically to a higher court for trial by jury after hearing the evidence, in this case we must ask for the Crown Prosecution Service to show that there is, indeed, a case to answer. He looked over at the prosecution desk. The CPS lawyer rose slowly to his feet.

"The prosecution will be offering no evidence whatsoever in this case," he said sorrowfully. David's man was on his feet again.

"I must ask for an acquittal, release from arrest and costs for my client," he rattled off. "And I must give notice that my client will be seeking damages for wrongful arrest."

"Acquittal, release and costs against the police granted." At this point the Senior Magistrate had to stop owing to an outburst of cheering, both from the public gallery and the street outside. He called repeatedly for order before continuing. "I will be sending the papers in this case to the Director of Public Prosecutions We have all been wasting our time due, it would seem, to malicious false evidence being given to the police, who then swallowed it hook, line and sinker." Further cheers.

"And if that man in the pin-stripe suit and the blue rosette doesn't stop shaking his fist at me," he added. "Then he'll be arrested for contempt. You have the apologies of the Court, Captain Vyvian."

"The court will rise!" again intoned the usher as the magistrates withdrew. David stepped out of the dock and went over to thank his recently assigned lawyer.

"All part of the service," the young man grinned back at him. "In view of the by-election tomorrow, you were lucky that Enstone recovered consciousness when he did. Being out on bail wouldn't have exactly aided your campaign, though, to be honest, the whole case stunk to high heaven."

David met up with the others in the hallway of the Court. Kaid, who had given everyone at the Hall a sleepless night with his howling, was so overjoyed to see his Boss again that he went so far as to forget his injured shoulder for a few minutes. David kissed Lara, very chastely in view of his split lip, and they went out into Speedwell Street and the reception that awaited them.

"A little light refreshment, Ladies and Gentlemen," enquired a voice to their right. David turned to see Ivor Digney, sweating slightly in a Norfolk jacket, proffering a salver on which were some goblets containing a mixture of port and brandy. Like many others of the Evenlode Brigade, he had been stood to earlier that morning by Tony Stark.

"They were staple fare in the Mess for NAAFI-break when the battalion was on Public Duties," he said aside to David. They all drank deeply and thankfully.

Since Speedwell Street was part of Oxford's complicated one-way system, its temporary closure had produced gridlock throughout the city centre. Mounted police had therefore been sent down from Kidlington in their horse-box, and were now deployed in keeping at least one lane in the street open for through traffic. This was made all that much harder by Caspar's Bentley, but such was the pack of resolute men with white rosettes around it, that the police thought that it was best left alone.

The by-election itself, given the government's paper-thin majority, was news anyway but, when mixed with the hilarious television debate of the previous evening and now the candidates' punch-up saga, was headline material. Consequently the press were again out in force, both with reporters and photographers. David, of course, realised that he was only the man of the moment, and that his news worthiness would have a very limited shelf-life, but it had all happened at a most convenient time for him.

"Last night my dog and I went to help an older man who was being robbed," he said modestly into the outstretched microphones, trying the while to present his undamaged profile to the cameras. " We were both slightly hurt in the process, and for good measure I was arrested and spent the night in the cells. All I want to do now is to continue with my election campaign before the polling booths open tomorrow morning. Thank you, Gentlemen."

Jack Kestrel had retrieved Caspar's hat and coat, and he, with help from Tony Stark, a pugnacious-looking Terri and some of their supporters, cleared the way for the party to reach the Bentley. Caspar, wearing his hat at a positively rakish angle, drove, with Yvette beside him, while David and Lara, with Kaid sitting in between them, were in the back.

'I am not sold on leather-covered car seats at the best of times,' Kaid thought watching the police horses that were flanking the car as it edged away from the courthouse. 'And I am bloody uncomfortable, to put it mildly, having to share the back seat with anyone.' He adjusted his position so that his hindquarters were on the seat, while his forepaws rested on the transmission tunnel and whined slightly, remembering his shoulder.

162

"I thought that we'd look in on Paul Enstone," said Caspar. "It's not exactly on our way, but not far off it." They drove out, across Magdalen Bridge, and up to Headington where the Colditz-like building of the John Radcliffe hospital stood atop a small hill. Finding it impossible to park anywhere near the main building, and with the likelihood of an unpleasant scene with the authorities over Kaid, Yvette and Lara elected to stay with the dog in the car while the men visited the doctor.

Paul Enstone was in fine fettle, having just rejected a midday tray of congealing fish fingers and some low-fat vanilla-flavoured yoghurt, described euphemistically as 'dinner'.

"How the hell do they expect an aspiring young politician, such as me, to work on the sort of crap that their private catering contractors dish up?" he demanded of the pair, having first thanked David warmly for his help outside the studios. "I'm discharging myself this afternoon and I'll give you a run for your money tomorrow, David."

"As for you, Caspar, don't you go and overdo things," he wagged a roguish finger. "Nearly time for you to go back to picking grapes and patronising the Frogs!"

After further banter, they left and were back at the Hall in time for lunch. As they pulled up, Nikki met them with a long list of people, both press and constituents, who were expecting a call back. As the pressure had built up during the morning, she had telephoned Robert Summer to ask if Tracy could come down for the final day and a half. He had agreed, so Tracy was even now driving down the M40 towards them.

Where the Hell was Stan, David wondered, not for the first time. He told Nikki that she, and Tracy when she arrived, should tell all press callers that he would be available for interview before the annual Chamber of Trade dinner at Fritton that evening. All potential voters should be reassured that their candidate had emerged from court without a stain on his character and looked forward to representing them in parliament after polling day. He went back to a stiff 'Lurcher's Revenge' before lunch.

"What's the form now?" asked Caspar. They had finished their meal (smoked trout with freshly grated horseradish and thin slices of buttered rye bread, followed by half a cantaloupe melon each) and were drinking coffee on the terrace. "Let me know what we can do tomorrow — after all I do know the area and most of the people in it."

"I've talked to Perry about this already," David replied. "It would be a great help if you could both ferry him around as many polling stations as you can during the day. Lara and I will be swanning around also. I've tactfully put it to Perry that Stella would be best left at home, and I think he's taken my point."

"Don't forget to pick up a list of all the polling stations from the office," he added. "And you can have a map if you feel that you need one."

"I managed to find my way to Sidi Barrani without one," grumbled Caspar. "I'm sure that I can get round a country that I've hunted over for years without help. Where's young Harcourt, anyway?"

Stan had gone to ground. Soon after Lara had called him early that morning, he had received a call from one of his 1922 Committee acquaintances. How, he was asked, could his candidate split the Tory vote when he was imprisoned and awaiting court on a serious criminal charge? Hadn't Stan realised that candidates needed their hands held at every stage? The way that things were going, Livkin would be back as front runner. This was not the method, his caller concluded, to bring down the present crew so that a Thatcherite phoenix could eventually rise from the ashes.

He really had meant to go to the hearing in court, knowing full well that beating up old men was not David's style. But the call had rattled him. Whatever chance he might have in a few years with a revamped Conservative party would evaporate fast were Livkin to be returned. Since he was clearly unable to influence events until, at best, after the hearing, he drove out to see one of his agricultural clients, who was feeling somewhat neglected, and heard the news of David's release on the car radio later on. Soon after he returned to his cottage he had another call, this time from a friend on the local Conservative party association.

"Stan, hopefully you recognise my voice as I am certainly not going to give it on an open line," said his friend. "Central

164

Office has as good as acknowledged that they made a big mistake in foisting Livkin onto us in the first place. After the debacle this morning in court, after which our man had to leave, I gather, by a back door, your chap seems the only one who could stop the Liberal Democrats from winning the seat." He paused, and Stan grunted to show that he was still there.

"If Vyvian could be persuaded, if elected, to support the party in the House, then we will throw what weight that we can behind him at this late stage," he continued. "Obviously, we wouldn't expect him to sit on the Conservative benches or anything, nor indeed to support the party should it decide to proceed with anything directly contrary to his manifesto; but my masters would be encouraged if I could reassure them that he was not out purely to bring the government down."

Careful, thought Stan, all may well not be lost yet. What had seemed, a few moments ago, to be likely to land him on the horns of a dilemma, could well turn out to be more a case of irons in the fire.

"I'll see what I can do," he replied. "My candidate is conservative by nature, though not very well disposed towards your party after the snide attacks on him in the *Morning Chronicle* and the lies told about him by your chap to the police. Leave it with me though, and I'll see what I can do." He rang off, poured himself a large gin and tonic and smirked. Short of the Labour candidate winning, he was home and dry with some faction or other, whatever else happened.

Stan had a pub lunch and then drove on to Party HQ, where he found David working on the plans for the morrow. He made some lame excuse about 'sounding local opinion' during the morning and then settled down to catch up on his work. They had decided earlier on that there was no point in having party tellers at all of the polling booths: however well they did or did not do, the County Party would be unlikely ever to contest a General Election. However, for the look of the thing, party supporters would be present at peak times. Ward bosses would have their telephones manned all day to service last minute requests for transport to the booths; while Nikki and Tracy would be on duty at Party HQ and would pass on any messages to the wards, or indeed to David and Stan, who could both be reached on David's car telephone.

Fritton's Chamber of Trade had, following modern custom, invited 'Mr David Vyvian and partner' to be the guests of honour at their annual dinner that evening. The members, who included livestock and dairy farmers as well as the odd fruit grower from the northern end of the constituency, had been much encouraged by David's stand on supporting agriculture and in particular the produce of the Vale. Their choice of David, admittedly in a rather restricted field, had been more or less unanimous.

Although he had managed a quick rest before setting out, David was feeling a bit frayed round the edges by the time that he, Lara and Kaid eventually were home again. There had been a few reporters about before the dinner in the church hall and the meal had been a pleasant enough affair. He had made a short speech afterwards, both apologising for the fact that he and his dog were not totally unscathed by the rigours of the campaign and hoping for their hosts' support at the polls. A rather weak joke about him immediately realising that the rotten fruit which had come his way could not have been grown in the Vale brought polite laughter, and they were away.

As they let Buraq into the garden for a final pee, David read a scribbled note that Caspar had left him on the console table in the hall. Stan had called earlier to remind him that he would be round at eight in the morning and also to let him know that the pundits had him level-pegging with Mileham in the latest telephone poll. 'Sweet dreams!' Caspar had written on the bottom of his note. David crumpled the bit of paper and glanced up at Lara who was walking upstairs to their bedroom.

Kaid's glance was upwards also. Buraq was too stupid to master the polished staircase, so spent the night downstairs, while he had his special place outside the Boss's bedroom door.

Chapter 12

WINNER'S ENCLOSURE

Although it seemed to David that his head had scarcely touched the pillow, he was woken by Lara gently edging close to him. Later, after she had got up, humming 'Party Time' rather tunelessly, he reached out to turn on the radio. The *Today* programme on Radio 4 — it had never been quite the same since Brian Redhead had died — informed him that it was a quarter past seven. He pushed the duvet aside and went through his dressing room to his bathroom Fortunately his cut lip had not bruised too badly, nevertheless a certain amount of skill was required with his safety razor to avoid the small wound.

Though he did not usually wear one on a regular basis, David donned his regimental tie which, together with his cords and tweed jacket, went with the image that he supposed that he was trying to create. A touch of Blenheim Bouquet after-shave and a clean handkerchief completed his preparations, then he went down to the dining-room for breakfast. Lara had already beaten him to it and was pouring them both cups of coffee. Kaid and Buraq were skipping around outside and no doubt waiting for the postman. He knew the Lurchers well, of course, but strangers coming to the Hall were often apprehensive at the rapid arrival of two large dogs.

David helped himself to a slice of toast, and liberally applied some butter that came from the neighbouring farm. He was sure that its production contravened numerous EU regulations, let alone those of the Environmental Health Officers, or 'Health Police' as they were known to the farming community. Some Cooper's Oxford marmalade, no longer made in Oxford, alas, went well with it, and after a couple of slices he was fit to face the day. Lara in the meantime was enjoying a freshly laid egg, boiled so softly that it should doubtless have also carried a government health warning.

Stan arrived shortly before eight, and willingly accepted a cup of coffee. He by now realised that matters were totally beyond his control, so was relaxed about the outcome. He still thought that, on balance, the Liberal Democrats would win. Paddy Ashdown, their leader in the House of Commons, had been down to the constituency on the previous day and had spoken warmly in Roger Mileham's support. On the other hand the Conservatives appeared to have lost heart over Norman Livkin, as had been evident from the call that Stan had received on the previous day.

Paul Enstone, the silver-haired Labourite, could expect some sort of sympathy vote following his Wednesday night beating; but Stan found it hard to see what help the Conservatives could covertly give to further David's chances at the polls. He produced an Ordnance Survey map of the area and unfolded it, laying it out on the far end of the dining room table.

"I've marked all the locations of the polling stations in the constituency, together with a suggested route which should take in as many as possible," he explained. "I suggest that we start in the village, where you, David, can cast your vote and then work our way up to the other end so that Lara can vote in her parents' ward where she is still registered."

"The girls in the office have done wonders in getting, hopefully, all-day cover from supporters," he went on. "Especially as the locations opened over an hour ago and won't close until ten tonight. On past form the count, which is always at Evenlode Temperance Hall, won't be completed before two in the morning; so I suggest that we all take the afternoon off, start again at around half five, when people have stopped work. We then put in another couple of hours, then meet up in Evenlode at about one tomorrow morning."

"Have you got a map for Caspar?" asked David. "He may well know the country like the back of his hand, but won't have a clue where the polling stations are."

"I told Nikki to leave a marked up copy on the front seat of the Bentley," Stan answered. "Though, on form, your father won't look at it."

They went out to the Mercedes to find that someone, presumably Jack Kestrel, had not only cleaned it, which was fine, but also fixed two County Party posters to the front doors with masking tape. David hoped that the posters would eventually come off as easily as they had gone on. Stan climbed into the front next to David, leaving the back free for Lara and Kaid. Normally Lara would have been in the front, but Kaid had developed a slight aversion to Stan in recent days. Terri, who was in mild disgrace after crashing the farm van into a ditch after a night at the pub, took charge of Buraq in the stables.

'Well, thank you, Anubis, that Sonny isn't coming too,' grumbled Kaid. *For choice he preferred the back seat all to himself, and had been most uncomfortable in the Bentley on the previous day. Anyway, he preferred Lara to old smarmy-head in front.*

David drove down to the village, and parking just beyond the polling station, observed a truly remarkable sight. For Ivor Digney had opted to take the first shift outside what was normally the church hall. Throughout his years of army service, he had always adopted the maxim that 'Any fool can be uncomfortable', and he was certainly no fool. He was seated on a garden chair, while beside him was a picnic table on which were laid out some newspapers, a radio-cassette player, some bacon sandwiches and a thermos flask of coffee. He was also being harangued by the tellers from the main parties. At David's approach he rose to his feet and removed his straw hat.

"Good Morning, Madam, Gentlemen," said the erstwhile Welsh Guards sergeant. "I am afraid that I appear to have upset these good ladies." He indicated the middle-aged tellers who were clucking around his table. Typical Pony Club mums, David thought.

"First they accused me of blocking access to the hall, so I moved my table a bit more to the side of the path," he continued. "And now they object to me playing my wireless!"

"Every time a voter comes along he plays a cassette of a stupid pop song," shrilled the Liberal Democrat lady. "It interferes with universal suffrage!"

"Nothing I can't handle," Digney continued breezily. "I'm tuned to Radio 4, but whenever I see a likely voter approach, I switch to a recording of 'Party Time' to concentrate their minds. My daughter set it up for me last night. Have you seen today's papers, Sir?" None of them had, so Digney produced a selection from his table.

The *Evenlode Echo* had delayed its weekly publication by a day in order to bring out an 'Election Special'. Though strictly independent of any political party, David felt that Roy Large had given him quite a good exposure in his roundup of the candidates and summary of their campaigns. The review of the television interview, and the court report from the previous day, certainly did him no harm either. But the biggest surprise of them all was the *Morning Chronicle*.

Not only did the tabloid lead on the court case (with a good picture of them all outside the building afterwards) but it went so far as to run a second leader on the by-election.

"We have been fairly consistent in the past over our support of the Conservative party," David read, under the heading 'Oxon Blues'. "But when we see efforts to ram a square peg into a round hole, then we say so.

"Although certain matters are still the subject of legal proceedings, in others Mr Norman Livkin has shown himself to be out of touch with the voters in today's by-election in the Vale of Evenlode.

"In these circumstances we feel that the country would best be served, and indeed the present government, if the Oxfordshire voters place their crosses today by the name of Mr David Vyvian, the right of centre independent." Wordlessly, David handed the paper to Lara.

"I suppose they would call Attila 'right of centre' as well," she said, trying to put on her serious historian's face. "The editor must have had a brain transplant after the rough ride that he's given you up till today."

"Indeed," said Stan, peering over her shoulder. So that was what the Conservatives meant by help. It looked like plan B after all.

David entered into the hall with Kaid and went over to one of the two tables that had been set up for the day. The jolly retired school mistress seated behind the table simpered "No need to ask who you are!" as she found his name on the voting register and handed him his voting paper. David had never been able to work out how the ballot was meant to be secret,

170

when the perforated number on the paper was recorded at the time on the register, not that it bothered him too much anyway. He went into one of the three empty booths and, using the pencil attached with string to the shelf in front of him, put his cross against his own name which, not unsurprisingly, was on the bottom of the paper.

He folded the slip and went back to the table to drop it into the metal box, sealed with pink tape, before asking the good lady if they had been busy so far. Quite a few of the young, she told him, and also commuters on their way to catch trains. They expected a slight surge at lunch-time and a busy evening. As he left the building, the still sulking Liberal Democrat teller came up to him.

"I suppose there's no point in asking how you voted," she said sarcastically.

"Not much," said the County Party candidate, tapping his rosette. He went over to thank Ivor Digney before they moved on to their next port of call. They left to the refrain of the chorus of the Number One hit. 'Come to me party! Come to me party!' was echoing around the village green as another potential voter was espied by their vigilant representative.

Apart from Lara entering the polling station in her own ward, none of them was entitled to enter any more, being as how they were overtly members of one of the contesting parties. The same rules applied to them as applied to the party tellers, so from then on it was mainly a case of cheering up their party workers and being friendly towards the voters. (Stan would keep on referring to them as 'the punters'.)

Kaid was quite enjoying himself, for a change. Most of the time was spent in the car, which he regarded almost as a second home anyway, and when he got out, by exaggerating his slight limp, people felt especially sorry for him.

Although their visits were largely repetitive, with David trying to remember the names of the members of the Evenlode Brigade at each station, while Stan consulted the notes that Nikki and Tracy had prepared for them concerning other volunteers, there were nevertheless moments of humour. As they approached the ward in which the Bladon's kennels were situated, there appeared to be a small demonstration in progress. John Crispin, the Master, had been true to his word and was providing cover for four wards in the area.

This particular polling station was manned by the hunt staff. Although all wearing the County Party rosettes, they had also seen fit to have some British Field Sports Society publicity material around. Spring Ur, broken ribs not withstanding, and some fellow new-age travellers were squatting in front of the two whippers-in and were chanting some unintelligible dirge. The whips were completely unfazed by these disgusting people, many of whom had links with the violent Animal Liberation Front.

Not so those manning the polling station who, thinking that the right of free access to the polls was being violated, had called the police. They, in their turn, were on the point of telling all concerned to disperse, when David had to intervene. He pointed out to the senior officer that the Bladon whips were volunteers who were acting as tellers for him in accordance with the Representation of the People Act. He had not, of course, any knowledge of the Act in question, but relied on the fact that they probably did not either. In the event, the hunt staff stayed, while the travellers went.

At another polling station, they met Paul Enstone coming away just as they were arriving. His silver locks were, to an extent, imprisoned by a large white bandage around his head. He grinned when he saw David approach and raised his right fist in mock salute. "Up the workers!" he muttered as he passed. "Let them eat cake!" David retorted and sketched a small fascist salute.

Then, mercifully, it was time for lunch. Since they were in the area anyway, Lara called her parents from the car, and they all met up for sustenance at the Red Lion in the next-door village. They sat at a table under a chestnut tree in the pub garden and had some rather good freshly cut sandwiches and lager. Simon Graham had been very happy to lend a hand in chairing a few of the meetings and had local men out at nearby polling stations. Both he and Ilona had wept with laughter when they had seen the interview in the television studios. The couple both promised to turn out for the result in Evenlode early the next morning.

After their light lunch, David drove straight back to the Hall, where they found that Carmen and Mirza had just arrived unexpectedly. Stan, who clearly had something on his mind, shot off muttering about being back as planned at half past five.

"Hola Amigos!" Carmen kissed both Lara and David on the cheeks and Kaid on the nose. "I had to get out of London, it was so hot, and the Maharajah here has to cover something called exit polls. Apparently they are not as disgusting as they sound, so here we are."

"Don't even joke about my title," chided Mirza, smiling indulgently. "The Beeb went ballistic when I was 'outed' by that glossy magazine." His coffee-coloured skin darkened in startling contrast to his blue Pathan eyes. "Those bastards also maintain that I mishandled the Oxford interview. They are trying to give me the chop. In the mean time, they just give me all the out of town assignments."

"Are you doing the count as well?" asked David. "If so, you're welcome to the use of a bed here to grab what sleep you can during what is going to be a fairly hectic night. The same applies to you, Carmen, if you want to witness at first hand how my *junta* will seize power tonight."

"I'm due to do the lot," sighed Mirza, casting the briefest of conspiratorial glances at Carmen. "They're sending down an Outside Broadcast van to Evenlode at midnight, so I'd really appreciate a bed. I hope that Carmen will, too, as otherwise I'll be stuck in the OB Land Rover all night. She is still my chauffeuse, you see."

The 'chauffeuse' nodded in agreement. She had finally taken pity on the First Secretary at the embassy, returned his Alfa Romeo to him and bought herself an Aston Martin in its place. In return, the diplomat had made sure that she was properly accredited to the embassy: apart from anything else, the CD plates were a great help over parking in the West End.

"Great," said Lara. "I'll tell Mrs Kerr to make up a couple of beds. We're going out again for an hour or so before supper and then again after midnight, which may tie in with your movements. Right now we are going to crash out in the walled garden for the afternoon. You are welcome to join us."

"Can I sunbathe topless?" asked Carmen innocently. "I never get a chance in London."

"Only if you promise to cover up when you hear Caspar's Bentley coming back," Lara laughed. "We could do without over-exciting him at this stage of the game." They all went out to the garden after changing into something more informal.

While the others draped themselves on garden beds in the heat of the June sun, Mirza reclined in a deck-chair under an apple tree with the two dogs. If his European friends wished to risk melanoma, and to fry their skins in order to appear non-white, it only proved to him that Noel Coward's line about mad dogs and Englishmen was about right. He was quite content to remain the same colour as he was and had no wish to resemble a Tamil. Soon the only noise in the garden came from Kaid and Buraq, who were snoring in close harmony.

Norman Livkin was not a happy man. He was aware that he would have to face an uphill battle when he had agreed to fight for the seat, but not against an Independent. His party, fickle as ever, appeared to have deserted him, and even his plea to Central Office that morning for support from a junior minister had been ignored. To him, the countryside and the peasants who lived in it, together with their barbaric obsession for killing animals and birds, richly deserved each other. He must do his best, he supposed, with an eye to future selections, but please let them be in the suburbs.

His wife, Esther, had found little if any support for her strident feminist views in the constituency. She had been booed at a WI meeting for suggesting that (male) farm workers should take time off work to do the housework, cooking and child-raising. She was also very angry with her husband for not having taken better care of Edwina, her cat, at the television interview. The animal now appeared to be doubly incontinent in a fairly random fashion.

On a whim, Stan telephoned Teresa Mileham when he was back in his cottage. He was in luck. Roger was out showing himself, pipe and all, around the polling stations, she said, and she was not. Half an hour later, in a welter of thrashing limbs,

174

Stan was in the process of having 'one for the road' with the lady, when he heard a step on the stairs leading up to the bedroom. With the practised air of one who had been caught in similar circumstances many times before, he disengaged (not without some difficulty) scooped up what clothes he could and bounded into the built-in cupboard.

He had knocked some wire coat hangers inside and they were jangling away like a chime of bells when Roger Mileham came into the bedroom. Also on a whim, he had become so hot on the trail that he had decided to pop home to change his clothes for something cooler. He ignored his panting wife, and going straight to the cupboard, he opened the door.

"What are you doing in there?" he demanded of the naked man, whose hair was smoothed back no longer.

"Waiting for a bus," replied Stan sarcastically. It was a line from a very old joke, but he really could not think of anything else to say.

"Don't be silly," said the aggrieved husband mildly. "I have realised from Teresa's demeanour over the last two weeks that someone was pleasuring her, but up till now, I had no idea that it was you." He paused to light his dreadful pipe, which enabled Stan to pull on his trousers.

"I only did it for the cause," sobbed Teresa from the bed. "He said he would help you to win."

"Shut up, Tessa," continued her husband evenly. "You always have to justify yourself somehow." He turned back to Stan. "We must be realistic and understanding about this. I love Teresa very much, but owing, she says, to my seemingly incurable problem of premature ejaculation, in no way can I —ah — satisfy her demands." He sucked on the pipe, which emitted curious gurgling noises.

"You seem to be a discreet sort of chap," an almost pleading look came into his eyes. "So I'm happy to let things continue as they are and wouldn't, in the circumstances, find it necessary to tell Mr Vyvian of his agent's apparent disloyalty." Without a backward glance and, alas without a change of clothes, he strode from the room and back to the campaign trail.

"Goodie! Goodie!" shrieked Teresa, patting the sheet beside her in an imperious way. "All systems go!" Stan groaned silently

175

and started once more to remove his trousers. Henceforth he would have to rise to the occasion whenever she snapped her fingers at him on pain of exposure, so to speak. 'He who lives by the sword shall perish by the sword' he thought miserably, misquoting St Matthew to himself in his stupor.

Back at Windrush Hall, the party had just finished tea on the terrace. Caspar and Yvette had rejoined them shortly before. Caspar was a bit vague over which polling stations they had visited with Perry. The others were rather left with the impression that the day had been largely spent in Caspar showing off Yvette to his old hunting and shooting cronies and to their doubtless disapproving wives. John Crispin had given them lunch, and it was evident that quite a few had given Caspar port as well.

Stan did not appear before a quarter to six and then was looking so pale and shaky that David suggested that he go home and rest.

"You've obviously been out in the sun for too long," he told his agent. "Try to get some sleep before tonight and we'll meet up in Evenlode later on as planned." Stan nodded dumbly and drove off.

In the end, it was only David and Mirza who went out, together in David's Mercedes. Both of the girls expressed a wish to be present when the result was announced in the early hours, but neither was enthralled by the thought of watching people go into polling stations for a couple of hours. Kaid, too, appeared to be suffering from election fatigue — besides it was his dinner time.

'I've spent the whole morning out on the trail and against veterinary advice,' the dog had thought. 'I'll come out again tonight to find out if the Boss has won a prize or something, but that's it!'

David dropped Mirza off at a busy looking polling station so that he could conduct his exit poll and promised to pick him up again at a quarter to eight. He then drove round some of the locations that he had not fitted in during the morning and spoke to his helpers. Despite working shifts, some of the older ones were flagging a bit by this stage. The stations were quite busy, with an encouraging amount of young, many of them exercising their right of suffrage for the first time. One or two even recognised him without Kaid!

He drove back to where he had left Mirza and picked up his friend, who asked if he could use the car-phone to call his news desk. He spoke rapidly into the hand-set before turning back to David, who was driving..

"I don't know how much you took in of that, which can't be put out until the polls close at ten anyway, but from my small sample, taken over about an hour and a half, you appear to have a significant lead over Mileham, with Livkin down with the 'also rans'," he said. "You might have seen the same on your rounds, but, as an old hand at your by-elections, let me tell you that far more young were turning out than is usual."

David and Mirza were back at the Hall in time for supper. Lara and Carmen had watched Central News while they were out and told them that there had been a small clip about bringing viewers the result of the by-election when if was known. Caspar was much cheered by that news, as it meant that Yvette and he could watch it all from the comfort of the library. He had had a full day and did not relish the thought of going out again in the small hours.

After supper David resolutely banished any thought of drinking the night away — besides he proposed driving to Evenlode himself later on, and had enough brushes with the police lately without being breathalysed on top of everything else. He firmly propelled Lara towards the stairs and suggested that Mirza and Carmen should also take the advantage of a three-hour break before they all had to go out once more.

"I don't think that I've ever been to bed so early in my life before," protested Carmen to Mirza as they climbed the stairs a few moments later. "Will you come and tell me a bed-time story, Rao Rajah?"

"Oh yes, *burra memsahib*," whispered Mirza Sind. "Oh my goodness gracious me, yes!"

David only slept fitfully and was in fact awake when the alarm call came through at quarter past twelve. He and Lara got up and tidied themselves before emerging onto the landing to rouse Kaid. They were in time to see Mirza quietly letting himself out of Carmen's room with only a towel round his waist. The Indian affected not to have seen them, stuck his arms out before him and stared straight ahead in a parody of a sleepwalker and marched back to his own room. He almost tripped over Kaid, who was stretching on being woken, but kept both his balance and his towel. He and Carmen would be going to Evenlode in her car in due course.

Downstairs they looked in on Caspar and Yvette, he quietly dozing in front of the television while she was contentedly leafing through a pile of magazines. They exchanged waves without disturbing Caspar and went out to the Mercedes. Half an hour later they found a bay in the small car park to the side of the Temperance Hall and went into the building where they found Stan, looking rested. He made no reference to his earlier fatigue, but started to brief them on the form.

"The official Returning Officer is the county's High Sheriff, but he usually delegates to the Chief Executive of the District Council to act for him in this constituency. That's him, over there." He pointed at a rather earnest looking individual who was adjusting a microphone on a raised platform at the end of the room.

"Although the turnout has been unusually high, because it's a by-election they have been able to put more staff on the actual counting, so we should have a result, they say, in about half an hour or so," he added, looking furtively over his shoulder. He wanted to avoid the Milehams at all costs.

He need not have bothered. A Liberal Democrat supporter had lent Roger Mileham an estate car for the closing days of the campaign, from the back of which the homely Tessa was distributing plastic mugs of herbal tea and carrot cake. Various supporters hung around, trying to keep up-wind of their candidate and his foul-smelling pipe, and bandied around such great names from the past, such as David Lloyd George, Joe Chamberlain and Jeremy Thorpe. Mileham's agent, who had been somewhat equivocal about their chances, would let them know in good time when the announcement of the result was due.

Paul Enstone had removed the snowy-white bandage from around his silver locks some hours previously, and was now sitting in the Evenlode Working Man's club nursing a pint of beer. He was aware that, as a professional man, he was to an extent distrusted by the rank and file, in much the same way as had been Neil Kinnock in the Eighties. He, too, would only enter the hall moments before the result was announced. He had no delusions: he knew that the opinion polls were right to within a small percentage of error, and that he was destined to come third.

Norman Livkin and Esther, she still defiantly wearing her Aids support red ribbon, had been persuaded against their better judgement to go into the hall by a group of Young Conservatives. These were of the 'Hurray Henry' tendency, many of whom came from without the constituency boundaries. They were, however, outnumbered in both quality and quantity by the army veterans from the Evenlode Brigade and other converts to the County Party. A rather weakly brayed chant of 'County Wonkers' (at least that was what it sounded like) to the chorus tune of 'Party Time' was quickly stilled by a surge towards the Young Conservatives headed by Tony Stark.

Mirza had met up with his Outside Broadcast unit and had positioned the hand-held camera and its operator opposite the raised platform so that the announcement of the result, when it came, could be beamed straight back to London for the live transmission across the country. In the meantime he had to put up with constant whittering in his ear-piece from his producer who wanted to know precisely when to interrupt the programme that was currently showing. Carmen had joined Lara in the meantime in the ranks of the County Party supporters.

Then at last Stan came to get David as the count was finally over. The Acting Returning Officer was certainly going to make the most of his brief moment on television, and certainly had no intention of starting before his full supporting cast was on the platform with him. David, together with Kaid, found themselves squeezed in between Norman Livkin, and Virginia Virago, one of the two Green fringe candidates.

"As Acting Returning Officer for the parliamentary constituency of the Vale of Evenlode, here are the totals of the

179

votes cast for each candidate in today's by-election," pontificated the official. "Enstone, Dr Paul, ('Labour' intoned Mirza into his microphone, his camera running) 7,626; Gerard, Hon Jonathan Quincey (Green Party) 250; Mileham, Roger Gladstone (Liberal Democrat) 10,179; Livkin, Norman Isaac — "At this point, the worthy was forced to break off.

Livkin, twitching nervously beside David and Kaid, had trodden on the dog's tail. Like lightening, Kaid had given him a retaliatory nip on the thigh, which had caused the man to scream with shock more than with pain.

'That'll teach him!' thought Kaid. He had recognised the blue pinstripe suit and the smell of cat from two nights previous, and here was the bloody man trampling all over him. He considered another nip.

" Livkin, Norman Isaac," repeated the returning officer, ('Conservative' muttered Mirza) "6,432; Virago, Virginia Lesbos (Lesbian Green Front), 14; Vyvian, David Lewis Overstone (County Party), 15,701, and that the said David Lewis Overstone Vyvian has been returned as the member for this constituency." Loud cheering broke out from around the hall, including some tuneless renderings of the adapted chorus line of 'County Party'.

"The boy is gob-smacked," said Caspar happily. David was indeed surprised. He seemed to have won, and won by rather a large margin, and now everyone was looking at him rather expectantly. The speech! Of course, he was expected to make an acceptance speech, and he hadn't prepared a word! He took the proffered mike from the Returning Officer.

"I would like to thank the Acting Returning Officer and his officials for burning the midnight oil tonight; the police for ensuring fair play, for at least most of the time (laughter); and my fellow candidates against whom I will bear no lasting grudge (Livkin was still rubbing his thigh)."

"My friends in the Evenlode Brigade and other local people who came to support our party gave invaluable help, as did my family, friends and, last but by no means least, Kaid." His dog wagged his long silky tail and grinned up at him.

Lara, who had been wondering whether she counted as 'family' or 'friend', both she hoped, joined David on the platform and they kissed, much to the disgust of Ms Virago. Mirza joined them, remote microphone in hand, and turned back for a moment to face his camera.

"I am now joined by Mr David Vyvian, the new member for the Vale of Evenlode, and also by his equally well-known dog, Kaid." Mirza turned to face David, taking care to obscure neither Lara, nor Kaid. "Congratulations, Mr Vyvian, on your comfortable majority. What message do you think that your victory spells out to parliament?"

"Thank you, Mirza," David replied. In the circumstances of having seen his interviewer in a highly compromising situation in his own house only a couple of hours before, he was damned if he was going to stick with the formality. "I think that it shows that voters, at any rate those in the Vale, which is where I live, are fed up with the traditional party system. Instead of sneering at such modest achievements and successes as we have left, we should take pride in them and build on them."

"Thank you, David," said Mirza quickly. His producer was telling him, via the ear-piece, to wrap the interview up. "This is Mirza Sind, BBC News, Evenlode." He switched off the mike and removed the ear-piece. Carmen joined them.

It seemed that most of the Evenlode Brigade joined them also. Luckily, thought David, the pubs were long since closed, and the lessors of the Temperance Hall would have taken a fearful view, had any liquor been introduced to their premises, so, after about half an hour of receiving congratulations from well-wishers, they were able to get away.

"I wonder where Stan was after the result was announced?" David mused on the way home.

"Now that you mention it, it was all very strange," Lara replied. "He was being chased from the building by that Liberal's wife, who was calling him a rotten swine."

Back at the Hall, Caspar had already put a bottle of his favourite Dom Perignon on ice. Mirza and Carmen were close behind them on their return, so they all enjoyed a quick drink before finally retiring. Lara even offered some to Kaid, who took a couple of polite slurps from her glass. She also removed his smart leather collar, together with the rosette, which he seemed

to have been wearing for weeks. The dog shook himself and rolled onto his back on the deep-pile carpet in front of the library fireplace.

'Well, thank goodness that is all over,' he thought, writhing on his back to have a good itch at the spot behind his shoulder-blades. 'The Boss has won his prize, or whatever, so we can now get back to normal at last.'

Chapter 13

WEDDING PLANS

David's sister Georgina telephoned at some ungodly hour on the following morning. She had been watching the young men from the estate practising their caber-tossing at dawn, she informed him, and had only read the news of his victory on her return for breakfast. Porridge with salt in place of sugar, kippers and cold haggis, thought David crossly.

Then Carmen and Mirza had left shortly after breakfast in her Aston Martin. Mirza was required to report in person to Broadcasting House.

"Which either means the sack, or being assigned to some disagreeable, hot and dangerous place," he told them. "Both the Beeb and ITN have the same notion, namely that if a reporter is not white, then he can slip into any Third World country without standing out like a sore thumb."

Carmen had no such uncertainties about her own immediate plans. Wimbledon fortnight would be starting soon, followed by the British Open Championship for the Cowdray Park Gold Cup in which Los Andes, the Ecuadorian polo team, would be competing. After that she intended to join the *MY Sybarite*, her father's yacht, for Cowes Week and for the attendant parties on shore. The yacht would then take them to Deauville for the racing, more polo and a little gambling. Further than that, she had not planned. However, she did hope that Lara and David could join her for a few days at either Cowes or Deauville.

Caspar and Yvette came down shortly before Carmen and Mirza left to announce that they, too, should be making tracks. "Got to keep an eye on the grapes," his father had said lamely. David suspected that Yvette had considered that four weeks of high living with old friends was quite enough for his parent, and had called 'time'. They were booked on a ferry for the following morning, so would drive to Newhaven that afternoon.

Then it was a day for clearing up and, if such a thing was possible for a newly elected Member of Parliament, getting back to normal. The farm staff, including a bleary-eyed Jack Kestrel and a cheerful Terri, were all out baling and carting the hay, though David managed to find time for a quick update from his farm manager. Tracy had returned to London on the previous evening after her brief but hectic stint in Party HQ, so it was left to Nikki, also bleary-eyed, to tidy up the farm office so that it could revert to its normal use.

Stan came over at around eleven o'clock, bringing with him an armful of the daily newspapers. David skimmed through them briefly. Although his decisive win was seen as another blow to the government's tattered reputation, he was fast becoming yesterday's news, as indeed he had anticipated. What, he asked his agent, was he expected to do now? He had gone along with Stan's plans as they had originally been spelled out to him, namely to keep the Liberal Democrats out, but he was now entering *terra incognita*.

"You're on your own here, David," said Stan cheerfully. "All I know is that you will be entitled to a desk and a telephone in or near the House of Commons and had better start thinking about a room for a weekly surgery somewhere in the constituency. Perry could probably help, as he owns various freeholds in Evenlode High Street. I suggest that you go up to London on Monday and report to the Department of the Clerk in the House to get your joining instructions."

"You'll find that the Tory Whips' Office will probably be courting you quite hard, so they should help about taking your seat," he continued vaguely. "To come back to the present, this is where I bow out and revert to being your estate management agent. Head Office is baying for me as it is."

"Oh, and by the way, Perry is holding a small get-together at d'Artois Court tonight for all of your party workers. It clearly takes us both to attend. Half past six for a couple of hours," he added. "And Livkin's lot have really blown it. They were on to Rock Hard Music to ask how much we had paid to get you onto their show. They'll be sued if they make any such suggestion in public."

Stan departed with a spring in his step. If he had failed his Thatcherite friends, at least he had established some vague credibility with the Conservatives and had not been exposed as a devious fraud to his client. Since, against all expectations, Roger Mileham had not won the seat, the couple would undoubtedly give up their rented cottage that they had taken soon after the local party had selected him. 'Good-bye and thank you, Mrs Mileham,' he thought.

Lara, sitting in the walled garden, had been reviewing her own position also. She did not doubt for a moment that David truly loved her, and would marry her in due course. But the fact that her man was now an MP, rather than only a comfortably off landowner managing his acres, put the future in rather a different light. She had originally thought that, once the by-election business was out of the way, with David as a gallant loser, she would return to work for Robert Summer at a reduced level until the wedding. She had a sudden pang for a pickled gherkin. Sneaking into the larder while Mrs Kerr was busy elsewhere, she satisfied her craving and returned to the garden.

David's win meant that he would inevitably have to spend some time in London when the House was sitting. But as a cross-bencher, or whatever, he would not have the need to pair with another member, nor, if she had anything to do with it, the need to pair with the young and nubile researchers and secretaries either. Saint Anthony himself might succumb to temptation in those surroundings! She also saw inherent dangers in any future relationship whereby they only met at weekends, or late at night after they had both had exhausting days away from the Hall. Besides, she mused, who would look after Kaid?

'Actually, I'm quite glad that you raised that point,' Kaid snapped at a passing butterfly in a half-hearted fashion. He and Buraq were under the usual apple-tree and, as ever, he was following Lara's thought processes. 'I'm very fond of Mrs Kerr and Terri, but I do expect some individual attention from the Boss and his mate.'

Lara went in through the French windows to David's office and reached Robert in his car. She had told him of her

186

engagement the day after David had proposed, so now could discuss her options with her employer quite openly. He was charm personified. He had never really expected her back, he said, and had planned to promote Nikki in her place, taking on another girl to work with Tracy. All that he wanted from her in due course, he had added, was the return of her mobile phone and an invitation to the wedding.

Lara's next call was to her London flat-mate, whom she telephoned at work. The place in Hays Mews had been incredibly convenient, together with its garage, when she was working for Robert, but was now no longer needed. She would pay her flat-mate, who held the lease, a month's rent in lieu of notice, and hoped that she would come to the wedding.

Finally, she telephoned her parents. Her father answered and they chatted away for a few minutes about the closing stages of the by-election. He would not, Simon Graham told his daughter, be driving down for a drink with the party workers at d'Artois Court that evening, but both Ilona and he wondered if she and David could make Sunday lunch on the following day.

"Be warned," he told her gloomily after she had accepted for them both. "Your mother wants to talk about the wedding."

The wedding: it seemed to be the one thing that everyone was talking about now that the by-election was over. Lara broached the subject with David later that day. Caspar and Yvette had left as planned after lunch and they had taken the dogs for a walk around the estate, an unaccustomed luxury in the past few weeks. They were sitting on a fallen willow by one of the streams, hoping for a glimpse of a kingfisher — a forlorn hope in view of the presence of the dogs — when she took the bull by the horns.

"Darling, you remember that I told you about lunch tomorrow with my parents?" she started. David grunted. He got on perfectly well with Simon Graham, even though he suspected that the Colonel, a former Green Jacket, regarded the cavalry as being too flippant for proper soldiering. He had his doubts, though, about Ilona, Lara's mother, who always seemed a bit leery whenever he was around.

"Well," Lara continued. "Apparently Mummy wants to know our wedding plans and all that sort of thing. There is no great hurry as far as I am concerned, but we had better have a united front before lunch at home."

"A registry office and a small party for close friends would suit me," David answered, idly watching the dogs who were wallowing in the stream. He fell silent when, in a flash of electric blue, a kingfisher darted along the reedy watercourse, oblivious of dogs and humans.

"But I realise that quite a lot of people will feel short-changed if we do it on the quiet. Besides, I imagine that your mother will expect some popish angle somewhere along the line," he finally added.

"Heretic!" Lara flicked his back with a willow shoot. "I realise that your divorce means that we can't be married with the full blessing of my church, but, providing we can get a priest to take some part under your rules, honour should be satisfied. Perhaps you could give your vicar a call this evening to find out the form."

David shuddered. Unfortunately, he did not have the living of his local church which, for all he knew, was being run by a woman by now, the diocese being in the forefront of the ordination of women priests. Caspar had marched out years before, both literally and figuratively, when the then incumbent had abandoned King James in favour of a more 'with-it' text of the Bible.

So, as children, David and Georgina had then been taken around most of the local churches by their parents before settling on the church of St Leonard in a nearby parish. Although the vicar was a bit too keen on the 'smells and bells' tendency for Caspar's comfort, the fact that he rode to hounds and could hold his drink counted strongly in his favour. David resolved to call him that evening before they went out.

The call, when David made it, was not entirely satisfactory.

"My dear David," the vicar had told him. "Under the present regime I can almost marry you, divorce and all, to another man and with the blessings of God the Mother. I certainly wouldn't object to any Roman involvement, in fact I have been taking instruction for some months now, with a view to going across to Rome myself."

"Your main problem," he continued. "Will be with my future masters. This women priests issue has set back any thought of ecumenism by several hundred years, and they tend to stick to their rules rather more firmly than, I am afraid, do we." David thanked the vicar and promised to come back to him in due course.

Lara was rather dismissive when David told her about it. She would speak to her mother on the following day, she said, who would sort it out with her own priest. Although God would have far rather preferred David to be a Roman Catholic, He was far too magnanimous to hold against him eternally that he had been born a Protestant and had sinned over the first set of his marriage vows. David seemed to remember that the Austrian-born former Mrs Tom Troubridge had been denied a church wedding in Vienna some years before when she wished to marry Prince Michael of Kent, but kept silent.

Sir Peregrine d'Artois, Bt, the chairman of the County Party, had the good sense to have invited not only the Evenlode Brigade's members who had helped during the election campaign to his evening drinks party, but also their wives. He thus ensured that all concerned left d'Artois Court not only sober, but also at a reasonable hour. David and Lara, now with both dogs on parade, circulated to thank as many people as they could, as did Perry and Stan.

"I'm so glad the Conservatives won in the end," twittered a voice at David's elbow. It was Stella d'Artois, high on half a glass of sherry. "I couldn't stand that shonky lawyer that the Socialists put up against you." David sighed.

"Thank you, Maris," he replied. There were times when it was just too difficult to explain. "It was all due to Perry's help." But Lady d'Artois, like the perennial gadfly, was already out of ear-shot and was attaching herself to other guests.

Kaid was out of sorts after having to share the back of the car with Buraq on the way over. And now he had to witness the sight of his son ingratiating himself with those very same people who usually made a fuss of him!

On Sunday morning David thought that he had better save a bit of time and line up two members to support his introduction to the House. Having no close friends who were already members, he thought that neighbouring MPs would be prepared to help in the circumstances, so started to telephone around.

Delighted, the Liberal Democrat told him from his constituency just across the county border. The more, the merrier on the cross-benches. No way! said the Conservative from the adjacent constituency, who was hoping for a PPS job in the near future. The government might need David's vote *in extremis*, but it was going to be political suicide to be seen even looking at him.

Piqued, David telephoned Paul Enstone and, after asking about his head wound, spelled out his problem. The doctor thought that it was a fine joke that someone as right-wing as David could not find a local sponsor from the so-called party of the right, but promised to get one of the few pro-hunting Labour members to fill the breach. David then drove Lara and the dogs over to the Grahams for lunch.

Simon Graham met them at the door of their farmhouse and, clearly acting under orders, took David off 'to look at the young stock before joining the girls'. They went to the post-and-rail fencing surrounding one of the paddocks and looked at the pedigree cattle and their followers, all contentedly grazing.

"Ilona has got some fairly strong views on the religious bit," said the prospective father-in-law rather apologetically. "We went to her church for Mass this morning, and I'm afraid that she had a rather difficult time with the Priest chap afterwards." He paused for a few moments.

"As you've probably gathered, the only reason that we are still living here after my Lloyds' losses is that Ilona's been so damned clever with these Bazadais cattle. Obviously, we'll do what we can over the wedding, but I'm afraid that any smart London bash would be way beyond us."

David reassured Simon Graham that they were both thinking about a simple country wedding anyway, but nonetheless was worried that the Catholic involvement was not proving as easy to resolve as Lara had thought. He was hardly reassured when they went into the house to find a tearful Lara with a grim-faced Ilona.

"Mummy's been on to Father Behan, who is the expert on canon law for this sort of thing," Lara told David. "The only way that my church will be involved at all in our wedding would be if you were a bachelor, either by Veronica being struck by the proverbial thunderbolt, or by you getting an annulment of your first marriage from your church."

David felt baffled. Here were he and Lara, living together as man and wife and wishful of entering wedlock, yet finding that nothing is ever as straightforward as they had hoped. Over lunch, which was not, in the circumstances, the most jolly of occasions, matters became slightly clearer, though not entirely flattering to him. Ilona made it quite clear to David that, though she had nothing against him personally, she would have preferred a Catholic single man.

However, the real stumbling block was Granny Tavcar. Now approaching her eighties, she had been overjoyed at the news of her only grandchild's decision to be married. Though hardly an Anglophile, she had accepted with reasonable grace that the wayward child was to become the wife of an Englishman. She therefore intended to break the habit of a lifetime, take a train to Klagenfurt and fly to England for the wedding.

So far, Ilona had not wished to spoil her excitement by telling her that her future grandson-in-law was not only a form of Lutheran, but also a divorced man. All that, Granny could probably stomach, David gathered, providing that the Roman rites were somehow involved. In an effort to defuse matters, David said that he would find out the form on seeking an annulment as soon as possible. Ilona said gloomily that she only hoped that the Church of England was somewhat more speedy in such matters than Rome, where the whole process could take years.

David and Lara left as soon as they politely could after lunch. During the drive back, David, whose own grandparents were long since departed, delicately tried to ascertain why the wishes of Lara's elderly grandmother were apparently so paramount to their wedding.

"I suppose its a form of guilt really," sobbed Lara. "She went through such a hard time during the war, bringing up Mummy on her own, and then after it under Tito. She was so kind to me, both before I went to Trieste and while I was there. And she never once reproached me when I was involved with Luigi, though she obviously disapproved madly."

When they were back at the Hall, David made a further call to Father Timothy, as he chose to call himself, the vicar of St Leonard's. The cleric was in the process of having an afternoon nap before preparing for Vespers, so was not best pleased to be disturbed. However, he listened as David spelled out the situation that he himself had anticipated on the previous day.

"Yes," he told David. "Annulment does exist within the Church of England, but nowadays, with divorce carrying none of the social stigma that it used to, it is hardly ever used. You can certainly petition for it on the grounds that, ah, Veronica declined to have children, or didn't fully understand the vows that she took, or anything else." He paused.

"One thing that you must understand, though, is that we are talking about months, or even years, rather than weeks here, and that a degree of co-operation from Veronica, though not mandatory, would help things along. Can I make a highly unusual suggestion?"

"Feel free," answered David, willing to clutch at any straw.

"Since time appears to be not critical for you both," suggested Father Timothy. "Let the annulment route be your main plan. But, if that gets bogged down or fails, try this for plan 'B'. You both get married in a registry office, then come along to my church. As your dear father never ceased to tell me before he moved away, the rites in St Leonard's are somewhat to the right of those practised in the Holy City.

"I then give you both an elaborate a blessing as I can legally do, with a choir, hymns and a bit of Latin thrown in for good measure. Since you tell me that the good lady from Slovenia has, at best, only a tenuous grasp of English, and since the church in her country is probably still not quite back in step with Rome, she should be satisfied.

"I'm not normally in the business of deception, but if we have to use this fall-back plan," Father Timothy concluded. "The end, with everyone happy, will surely justify the means.

Don't hang around for too long though, as once I have gone over to Rome, all deals will be off."

David marvelled at the pragmatism of this splendid man and went to find Lara. For her part, another craving had sent her running to the larder where, oblivious of the tut-tutting from Mrs Kerr who was preparing tea, she wolfed down two further pickled gherkins. As she wiped her lips with her handkerchief, the realisation suddenly struck her that she must be pregnant.

Lara had not set out to trap David into marriage — far from it. She had to admit, however, that since they had become formally engaged, she had ceased taking her birth-control pills and had eventually thrown the remainder of the sleeve into the rubbish bin. Besides, she was, now that she counted it out, overdue anyway. Deep down in her mind was the firmly held belief that loving David was not a sin, but preventing herself from bearing his child would be one.

They met in the hall. David was clearly bursting to tell Lara how he had fared with Father Timothy, so she let him spell out the two options first. In a way, she was glad that the decision had been taken out of her hands. She moved across to him and pressed up against his chest, her arms around his waist.

"David," she said quietly. "It's going to have to be plan 'B'."

The realisation of what she was saying registered with him quickly. He held her to him and looked into her eyes.

"Are you sure?"

"I'll go and see a gynie in the next day or so, but, yes, I'm sure. A budding little politician, perhaps?"

David grinned. "I think one in the family will be quite enough, but seriously, I'm so, so happy for us." He kissed her.

'I think I get the drift of all that,' thought Kaid, who had followed his Boss into the hall. 'I fathered six at my first go, only five of which, alas, were given away. I wonder if they will keep one?'

After tea, and indeed for the rest of the day, they were heavily involved in the details of plan 'B'. The last Saturday in July would not only give them six weeks, less a day, to organise everything, but would also enable them to get the invitations out in good time. Parliament, David had gathered from his conversation with the Liberal Democrat MP on the previous day, was due to break for the summer recess at the end of the following week and, more to the point, Carmen would have sailed for Deauville by then.

A call to the long-suffering Father Timothy after he had returned from Vespers established that both St Leonard's and he would be free on the date in question, and that he would be delighted to discuss the order of service with either or both of them in due course.

"I suppose you'll be bringing your heathen dog," he concluded.

"Of course he's not heathen!" protested David. "He goes to church as much as I do."

"And that, dear boy, is a *non sequitur*." said Father Timothy dryly, replacing his hand-set.

Having cleared the major hurdle, it was then a question of deciding on the format of the day. Neither of them knew, hardly surprisingly, if Register Offices were open for marriages on Saturday mornings, but Lara would telephone the Superintendent Registrar at Evenlode on the following morning. At worst, the civil ceremony could take place on the Friday.

Then there was the matter of the reception, which required delicate handling. Traditionally, it would be for Simon and Ilona, as the bride's parents, to arrange and pay for that, but David had no wish to add to their financial worries. He asked Lara if she thought that her parents would feel insulted were they to hold the reception at the Hall.

"Darling, you've got to be joking!" she laughed. "Don't forget that Daddy's a Scot, and even if he were stinking rich, the thought of someone else paying would be like Ambrosia was to the Gods."

David left Lara to speak to her mother about the reason for the sudden escalation of the wedding plans, which was not for general consumption, and to suggest that Ilona might have both Simon's parents and Granny Tavcar to stay for the wedding. He contented himself with a quick call from his office to Georgina, to warn her well in advance to keep the day free. He also dashed off a quick line to Caspar, who would be somewhere between Dieppe and Cannes as he made his way leisurely home to the Alpes Maritimes in the Bentley.

Finally, he sent a short fax to the office of the managing director of Ivanhoe Publishing, the Oxford firm which had done all the election printing for the County Party, advising him that a rush order would be arriving within the next couple of days for the thermographic printing of the invitations. He the rejoined Lara in the library, where she was just finishing a call to Carmen.

"Mummy was quite understanding in the circumstances. In fact, she was utterly delighted by the news that she was becoming a granny. From now on, I think she'll be totally on our side" Lara told David happily. "She thinks that Granny Tavcar will buy it, especially as civil ceremonies are de rigeur abroad. Simon's parents may well not come, since they have a rather Calvinistic view of divorce. By the way, will we be doing the catering from here?"

"No, Mrs Kerr isn't into mass catering, and you know how much she loathes strangers in he kitchen," David replied. "I thought I'd get David Frost, an old friend who runs his own catering business over at Cirencester, to do the drink and eats. Ivor Digney I am sure can take care of the rest, like car parking and a marquee for the garden in case it is too hot, or rains. For choice, we'll try to keep guests out of the house."

They spent the rest of the evening, apart from a short break for supper, in deciding a guest list with a top limit of about 200. David was insistent that his estate staff, such as they were, should be invited, together with quite a few locals whom it would be churlish not to ask. His relatives were mercifully few, apart from Georgina and her brood, and there were a few friends around from his army days.

Like David, Lara was not overburdened with relatives, apart from dear Aunt Virginia. There were some Graham cousins in Scotland, with whom she had largely lost touch over the years and a few friends from the filming world, headed naturally by Robert Summer. She had stayed in contact with some of her friends from her Lycée days, and a handful from Eton such as Pippa Grace, and of course Carmen. They both agreed to invite Lance Thrust, Mandy and Cat.

The following morning, David was due to go to London to book in at the House of Commons. The post arrived before he left, and among a pile of letters that turned out for the most part to be congratulations on his election to parliament was a pale blue envelope. It was written in a hand that, even after a gap of a few years, he recognised. He tore it open.

'Dear David,' he read. 'Congratulations on your election. I have always thought that parliament is a glorified asylum for social and emotional cripples, so I was right all along. By the way, now that you will be in receipt of a fat MP's salary, I expect you to up the alimony. My God, you live the life of luxury with your hunters, your dogs and your bimbo! Schuster and Schneider will be in touch soon with your Gresham Street people. Yours, Veronica.'

The bitch! Veronica clearly imagined that the draconian powers of the Child Support Agency extended to a form of ex-wife hand-out scheme, thought David. He put it down to pure malice rather than a serious attempt to prise more money out of him. Besides, at best he would draw a parliamentary salary for a mere two years as, come a general election where the voters tended to follow party lines, the County Party was sure to be extinguished.

He chucked the letter into the pending tray on his desk for later filing. He also noted with some alarm that quite a handful of letters were from constituents who had clearly been awaiting the election of a new member in order to resurrect old grievances. Most of these would be a matter for the local authority, rather than for him, but he realised that they all needed answering. He drove to Evenlode, where he left his car at the railway station and caught a train to London. Kaid, alas, was left behind. David planned to get him into the House by hook or crook at some stage, but his first day was hardly the right moment.

'Well, thanks very much! I get you first prize in your election, Boss, and all you do is leave me at home with that dreadful Sonny.' Kaid put on the doleful act as David firmly closed the front door in his face, then wandered into the walled garden. To cap it all, Buraq was lying under his favourite apple-tree!

Lara in the meantime was finding the organisation of her own wedding a mere bagatelle after years of running Clyne

Films for Robert Summer. She settled down by the telephone in the library and spoke to David Frost, the caterer, Ivor Digney, the Master of Ceremonies, and to Ivanhoe Publishing about the invitations. The Superintendent Registrar in the Register Office in Evenlode was most helpful. Yes, they were open for business on Saturday mornings, she said, and gently pointed out that she would need to see a copy of David's decree absolute before the ceremony.

The put-upon Father Timothy, who always liked to regard Monday as his day off, agreed to see Lara in a couple of days to talk about the order of service for their blessing. He chose to call it a service of benediction combined with a celebration of the feast-day of Saint Christophorus, which was fine by her.

Her final problem was what to wear. A linen suit would be in order for the register office in the morning, which Lara regarded as a legal matter. But, for the church and the reception afterwards, and at what she fully intended was going to be the only wedding of her life, something special was called for. Virginal white with a veil would obviously be a bit ridiculous, as indeed would be the suit that she would be wearing earlier in the day. Lara telephoned her mother for inspiration.

Ilona had for many years kept in a bottom drawer the wedding dress of her mother, Franzesca. Although her own wedding had taken place in church in London, it had been a very quiet affair since her husband-to-be, Simon, was the only Englishman whom she knew at the time. Thus she had never the opportunity to ever wear the garment, originally the property of Josip Tavcar's mother.

"Yes," she said to her daughter. "I think that I have just the answer. Come over for tea today and we'll talk about it."

Chapter 14

AND GRANNY CAME TOO

Meanwhile David's taxi had deposited him outside the Members' Entrance to the House of Commons. Feeling rather like a new boy arriving at boarding school, his first problem was to get himself into the building. The doorkeeper was polite, but firm. No pass, no entrance. Eventually someone from the Serjeant at Arms Office was sent for, and after examining David's passport which he had sensibly brought with him, escorted him to the office of the Department of the Clerk.

The staff were kindness itself, having done this sort of thing many times before. David was given a thick booklet of joining instructions and taken on a conducted tour while the necessary passes were prepared for him. Any ideas that he might have harboured about taking on Reggie Token's old office, said to be quite spacious, were swiftly deflated. He was offered either a sort of broom cupboard under one of the staircases in the House, or a half-share of a slightly larger office in an adjacent building. He opted for the latter.

David had no cause to regret his choice when he found that he was sharing with one Richard Riley, a recently elected Independent who represented a north midland constituency. He owed his presence in the House to much the same reasons as David, though in his case a proposed motor-way through the heart of his constituency, backed for some reason by the Conservative candidate, had cost the Tories another shire seat. He was a congenial man of about David's age and he took it upon himself to explain the form to the 'new boy'.

"That will be your desk over there," he started. "The Serjeant at Arms Office will sort out some stationary and let the switchboard know what extension you are on. Unless you've got other plans, I suggest that we share a secretary. I inherited an efficient lady, Mrs Watt, with the office, and I have her for eight hours a week, so she could easily look after you as well.

"I have a surgery in my constituency every Friday, so I bring up any letters that need doing as a result on Mondays and dump them on Mrs Watt. She is also authorised to collect my mail from my pigeon-hole in the House, plus all the bumf from the Vote Office, like Hansard, order papers and so on. The allowances, by the way, are pretty generous and cover, for instance, secretarial help, postage and travel between here and the constituency. The telephone is free for inland calls.

"I suggest you dump your joining instructions on your desk," he concluded. "We'll walk over to the House and have a spot of lunch and I'll introduce you to some of the others."

Though the chamber of the House had been deserted when David had been shown it in the morning, the House never sitting before half past two, the bars, and later the Members' dining room, were packed. David felt that, though quite a few members knew who he was, presumably from his over-exposure in the media during the past four weeks, none put themselves out to be particularly welcoming. He mentioned this to Richard, who laughed.

"Don't worry about it," he said. "You and I, plus one or two others, are the parliamentary pariahs who have bucked the cosy three-party system. If it comes to a crucial vote, both the government and the opposition whips will be licking our boots to get us into their lobbies."

After a reasonable meal — not quite up to Mrs Kerr's standards — David went back to his new office to tie up his introduction to the House for the following day. He then read his guide for new members for a time before catching a train home from Paddington.

Lara in the mean time drove herself in the BMW with both dogs over to her parents' house for tea, as planned. Her father was out on the farm when she arrived, but her mother met her at the front door.

'Doesn't Lara yet realise that I would far rather stay at home with Terri than share the back seat of this small car with Sonny?' Kaid had eyed his offspring with disfavour. 'He has been known to be sick in cars before now.' He did

199

consider scrambling over to the front passenger seat, but rejected the idea. Besides, Lara might strap him in.

Actually, Lara's thoughts were elsewhere, for she was intrigued. She had never seen her mother's wedding-dress, which in the circumstances she would hardly have expected to have been an elaborate affair. Her mother had sounded half mysterious, half embarrassed about her idea on the telephone. Ilona had inspected her daughter on arrival.

"I could have told straight away that you are pregnant. You look wonderful," she said with the gift of hindsight. She embraced her daughter lovingly and kissed her on both cheeks. "Anyway, come upstairs and see what I have got. It may be a bit much for the Vale, but see what you think."

Lara, who had half expected some white Fifties-type ball-gown with a veil, gazed in amazement at what her mother had laid out on the matrimonial bed.

"It belonged to Josip's mother," Ilona said by way of explanation. "She came from the Vojvodina. From what I remember, she was of the same height and build as you are."

On the bed lay a gorgeous dress, at least eighty years old. The lace-up bodice, faded with age to sage-green and undershot with tarnished silver threads, was set off against a full skirt of deepest garnet. Next to it, Ilona had laid out a short cropped blouse with sleeves puffed-up to the elbows tapering into long buttoned up cuffs. The low-cut white linen blouse had yellowed with age and appeared to be designed to be fastened with a bit of string beneath the bust.

"Of course, you ought to be wearing Puszta boots with this," Ilona told her, looking at her daughter doubtfully.

"Oh, mummy, I have got some wonderful black Slovenian kid boots, with beautiful stitching," Lara replied enthusiastically.

"And there is the jewellery," Ilona drew Lara's attention to her dressing table. She had put out an intricately worked wide silver and garnet choker, and, the *pièce de résistance*, a traditional Central European bridal *Brautkrönchen*, filigree silver studded with twelve garnets. "Granny Tavcar gave those to me, but I have never had the opportunity to wear the coronet, nor of course the dress."

Lara slipped out of her Gucci shirt and jeans and gingerly tried on the ancient garment. It fitted perfectly. The effect of the green, silver and garnet combined with Lara's fair hair and lightly tanned skin was startling.

"Yes, mummy, I'll wear this," Lara said, admiring herself in the long cheval mirror. Then she pondered. "What if the baby will show just a bit in six weeks time?"

Ilona laughed. "Darling, at home in the country most brides were pregnant. That's why the bodice is lace-up and the skirt is so full."

Lara thought that she would have to consult Brian, her hairdresser in Motcombe Street, about how to fix the coronet, and book him to come down to the Vale to do her hair between her visit to the register office and the blessing.

She changed back to her ordinary clothes, laying the beautiful dress carefully back on the bed, and followed her mother down to the kitchen for a glass of tea and lemon. Her father, Simon, joined them, but was somewhat preoccupied with problems of wild oats in the spring barley. She managed to get out of him that his parents were unlikely to attend her wedding as it would be, for them, a bad time of year. A clash with the opening of the haggis season, Lara thought to herself, knowing that her Graham grandparents were by now drawing their pensions.

Lara was back at the Hall shortly before David, who was greeted by Kaid with the well rehearsed drill of 'Boss-I-never-thought-you-were-coming-back'. This was followed by a thorough sniffing routine to check that David had not been consorting with other dogs. Finally satisfied, Kaid returned to his normal lair in the garden.

Lara gave David a summary of what she had achieved earlier in the day and listened with feigned enthusiasm as he described his first visit to the House. The main advantage, as she saw it, to his new job was that 'nine to five' in his case seemed to mean leaving the Hall at around nine o'clock and being home by five, and then only four days a week. She was extremely relieved that her man was not responsible to any Whips, who could otherwise compel him to remain hanging around the chamber until the small hours. Nevertheless, she realised that there could be the odd occasions when David might feel honour bound to see a debate through.

"David," she said, thinking aloud. "You will be totally faithful to me once we are married, won't you? I certainly shall be to you. I know that I'll be able to cope with whatever comes our way but, not being your typical Englishwoman, I really couldn't bear it if you had another woman."

He came over to her and kissed her gently. "Of course, darling. We've both made mistakes in the past, and I hope have learned from them. I'm never going to risk losing you." He kissed her again. Caspar and his mother had had a happy marriage, and he realised that this was probably not unconnected with their mutual fidelity.

"And you won't mind if I wear my great-grandmother's wedding dress for the church and reception?" Lara thought that the moment was probably right to bring the matter up at this stage. She wanted to break David in gently to the idea that her wedding apparel could be regarded by some as Ruritanian, rather than Slovene.

"As long as it holds together for the day," David grinned at her. "By the way, I thought that we might ask Carmen and Mirza to be our witnesses for the register office, unless you have any better ideas."

Lara had not, so they took the dogs for a good walk before returning to the Hall for a bath before supper.

The next few weeks passed very quickly for both of them. David was in no hurry to make his maiden speech in the House, so contented himself with trying to learn the workings of parliament, and indeed the geography of the place. By arrangement with Perry, he had leased the ground floor of an empty shop in Evenlode, where he would hold a surgery every Friday evening, to which his constituents were beginning to come.

The motherly Mrs Watt, whom he shared with Richard Riley, took care of all his correspondence with great efficiency, and some of his fellow members even started to talk to him. A distinctly end-of-term feeling seemed to permeate the

Corridors of Power as the end of July, and indeed of David and Lara's wedding, approached. Then, with only three days to go, the Opposition tabled a vote of no confidence in the government.

This was not a problem for David, as he and Lara had not planned to leave on their honeymoon before parliament went into recess at the end of the following week anyway. However, for those members who had already sloped off on holiday, having paired with a member of the opposing party, the imposition of a three-line whip for the first week of August was, to put it mildly, inconvenient.

He discussed the vote at some length with Richard Riley who, like him, was under no delusions as to their fate if the government fell and a general election was called. They were both on borrowed time.

"It cuts both ways really," said Richard. "The government might like to think that we'll support them in order to keep our jobs for, at the most, another two years. But the more farsighted ones must realise that, as a QC, I'll never want for a crust, neither will you with your rolling acres."

"My paper spelled out the maths involved this morning," David told him. "The Lib Dems will obviously go with Labour and it's thought the Ulster Unionists will this time as well. By their reckoning, the Conservatives, without any help from our ilk, will scrape home by a majority of one on Tuesday. They can, of course, afford a tie as the speaker's casting vote always goes to the party in power."

David was still working on plans to get Kaid, who when all was said and done was largely responsible for his election, into the House. There was no problem over his office, because it was outside the precincts of the main Palace of Westminster, and he had brought Kaid up by car on a couple of occasions. The dog had not particularly enjoyed it, especially when he was left with Mrs Watt, who tried to feed him chocolates which Kaid loathed, for a couple of hours while David went over to the House.

He had been rebuffed when he approached the Serjeant at Arms, quoting the Shadow Secretary of State for Health's guide dog and the police sniffer dogs as precedents. David Blunkett's dog was necessary for his mobility and had only been allowed after lengthy discussion with the Service Committee, while the police dogs were essential to deter any latter-day Guido Fawkes, he was told. Blunkett himself was quite amusing about it when David met him. Offa, his earlier guide dog, was only allowed in on the understanding that he would make no noise at all compared with the other occupants of the Chamber!

As a parting gesture and on impulse, David sent a note to the Speaker's office stating that he wished to be called on to deliver his maiden speech during the no confidence debate on the following Tuesday. He then left for the country.

Lara in the mean time had been quietly getting on with all the arrangements for the wedding. The invitations, with help from David in the evenings, had all gone out within the first week; the food and drink had all been settled with David Frost; Ivor Digney had been over on a few mornings to talk about tentage and car parking; and the order of service had been finally agreed with Father Timothy, which included Lara's cunning plan for a choral rendition in English of Beethoven's *Ode to Joy*.

The most relieved person of all at the way the wedding plans were developing was Jack Kestrel. As the part-time gamekeeper remarked to the homely Mrs Kerr in her kitchen, he had only been to London once in his life — by hired coach for his employer's first wedding — and had felt physically ill throughout the experience. He never intended to repeat the dreadful culture shock again.

Lara had decided early on that the local flower shop would be invited to decorate the church. They would receive good notice and would be asked to produce pink hydrangeas and old-fashioned roses. Hopefully, they might be able to get some Turk's cap lilies, which she used to see growing wild in Slovenia and was very fond of, as well.

Mrs Kerr had diffidently volunteered her daughter to help who was, apparently, 'ever so good with flowers'. Lara accepted the kind offer though, in truth, very little was needed for the reception as the marquee would incorporate much of the walled garden, together with its summer borders. These would be resplendent with single-flowered hollyhocks in the most exquisite pastel shades, white and blue Canterbury bells and huge marguerites. Perhaps the daughter could make up some table decorations from wild flowers, such as field scabious, ox-eye daisies, orchid-like marsh helleborines, sweet-smelling camomiles and blue corn-flowers. All of these grew in odd corners of the estate, especially on the set-aside land.

Then, as the replies to the invitations started to come in, there was the question of where to put up close members of their families. Caspar and Yvette, who planned to fly over on the day previous and return on the subsequent day, would clearly stay at the Hall, as would Carmen and Mirza. Similarly Granny Tavcar would be met at Heathrow by Ilona and would reside at her and Simon's farm for the wedding,

Lara's Aunt Virginia would be driven down and back again for the day by Buff Mainwaring, who had accepted promptly. Lara had fully expected to have had the Ardkinglases as guests at the Hall, but Perry d'Artois had preempted her by asking Dougal and Georgina to stay with him and Stella. All of the girls were scattered across the face of the earth, thus Hamish would be the only sibling to attend, so Lara asked him to have a bed with them. David noted in passing that Major John Crispin, master of the Bladon, and his wife had both declined: she due to Pony Club camp and he due to a hunting convention in Virginia.

Lara also had ample time to cast a critical eye over the hall and its surroundings. Not that she planned any changes for changes sake nor, in the event, did she find that Veronica's influence had been more than merely ephemeral. It had hardly extended beyond the door of her boudoir, which Lara planned to turn into a further, and much needed, guest bathroom. Mary Vyvian, when she was alive, had clearly possessed the good taste that can be ageless.

Obviously, David and Georgina's old nursery, used as a spare room for many years, would need to be reconverted, but that could wait for a few months yet. Lara also had one or two ideas for modernising the kitchen but, although she had Mrs Kerr's trust, she realised that she would need to tread very carefully indeed in that particular quarter.

Outside, she limited herself to ensuring that the part-time gardener, who came in two days a week, knew what was going on. She also had a word with the farm manager to ask if Jack Kestrel could be persuaded to leave the Land Rover in the barn in future so that she could park her BMW in the double garage next to David's Mercedes.

Then, suddenly, it was the last Thursday in July, two days before the wedding. David came home at a reasonable hour and they spent the evening in having a final check on the numbers and in opening and listing the various wedding presents that they had received. Most were fairly prosaic, though nonetheless welcome, but three stood out in particular.

Robert Summer had made an offer quite early on to make a film of the wedding. David had jibbed at the idea, having seen some truly dreadful videos of other weddings, but Lara had sufficient faith in her former employer to know that his filming would be neither intrusive, nor second-rate. Thus they accepted his kind offer, having first cleared the idea with Father Timothy.

'I am quite keen on this filming idea myself,' Kaid had thought when the plan was first mentioned. 'As an old hand, I will ensure that I am in the frame for much of the time.'

Mirza must have been to some trouble, and no little expense, to lay his hands on a late 18th Century Mogul miniature of the Rajput school depicting a game of polo. They had resolved to hang it in the library.

Carmen had faced the problem head-on and had actually walked from Park Lane to Berkeley Square. She found the Sladmore Gallery in Bruton Mews without difficulty. Once inside, she informed Edward Horswell, the co-proprietor, that she wished to buy an original 19th Century bronze of a lurcher by none other than Paul-Raymond Gayrard, one of the father figures of *Les Animaliers*. The matter of price was raised and disposed of, and within ten days her weighty present was delivered by Securicor to the Hall.

Kaid did not think much of the bronze, which he thought was more like a deerhound than anything else., so reminded him of his late Uncle, Sidi. 'Some people are easily satisfied,' he reflected.

There was also a pleasant set of hunting prints by Gilbert Holiday from Georgina and the rest of her family; Caspar had promised a quantity of yet-to-be-pressed wine from his vineyard in the Alpes Maritimes; while Stan, perhaps exercising his devious Wykhamist sense of humour, gave them a double gun-rack for the back of the Land Rover.

On the following afternoon David drove Lara to Heathrow where she met her mother in the Arrivals lounge of Terminal 2. Together, they would take Granny Tavcar back to Simon and Ilona's farm and Lara would stay there for the night, and be married, for Granny's benefit, 'from home'. David thought that it would be time enough to meet his grandmother-in-law on the morrow, so made himself scarce. He bought a copy of the *Evening Standard* to while away the time before Caspar and Yvette's Air France flight arrived an hour later.

Some minutes later he was aware of someone standing before him. He looked up to see Pearl smiling down at him. He rose to his feet. She really was stunningly beautiful but, he fully accepted, strictly off limits now.

"I thought it was you," said she. "Buffie tells me that you are to be married tomorrow to that beautiful blonde that you had with you at Eton. Congratulations. Must dash." She glided across the marble to where a florid-faced portly man was waiting impatiently by one of the Departure gates and was gone. Dear God, thought David, for her companion was none other than John Crispin, complete with dark glasses, cravat, and straw hat with a Guards' ribbon round it. He hoped that the MFH was capable of the stamina that clearly kept Buff Mainwaring going. Another 'Uncle', he supposed.

The Air France flight was on time, as had been Granny Tavcar's Austrian Airlines flight from Klagenfurt, he had gathered from the Arrivals board. He pushed Caspar and Yvette's baggage trolley across the elevated walkway to the multi-storey car park and before too long they had joined the Friday evening rush-hour on the M4 and then on the M40. Caspar was in fine form due, Yvette told David, from having spent the entire month sipping rosé beside the swimming pool at the villa. They entertained a little, mostly near-neighbours who were mainly French. The coast they always abandoned to the tourists in July and August, when it was too hot at sea-level anyway.

Hamish was already at the Hall when they eventually arrived and, with Etonian self-confidence, had by then helped himself to a stiffish whiskey-and-soda, David noted. He was due to go up to Cambridge after his 'gap' year and had acquired a small car in the meanwhile. They gathered that his parents' camper had finally given up the ghost, so Dougal had bought a Saab, which he was convinced was manufactured in Devon.

Carmen's Aston Martin was close behind, and had gathered a slight dent in the front bumper. She was a little vague when asked about it, but Mirza later told David that there had been a display of Latin temper when a parking meter had declined to accept an Ecuadorian coin.

The tentage had been erected during the afternoon, evidently to Ivor Digney's satisfaction. Earlier, Lara had taken Mrs Kerr's daughter around a few of the fields to show her which flowers to pick for the table decorations, which would be left until the following morning.

David took his nephew out with the dogs early on the following day as he intended Hamish to be in charge of them during the church service when he and Lara would be otherwise occupied. He left the dogs with Hamish also when, later in the morning, he drove over to the Graham's to pick up Lara for the Register office ceremony. Carmen, with Mirza followed on behind as she planned to help her friend prepare for the wedding in the afternoon.

Both David and Lara had decided that the civil ceremony would be deliberately low-key, so their two friends, who would be acting as witnesses, would be the only ones to attend from either camp. David had already met the Superintendent Registrar during the previous week when he had produced a copy of his decree absolute. On this occasion she conducted the brief service in a mature and friendly way. David had rather dreaded the cloying and familiar fashion sometimes used by vicars during church weddings.

After the service Carmen drove Lara back to her home to lend moral support, while David and Mirza went back to the Hall.

Chaos seemed to be reigning in the walled garden, kept in check by the authoritative figure of Ivor Digney. Inside there was comparative peace, broken only by the sound of hiccups from the drawing room. It appeared that Caspar had been plying his grandson, Hamish, with the Dom Perignon that had been set aside for lunch. David firmly cut off further supplies and led them to the dining room where Mrs Kerr had set out a cold buffet.

"Well, Mirza, do you think David's ready for the monogamy bit at last?" Caspar queried later, while spreading a slice of cold tongue with Mrs Kerr's chutney. "Trouble is, men are designed for multiple relationships, as your people are clever enough to recognise." He added a piece of baked potato to the meat and contemplated the mouthful thoughtfully. He then winced as Yvette kicked him beneath the table.

"My grandfather, who ran quite a harem in his day, always used to tell me that there are more ways of killing a cat than by stuffing it with cream," replied Mirza inconsequentially, certain in his own mind that Yvette kept Caspar on the straight and narrow path. "Anyway, you wouldn't thank David if half the toddlers in the county shouted 'Grandpa' after you when you come to visit him."

"Most of the boys in the area shout 'Hi Dad' to him as it is," laughed David. He turned to Yvette. "I'm sure you keep a close eye on him at home, Yvette."

"Do not worry about that," she answered, joining in the gentle teasing of Caspar. "I have let it be known that he has had the, how do you call it, prostrate operation, so functions no more."

Caspar's outraged denials were cut short by Mirza who suggested that, to avoid a rush, they should perhaps change sooner rather than later into their wedding finery. Meanwhile Jack Kestrel, who would drive David and Mirza to the church, was giving the car a final polish.

Kaid was not completely certain what this wedding thing entailed. He assumed that there was probably some walk-on part for himself and Sonny, as Terri had brushed them both in the morning and had polished their smart leather collars.

Lunch at the Graham household had not been the easiest of meals. Granny Tavcar had decided to act up. Simon Graham had conveniently forgotten his limited Serbo-Croat, and Carmen's efforts to engage the old lady in Italian were firmly rebuffed. Reduced to speaking only to her daughter and granddaughter, her main complaint was that there was no Slivovitz in the house. It was not, so she told Ilona, that she drank a great deal of it, but surely it was the least that her daughter could do to provide some for this, her first visit, to their house.

Since much of the day had been organised around Granny, who now seemed in spoiling mood, Lara was close to exasperation as she explained the problem to Carmen.

"Don't worry, Lara, I fix," she said in the tone of one used since birth to getting her own way. Excusing herself from the table, she telephoned the Hall and asked Mrs Kerr to get Ivor Digney. She had only met him the once, at the amusing dinner party back in May, but assumed, correctly, that Mrs Kerr would remind him who she was. Her instructions to him were brief and to the point. How the former Welsh Guardsman was expected to lay his hands on a bottle of Slivovitz in the Vale of Evenlode on a Saturday afternoon was his problem, not hers. (To Ivor Digney, the problem was a mere bagatelle to some that he had faced in the Officers' Mess: there lived an old Hungarian, György, in the village who had come across after the abortive uprising of 1956. He practically existed on the stuff. Thither Digney's daughter was despatched.)

Carmen's return to the dining room coincided with the arrival of Brian, Lara's hairdresser from Motcombe Street. Together they removed Lara from the now icy atmosphere that emanated from Granny and bundled her up to her bedroom to prepare for her wedding. Since temperance had been the order of the day at the early lunch, due to Granny's perverse refusal to try any alternative to her favourite tipple, Carmen grabbed them all stiff vodkas and tonic from the sitting room on the way. Lara was soon restored to her usual good nature.

She was further boosted by the rapture which was shown by her friend and by her hairdresser when, an hour and a half later, she was fully clad in the ethnic outfit. Even Granny, when they came down, emitted a sort of grunt that could be taken for admiration at both the dress and her jewellery.

They were all changed and ready by half past two, so Carmen set off with Brian, immaculate in a grey morning coat, who was to be in attendance throughout the day. Ilona followed with her mother, whose whingeing had by now reached a high decibel count. Granny Tavcar was clad in a black taffeta suit, her standard apparel for church occasions, but as a concession to what was supposed to be a joyous event, wore a high-necked white blouse with it. Simon Graham, who was to give his daughter away, and Lara brought up the rear in a hired limousine: it would eventually convey the bride and bridegroom back to the Hall after the church service.

Though the bride's car proceeded at a sedate pace in order not to be early at the church, the others were in good time and found that the party from the Hall were just ahead of them. Ilona was a trifle surprised when Mirza Sind, whom she had only met briefly, edged up to her and handed her a large hunting flask.

"Your mother's cough mixture, Mrs Graham," explained Mirza. He gave her a conspiratorial wink. The penny dropped. Ilona whisked her fractious mother behind a large tombstone in the churchyard and handed her the flask wordlessly. Franzesca Tavcar took an enormous swig, cackled, belched gently and reapplied the flask to her lips.

"Jeezus," remarked Robert Summer to his cameraman — they were filming discretely from behind another tombstone — "Get a shot of the old broad hitting the sauce like there's no tomorrow!"

Granny Tavcar, her metabolism now restored, allowed Ilona to lead her into the church, though she firmly resisted any attempts to remove the flask which she had secreted somewhere about her person. Stanton Harcourt, his hair especially sleeked back for the day, who was acting as an usher, showed them to the front pew on the left-hand side. The Ardkinglases, with Hamish and the dogs at the far end, were in the pew on the other side of the aisle, together with Caspar and Yvette.

"Have you got the ring?" A suddenly nervous David asked Mirza, now co-opted as Best Man.

"No. You placed it on Lara's finger this morning, you will recall, in the Register office." Mirza replied. He slipped out of the church just as Lara arrived and recovered the 'pledge of David's troth' in time to rejoin David just as the processional hymn began.

"Glorious things of thee are spoken," sung the choir and the congregation to the tune by Haydn. "Zion, city of our God."

"Gott erhalte, Gott beschütze," warbled Granny Tavcar, recognising with delight the Imperial Habsburg anthem. *"Unsern Kaiser, unser Land."*

"Caspar, why are they playing the Bosche tune?" asked Yvette.

There were more than a few eyebrows raised as Lara came down the aisle on the arm of her proud father, but all were forced to admit that she looked truly stunning. Not for her the demure veil demanded by tradition. Her fair hair had been skilfully swept up by Brian and was crowned by the slightly barbarian coronet, matching the garnet-studded choker. The women in the congregation glanced incredulously at her kid boots, just visible below the sweep of her skirt. Mandy Thrust whispered to her pop star husband, Lance, that only Karl Lagerfeld could have designed such a creation. (Lance himself had caused a mild sensation earlier by attempting to enter the church while smoking a cigar.)

Well done, Rudolph Rassendyll, thought Stan as she passed him. No doubt Anthony Hope had a get-up such as this in mind when he penned *The Prisoner of Zenda.* Mrs Kerr, who had obtained a lift with Terri, shed a tear. Georgina, less charitable, pursed her lips and thanked God that her mother was not there to see it. Her spouse had worn the kilt for their wedding admittedly, but that was different.

Lara and Simon came to a halt beside David as the final lines of the hymn were sung. Final for most, perhaps, but as the singing stopped, Granny Tavcar, working to her own timing, was still hard at it.

"Ewig sei mit Habsburg's Throne, she piped. *"Österreichs Geschick vereint."*

In fact Father Timothy really did them well, David thought afterwards. The service of blessing was strung out to span about forty minutes. There was a little bit of Latin and Marian worship for the Romans, as well as Psalm CXXVIII, customary at weddings under their rites. David gave Lara a gentle nudge, noticed of course by Stan, when they sang the verse about 'Thy wife shall be as a fruitful vine'. Then there was 'Onwards Christian soldiers' for David's army friends and such members of the Evenlode Brigade whom had been invited. And there was Lara's translation of Schiller's Ode to Joy sung to the tune of the finale of Beethoven's 9th Symphony by the choir as an anthem.

"Joy resplendent, spark divine, Daughter paradisiacal. Drunk with fire, let us enter, Heavenly child your holy shrine," sung the choir.

Granny Tavcar recognised the tune, but not the words. She took the opportunity to study her grandson-in-law to check that he was good breeding stock. She also surreptitiously took a quick pull from the flask under cover of her hymn sheet. Robert Summer, now in a side-chapel with his small crew, again was able to capture the motion for posterity.

"Your magic powers bind forever, what earnest fashion did divide. All mankind shall be as brothers, where your downy wings reside," continued the choir.

"Isn't that Neil Kinnock's old tune?" asked Lady d'Artois of her husband. A few pews further back, the silver-haired Dr Paul Enstone smiled as he recognised the new European anthem.

"Be embraced, you countless millions, let us kiss the whole wide world! Brothers — in the firmament, an all loving God abides," thundered the chorus. Lara thought that she had really been quite clever. Alas, her talent was not recognised by her dog. Buraq, unused to church music, raised his head and howled to the ceiling during the chorus. Hamish, who was meant to be in charge of the dogs, looked suitably embarrassed.

'At least no humans have been stupid enough to bring immature infants along,' thought Kaid crossly . He gave a low growl in Sonny's direction in an effort to silence him.

When the bride and groom finally left the church, it was to a medley of Etonian songs played on the organ. The flower arrangements inside had been lovely — so lovely that they had almost distracted Granny Tavcar from noticing the otherwise somewhat austere Protestant interior.

Hamish handed over the dogs outside the porch, so they returned to the Hall on the floor in the back of the hired limousine where there was ample room. Digney was on hand to greet David and Lara as they arrived at the front door and provided two glasses of rather good champagne.

"Madam, Miss Alberdi told me of the slight problem about your grandmother's refreshment," said their major-domo deferentially. "My Hungarian friend nearby has loaned me two bottles of the — ah — ethnic drink, some of which Mr Sind took down to the church, and also some salami from the Banat and some pickled chilli peppers. It's all on a little table in the left-hand corner of the tent where the good lady will find it."

The good lady was, in fact, hot on their heels, so they installed her at the little table in the corner where she seemed most happy. As the reception progressed, both Lara and Ilona took time to check on her, but her greatest success was with Father Timothy. Though the priest was considerably younger than her, they had German in common. Father Timothy, with his enquiring mind, could not hear enough of the problems encountered by the church in the former Yugoslavia when under Tito's rule.

At one point Robert Summer, monolingual as ever, felt that he must sample some of the liquid that the old lady was steadily consuming with no apparent effect. With Ilona translating, Granny Tavcar fixed the film producer with an unblinking stare while handing him a half-full tumbler of Slivovitz and a pickled pepper.

Uncertain what to do, Robert downed the drink with one gulp immediately preceded by the fiery pepper in what he imagined to be the approved form. His crew in the garden took great delight in filming him stumbling from the tent, gasping for air and with tears streaming down his face. Granny Tavcar laughed so much that Buraq was able to remove several thick slices of Hungarian salami from her plate undetected. Kaid, in the mean time was successfully trying his pleading look with Brigadier Buff Mainwaring and Lara's Aunt Virginia. He was especially partial to smoked salmon.

David and Lara had decided in advance to dispense with formal posed photographs outside the church, a reception line and speeches. David alone would make a short address towards the end of the reception, if only to give thanks where they were due and to advise their guests that there would be no going away as such. There would be a wedding cake, of course, and guests would be eventually dispersed by cutting off supplies of food and drink.

In the meanwhile the couple circulated and introduced each other to their own friends, where necessary. They were both amused to see Stan making a play for Joanna Matheson, whose 1922 committee husband, Leo, had pointedly declined to attend. Jack Kestrel and Tony Stark, hunting as a pack, had cornered Nikki and Tracy and were making proposals to them that David hoped were not too indecent. Mrs Kerr was enjoying a cup of tea at a table in the shade with Paul Enstone, while Terri, fired up with the champagne, was talking non-stop to the inarticulate and near leg-less Robert Summer.

They both noticed with some amusement that Richard Riley, the MP with whom David shared the Whitehall office, was in deep conversation with Georgina, Dougal being distracted by talking about the Historic Homes Association with Perry. Also Hamish had been taken over as a sort of toy-boy-for-the-afternoon by a slightly inebriated Mandy Thrust, to the evident amusement of Lance and to the horror of young Cat.

'There's my friend Cat,' thought Kaid with pleasure. 'If he's not good for a canapé or two, I'll dump him back in the river!'

Then, all too soon it was time for the cutting of the cake and for David's short speech of thanks. Shortly afterwards he had a quiet word with David Frost, who told his staff to stop serving food and drink, not that there was much left of either by then. The guests gradually left, thanking David and Lara on the way out. Nikki and Tracy decided to put duty before the rather traditional pleasures on offer from Jack and Tony, so elected to drive Robert Summer back to London.

The last to leave was Granny Tavcar. It was only by allowing her to take with her what was left of the second bottle of Slivovitz that the Grahams were able to extract her at all. On

215

the way out she gave David a smacking kiss on both cheeks and muttered something at him in Slovene.

"What did she say?" David asked Lara when he had recovered from the waft of high octane fuel that surrounded his grandmother-in-law.

She blushed lightly. "It's an old country blessing meaning roughly that your loins will bear me many sons," she told him.

They went to thank the likes of David Frost and Ivor Digney for all their help and then went into the Hall to change into more comfortable garb. When they came down, it was to find that Caspar had arranged for the rest to go for drinks at d'Artois Hall, followed by dinner in Woodstock. The only catch was that Caspar wanted to borrow the Mercedes, the Bentley being at Nice Airport. A compromise was reached whereby the near-teetotal Mirza would drive.

After an early supper of spicy moussaka and hot garlic-bread, prepared on the previous day by Mrs Kerr to soak up the champagne, David and Lara went upstairs. It had been a long day for them, but they were not quite ready for sleep. Much later on, when they were both very drowsy, Lara turned to David.

"Thank you, Darling," she said. "You must have given Granny the best day of her life."

Chapter 15

A LURCHER IN THE HOUSE

"I suppose that it can't have been much more than ten weeks or so ago that I was lying in this self-same spot under the apple-tree and wondering what Stan was talking the Boss into. Anyway, it seems like an age to me, and has seen me transformed into a really political animal.

I quite enjoyed the parliament bit, which we'll come to later, but I hope that the Boss, having made his point, will leave me out of politics from now on. When all is said and done, I'm a country dog at heart. Also, those journeys to London bore me rigid. Quite a few other MPs have dogs, which are confined to their owners' offices and then only if they are outside the main 'Palace', but I don't get to see them all that much.

The wedding, which you have heard all about anyway, was a week ago now, and the Boss and Lara went off yesterday to stay on Carmen's boat for a couple of days before moving on to Austria. You may also remember that Sonny, a throw-back to my great-grandfather I am afraid, nicked half a plateful of Lara's Granny's foreign sausage at the reception. Well, I had been saying good-bye to guests with the Boss at the end — it is my home too — and went back to the garden afterwards. There I found the little bugger heaving and retching right in the middle of the lawn. No self control, the young. At least I held on to the smoked salmon that I scrounged.

The Boss and Lara went up to bed with indecent haste, if you ask me, after dinner without even putting us out. It didn't matter as it happened because the Boss's dad had taken the rest of them off to dinner in Woodstock, so Mirza let us out for a final pee when they all came back. I have to say that Hamish was looking a bit cross-eyed when they returned: I just hope that he didn't emulate Sonny!

Everyone was bright and breezy at breakfast the following morning and soon afterwards they all were on their way. Jack drove the Boss's dad and Yvette to the airport in the Mercedes, while Carmen and her 'Maharajah', as she calls Mirza, headed for London. Hamish drove off to Eton for lunch with some old friends who lived nearby. The tent people took away their marquee and by lunch time we were all back to normal, or so I thought."

Kaid yawned, rose to his feet, and wandered into the Boss's office. After a moment of reflection, he climbed onto the small sofa. He knew that he was not allowed there, but he also knew that, with the Boss away, Mrs Kerr would condone his misbehaviour.

"We went to London on Monday morning. Sometimes we go by train, which is quicker but I am not allowed on the seats: at other times we go by car which, although more comfortable for me, seems to take for ever and a day. Either way, it has the tremendous advantage that I don't have to put up with Sonny during the day. He is currently so lacking in filial respect and is so self-opinionated that I can fully understand why so many of my forefathers tended to do a runner soon after the procreative act.

He has also started to ask awkward questions about dear Flicka, his mother. With the best will in the world, I can't help him there. As I remember, one day she was there, the next she was not. Although I can understand what the Boss is saying, and to a certain degree what he is thinking, it is largely a one-way traffic, so I can't ask him what befell her. I told Sonny, in an effort to silence him, that she always said how well-bred she was: a mistake, as I now see him comparing his close-cropped hide with my long silky hair.

Anyway, when we arrived at the Boss's office, we found the good Mrs Watt in something of a state. Richard Riley, who shares the office with us, had called earlier to say that he was unavoidably tied up in the constituency, she told the Boss, and the telephone had been going non-stop for them both since her arrival. It rang again at that point and the Boss took the call. I gathered that someone from the government Whips' office needed to see him urgently.

Although I hadn't, at that point anyway, been allowed into the main building where it all happened, I was beginning to get the big picture. The largest pack, which therefore called the shots and was the government, were named the Conservatives. They tended to speak as though English was their second language, a bit like Mirza perhaps, but unlike him they exaggerated their would-be Oxford English so that it came out as 'Wah, Wah, Wah'.

The smaller pack were mainly Labour party members, with a bit of the Celtic fringe thrown in. They tended to speak with the accents that they were brought up with at home, and frankly sounded rather like that mixed collection of farmers that we encounter at Banbury Market.

Apparently decisions which could effect the destinies of the hundred million-odd humans and dogs in the Kingdom were decided simply by counting the heads of the two packs as they passed through lobbies. Providing that the government had done the sums right, they won the day. And that seemed to be in question when the Wah-Wah man from the Whips' office came round.

'What with Cedric's inexplicable death over the weekend in somewhat bizarre circumstances and our member for Bagshot's stroke, we are rather counting on you, Vyvian, to save our bacon,' said this patronising fellow. 'After all, you don't want to vote yourself out of a job. Nice dog,' he continued in the same vein. 'Saluki?' Stupid bastard! I gave him the unblinking stare treatment.

'Three months ago, I hadn't even considered running for parliament, so the loss of my seat will hardly cause me loss of sleep,' replied the Boss with some heat. 'You've raised taxes, castrated the Armed Forces and mismanaged both Health and Education, while Law and Order is about as big a joke as Back to Basics. Give me one good reason why I should keep you in power.'

'Wah, Wah, Wah,' said the patronising one. 'Tamworth Manifesto, Churchill, Wah, Falklands, Wah, Old School tie, Wah, Gulf,' he then stopped, before continuing in an almost normal voice. 'I'm not getting through to you, am I? Tell me your price.'

I thought that the Boss was going to hit the man for a moment, but then he just laughed out loud. 'My dog — a

Lurcher by the way — largely is responsible for my presence here. I am due to make my maiden speech early on in the no confidence debate tomorrow, and I want him in the chamber with me, just for the day, and with access to all parts of the Lower House that are open to members.'

'Wah, splutter, Wah,' was all that the man from the Whips' office could manage for a time. He then managed to formulate a coherent sentence. 'Are you seriously suggesting that the future of the present government depends on your fucking dog?'

'If you choose to regard it that way, then yes,' said the Boss coldly. 'As I said before, it is a matter of complete indifference to me whether your leaderless bunch, which seems to be run from the NAAFI, is replaced by an equally leaderless opposition. Besides, I am psychologically dependent on my dog.'

I can't say that I fully understood that last remark, but it seemed to be some sort of a lifeline to our visitor, who left. The Boss then called Riley on his private number at home to find that the crisis or whatever was clearly over as his wife had to go out to their swimming pool to get him.

'Listen,' said the Boss. 'The government really needs us to survive. I have stuck out for getting Kaid into the Chamber tomorrow as my price, so why don't you extract a promise from that fat chap who runs roads to grant you a full Public Inquiry over that by-pass that threatens your constituency?'

They chattered on for a bit, ending with the Boss asking Riley to join Lara and himself (and hopefully me) for lunch in the House before the debate on the following day. He then left for the House, telling Mrs Watt that he was off for a bite of lunch and to fix a pass for Lara, now that she was a fully fledged 'spouse'. He also intended, so he said, to book her a seat in the Special Gallery for the debate. Lucky Lara!

So I spent the next couple of hours with Mrs Watt, a kindly soul, but not a patch on the apple-cheeked Mrs Kerr. She feeds me chocolate-covered digestive biscuits, which are all very well once in a while, but not as a staple diet. She also puts out a bowl of water for me but, to be honest, the taste of London water is so disgusting that I prefer to go thirsty. The Boss once said that, by the time that it gets to London, three people have already drunk it. Yuck!"

The thought clearly reminded Kaid of his present needs, so he wandered out to the loo off the hall, checked it for Domestos, and noisily slaked his thirst before returning to the sofa in the Boss's office.

"Dr Enstone, the chap I was beaten up with that night outside the television studios, was on the train home, so he and the Boss chatted away about such mind-numbing topics as preserving local schools at village level and more bobbies on the beat. As we parted to go to our cars in the car park at our destination, the good doctor had a final piece of advice for the Boss.

'Listen, David,' he said. 'Unlike you, I've never been an MP, and whatever deal you may've done with whichever party over the vote tomorrow is your affair. Just try to make certain that they stick to their end of it. Never trust the buggers of whatever hue.'

We came home to find an exhausted Lara, who had only just returned from taking her Granny to Heathrow. This had entailed a journey to take in Oxford, Henley and Windsor, all of which the old lady had heard of at some point and now wished to see for herself. Nothing that she saw, naturally, compared remotely with the past glories of the Habsburg Empire. Though Lara loved her Granny dearly, she told the Boss, she was quite relieved when the Austrian Airlines flight was called.

Not that I can read, but the papers on the following day caused a certain amount of mirth at the breakfast table. It seemed that the Boss and Riley had it within their power, depending on how they voted at the end of the debate, to either topple, or to prop up, the government.

'It could be argued that an element of farce is present,' the Boss read out loud to Lara from his paper. 'When the members of the jingoistic County Party and the Ban the M34 Alliance can hold the government to ransom, but that is one of the quirks of the democracy that we uphold.' Indeed!

We went to London by car on this occasion and parked in the underground House of Commons car park. We then walked over to our office to meet Richard Riley as planned. I had sensed that something was worrying the Boss, so I was not too surprised when he asked Riley (he looks a bit like Stan, by the way) what he planned to do.

'Oh, I'll vote for them in the end, I suppose,' he said languidly. 'They've promised me a full Public Inquiry over that damned road in return.'

'In writing?'

'No, just the chap's word.'

'Look,' said the Boss. 'Just a hunch, but a chap's word is about all that I've got. Let me go over to the House with Kaid. If I get in, I'll call you here and you can join me. If not, I'll come straight back here and proceed to raise the roof.' We didn't and he did.

The doorkeeper had been very polite but firm. He had received no instructions about me from the Serjeant at Arms, nor from the Service Committee. So we returned to our office and the Boss called the government Whips' office. I could just hear the Wah-Wah noise at the far end.

'Don't you "old boy" me,' shouted the Boss. 'I am returning to the House in five minutes and, if my dog is again denied entry, I will have to advise Mr Richard Riley that the promise made verbally to him could prove equally worthless. He would like it in writing in the circumstances.' He put the telephone down which was now emitting a very high Wah rating.

When we returned to the Members' Entrance, things were very different. The doorkeeper, an old soldier with lots of medals, saw the King's Lancers cap-badge on my smartly polished leather collar and actually gave me a salute! He also had Lara's pass and reserved seat ticket ready for her and an envelope for Riley. In high good humour, we went to the particular dining room where members can entertain guests.

I suppose that I am a bit spoiled by the peacefulness of meals at home, but lunch in the House really was something different. I think that the main reason why most of them go into politics in the first place is the pleasure that they get from hearing the sound of their own voices: it was amazing to me that they found the time to get food and drink into their faces.

One of the waitresses recognised me from my media exposure and brought me a dish of roast beef. I don't usually eat at lunch-time, but ate it up out of politeness anyway. Also Riley was quite amusing. He prattled on about his own dogs — Labradors — which he uses for shooting. He never brought them to London because they basically lived out in kennels, poor sods, and also he had that much further to travel than we did.

After the meal we took a little walk on the terrace overlooking the Thames. It is quite a bit wider in London than it is at home, so I wouldn't give much for Cat Thrust's chances were he to fall in by Westminster bridge! The Boss then muttered something about getting a Prayer card (?) to enable him to reserve a seat for himself in the Chamber, so disappeared for ten minutes or so. In the meanwhile I had been attracting some curious glances, especially from a black guide-dog who should have been pleased to see another canine face around.

When the Boss came back, he said that it was time for us to go down to the Chamber. Riley said that he would join him later and would take Lara to the Special Gallery for her to claim her reserved seat.

The Chamber itself is rather like a church, except that the pews, which are of padded green leather, face inwards across a central aisle. Also, in place of an altar, there was a carved wooden throne with a long table in front of it. The Boss took his seat on the right-hand side of the aisle fairly near to the entrance, I sitting on the carpet at his feet, and the Chamber started to fill up further. Then, as the big clock on top of the building chimed the half-hour, a small procession entered, consisting of a jolly looking lady who was later to be in charge of proceedings, an elderly cove carrying a great golden club and a parson.

Once they had taken their places, the golden club being placed on the long table, the reason for the Prayer card became clear. The humans all indulged in about four minutes of Jesus-worship. I tried to look serious, while sending a quick prayer to Anubis, and then we were under way. What a yawn! No wonder that several of the members nodded off quite soon. Some chap near the far end on the other side was seeking leave to introduce the first reading of the Inland Waterways (protection of endangered species) Bill, or something equally obscure.

He droned on for about half an hour, and towards the end the Chamber started to fill up. Then the Prime Minister and the Opposition leader came in, together with the various faces that one sees on television from time to time lying in their teeth. There then followed a quarter of an hour of what was, to me, sheer farce. From listening to the Boss talking to Lara afterwards, it was the twice-weekly Prime Minister's Questions.

Only about ten members were able to ask questions in the short time allocated and apparently they were each allowed two. Of these, inevitably they chose to waste the first one with such idiotic queries as to the official engagements that were due to be carried out by the Prime Minister on the following day. The incumbent would rise briefly to his feet and would refer back to the answer that he had given only minutes before to an identical question from another member. Indeed, some of the members' questions reminded me rather of Sonny's brainless waffle."

The thought of Buraq caused Kaid to stir uneasily on the sofa. It could only be a matter of time before the little sod came bounding into the office to disturb his reflections.

"The sting, if any, seemed to come in the second questions, which tended to be on the lines of 'In the course of his engagements, would he consider abrogating the Treaty of Rome (whatever that was) in view to the French farmers' attitude towards their counterparts in the Ewkay (wherever that is)'. Given that the leader of the government pack didn't look too bright, he nevertheless fielded these questions quite adroitly, but never by giving a direct answer. That didn't seem ever to bother the questioner: after all, those of his constituents who bothered to watch the proceedings on television would have seen their man tackling no less than the Prime Minister.

Then we were on to the main business of the day. The chap who leads the opposition pack rose to his feet and begged leave to introduce a motion that the house had no confidence in the present government. Leaving aside the fact that I thought motions were vet-talk for having a crap (rather than just talking crap) he then went on to make rather a good speech on the lines of those made by the Boss when he was on the stump. He then sat down to cheers from his own pack and quite a lot of Wah-Wah-Wah from the other side.

Then the Prime Minister got up and went on about how much worse the country would have been under the opposition; and how we were leading the World in practically any field that you cared to mention (less cricket) et cetera before he sat down to lukewarm applause from his side and a form of Yer-Yer-Yer chant from the others. At this point most of the bigwigs on both sides left the Chamber, to research their nubile researchers I shouldn't wonder, leaving the rank and file to have their turn in the debate.

The jolly lady seemed quite competent at keeping order as she called on speakers, first from one side and then from the other. I knew that the Boss was due to speak from what he had told Lara over the weekend and, sure enough, after about an hour she called 'Mr David Vyvian'. The Boss rose to his feet, but before he could utter, some portly wino on the other side shouted something about spying strangers and pointed at me!

Well, clearly nobody had marked his card for him. One of the Whips bounded up to where he was swaying gently and pushed him back onto the bench, while the Chief Whip went up to the jolly lady and told her that the Honourable Member had only said that it was outrageous, or something. Anyway, it all took a few minutes to sort out before the Boss eventually started.

I won't bore you with his full speech — I can't remember it all anyway — but he started reasonably enough by introducing himself as being the County Party member for the Vale of Evenlode, previously held for the Tories by his old and respected friend, the late Sir Reginald Token. (Cries of 'Hear! Hear!' from the benches opposite.)

His constituents, he said, were worried people, so worried in fact that they had failed to support the Tories for the first time in memory at the recent by-election. The farmers, when not battling with their IACS forms, were worried by the implications of being bullied into Gatt by the Americans; there was no longer a local regiment for the young men who were so inclined to join; the Post Office in his village had been robbed in broad daylight; and one of his constituents had been kept waiting with a broken arm in casualty for over six hours.

Warming to his theme, he went on about the humiliation of the government in Brussels, VAT on heating oil and electricity, and the bewilderment of teachers at schools in the Vale by the constantly changing parameters of the so-called National Curricula. Most of all of this was Greek to me, of course, but it sounded good.

Having endeared himself to the government pack, he then turned on the opposition whom he described as Sançerre Socialists who had seemingly abandoned many of their old and sincerely held principles in favour of slick suits and gaudy ties. If he thought for one moment, he said, that their thinly disguised politics of envy, which proved popular only with certain sections of the urban population, would work, then he would support them. As it was, the government had been democratically elected to serve a full term, and so should be given a chance to redeem the situation.

In the circumstances, it was hardly surprising that, when the Boss ended and sat down, it was to silence, broken only by the portly wino who was singing (rather badly) 'How much is that doggie in the window?'. The jolly lady then called on a member of the government benches to reply, and I have to say that he was really quite rude. How lucky were they, he intoned sarcastically, not only to be promised so generously the support of the entire County Party, but also to have been given the benefit of the views of one so experienced as their leader, the Honourable Member for the Vale of Evenlode.

He went on for a bit in the same vein — he looked a bit like that dreadful Livkin man whom we had such trouble with in the by-election — while the Boss just had to sit there and take it. When he had done, we left the Chamber, collected Lara from the Special Gallery, and went to have tea. Afterwards, Lara went off to see her Aunt Virginia while we returned to the fray. I pretended to see a cat on the way back to the Chamber which gave me the opportunity to have a quick whiz along one of the long corridors. In so doing, I nearly knocked flying some woman whose frequent appearances on the television make both the Boss and Lara snarl with rage. 'Sorry, Mrs Bumley,' said the Boss in an offhand way as he called me back to him. It was her turn to snarl.

We had to put up with another couple of hours of 'Oh yes you did — Oh no I didn't' before we left again to meet Lara for supper. Riley joined us and was quite amusing about the Boss's speech. He had gone to one of the many bars after it, and maintained that if the government lost the vote later on, it would be on account of the degree of apoplexy suffered by the older Tories. Apparently words such as 'class traitor' and 'deserves to be horse-whipped' had been bandied around. Luckily for me, the nice waitress was again on duty, so I had some more roast beef for my dinner.

The bigwigs had returned to the Chamber by then (Riley told the Boss that they had probably been discussing Uganda with their researchers or something) and the place was pretty full. 'Order! Order!' shouted the jolly lady, by now a bit frayed, as the 'Wah-Yer' contest raged across the central aisle. Then, way past my usual bedtime, the House was called on to divide. Over 600 of us had to go through one of two doorways, so there was a bit of a queue for both. I suppose it was because I was half asleep, and I had also seen the guide-dog going through the other door, which was why I gave the wooden throne a token spray in passing.

'You can't do that here!' said the man, who was checking us through with a hand-held counting device, to the Boss.

'I didn't,' said the Boss. 'It's regarded as frightfully lucky in my constituency, anyway.'

Well, you all know the result of the vote: the opposition motion of no confidence was defeated by two votes. The papers on the following day made a certain amount of fuss, after doing their sums and counting all of the names, about the majority only being one, not two, so they reckoned. It could have had something to do with the teller in the Noes Lobby (the chap who objected to me leaving my card, so to speak) clicking his counting machine in the heat of the moment as I passed him. If he couldn't tell a dog from a human, he should wise up: we're the ones with the brains."

Kaid now rolled onto his back, stretched all four feet in the air and fell into a deep and untroubled sleep. He did not even stir when Mrs Kerr, peering around the door to check on him, tut-tutted at the brazen display of his 'naughty bits'.